Love Byte

David Atkinson

buried
river
press

ISBN 978-1-910208-01-4

Buried River Press
Clerkenwell House
Clerkenwell Green
London EC1R 0HT

www.halebooks.com

Buried River Press is an imprint of Robert Hale Ltd

2 4 6 8 10 9 7 5 3 1

Printed in Great Britain by Berforts Information Press Ltd

Love Byte

For my girls, Erin and Emme

CHAPTER ONE

It was a magical moment. My gorgeous, glamorous girl-friend was about to become my gorgeous, glamorous wife. Resplendent in her flowing ivory wedding dress, and backlit by bright sunshine, Lindsay appeared to float through the gardens of the ancient churchyard. Long grass whispered at her ankles, she held her head high, and the small bouquet clasped in her hands trembled gently. Beside her, brightly coloured flowers swayed in the warm breeze and a white butterfly that followed her progress appeared to dance with joy in the summer air.

As the string quartet struck up the first notes of 'Eternal Flame' the guests all turned, gazed and smiled as Lindsay glided between them. My best man, Jamie, and I looked on, feeling almost like bystanders. We had spent ages grooming ourselves and donning our green Hunter tartan kilts, but compared to this approaching vision of loveliness, we were but tramps. Andrew Gillen, the Church of Scotland minister, stood ready and the brides-maids, Ellie and Andrea, glowed in pale pink and bustled along behind Lindsay to prevent her dress from snagging on anything.

Around us were ancient gravestones, the inscriptions

worn away by time and harsh winters past. The contrast between life and death was not lost on me and somehow the presence of these silent and long dead witnesses made me feel more alive, keenly aware of how lucky I was to be living and revelling in that moment.

To take advantage of the fabulous weather, the ceremony had been moved to the churchyard, and as my wife-to-be stood by my side I couldn't help smiling. I was so proud and happy; I was fit to burst. It truly was the happiest moment of my life, and I reckoned up until then I'd had a pretty good existence.

The minister, plump and grey before his time, was a serious man in his Sunday services. Throughout the winter and spring we'd attended nearly every week to ensure that when we came to be married, he would look upon us as parishioners rather than interlopers just wanting to use the grand thousand-year-old Edinburgh church for our nuptials.

We'd endured lectures on the evils of drink whilst nursing hangovers from the previous Saturday night. Lindsay had nodded sagely, agreeing with the sentiment that tobacco was a dangerous drug and should be banned – whilst quietly pushing her Benson & Hedges to the bottom of her handbag – and we'd both squirmed guiltily as he'd lectured us on the folly of pre-marital sex, having arrived late, and glowing, to the service from an extended Sunday morning bout of love-making.

On this day, however, he had beamed at us and began by addressing the congregation with a potted history of the church and its place in Edinburgh's violent past. My attention drifted and I became acutely aware of the surroundings. I was conscious of the wind that rustled the leaves on the trees, I listened to a bird that chirped cheerfully from an ancient stone wall and I detected the bright but faint tinkle of an ice cream van that advertised its arrival on some distant housing estate. Honeysuckle and lavender shrubs produced a heady scent that drifted across the churchyard and bees busily buzzed on the flowers, gorging themselves on nectar.

My gaze wandered over the reverend's shoulder and tracked across the still and tranquil loch that formed the spectacular backdrop to the ancient church that made it such a popular choice for photographers and painters. As I watched, a swan gracefully spiralled down and settled on the surface, sending small ripples across the water. It was hard to believe that we were in the middle of a modern city; it looked and felt like the Scottish Highlands.

Standing in the dappled shade provided by an ancient oak tree, I slowly became aware that the Reverend Gillen had ceased speaking to the assembled guests and was now addressing me. I took my girlfriend's hand for the last time as a single man and the formalities began.

As the camera of Alistair Swanson, the DVD maker, panned across the rows of smiling faces and focused in on an elderly relative, my 2½–year-old daughter Amy suddenly piped up.

'Ooz that?'

Dragged back to present reality with a jolt, I peered at the TV screen. The camera had focused onto an old woman smiling with crooked black teeth.

'Ooz that?'

I tried and failed to recall the old crone's name. She was a former church elder who, ironically enough, became too old and decrepit to remain in her position. Abruptly the camera moved again to show an old man perched on a chair. He was twisted and bent, obviously in pain, and looked to be leering at my bride.

'Ooz that?'

I smiled at my daughter.

'Ooz that?' she enquired again.

'I don't know,' I admitted honestly, knowing full well that this explanation would not be enough.

'Ooz that?' This time she was louder and more insistent, as if raising the pitch of her voice might jog my memory into an answer.

I sighed. I sighed a lot when Amy was asking me questions.

'I don't know his name, Amy. Anyway, he's probably dead.'

I had no idea if the old man was dead or alive. I didn't know who he was. I didn't care too much either.

Amy's infant brain tried to process this statement. She had little concept of death. The scene on the TV changed and focused onto another guest.

'Ooz that?'

'She's dead as well.'

Another guest came into focus.

'Ooz that?'

'Dead.'

'Ooz that?'

'Dead.'

'Ooz—?'

'Dead.'

'Ooz—?'

'Dead.'

Soon most of the guest list had departed this earth, at least for Amy's benefit. At some point in the next week or two, either in the street or at a playgroup, we would bump into someone I'd snuffed out and Amy would smile with recognition, point at them and shout, 'Dead.'

I should have known better than to play the wedding DVD when she was still awake, but she'd started to grow tired of *In the Night Garden* and as it was only 6.30 I was trying to eke out another half an hour of peace before the manic evening bedtime routine kicked in. So instead I was plonked on the cool wooden floor of my expansive living room, staring at my past.

The camera lingered on the serene and smiling face of my wife Lindsay, her luxurious black hair moving gently in the breeze, dark eyes shining with joy, frozen in time within a scene that would be forever summer.

Amy stared intently at the screen. 'Ooz that?'

I sighed again. 'That's Mummy.'

Amy turned to me, flicked her hair from her face and blinked her dark-brown eyes, full of innocence and trust.

'Dead,' she said with certainty.

I nodded sadly. 'Yes. She's dead too.'

CHAPTER TWO

Half an hour after Amy was asleep, I had settled on the leather couch with a glass of Australian Shiraz and was channel surfing through SKY TV's finest. After flirting with *Wheeler Dealers* for a minute or two, I plumped for an old episode of *Grand Designs* where a middle-aged couple were insanely trying to restore a ruined castle. It had been a long, tiring day, as were most days spent running after my toddler. Sometimes I even looked forward to going into the office for a break. As the wine started to seep into my system I slid further down the couch and began to feel my eyes closing. Suddenly I was jerked awake by my mobile phone blasting out 'Firework' by Katy Perry. It had become my ringtone only recently. I had selected it randomly from the stack of music files on my phone.

The screen on the iPhone told me it was my mother-in-law, Pauline, with her regular evening phone call to make sure her precious granddaughter was safe and sleeping. I knew she sometimes worried about me too and how I was handling everything. I personally thought I was doing remarkably well, but Pauline wasn't convinced and was waiting for me to have some kind of breakdown. I occasionally suspected she was disappointed that I hadn't, but I wasn't a breakdown sort of guy. Pauline was highly strung and always on the go; I was pretty laid-back and relaxed, and she didn't get that at all. Yeah I was still hurting, angry, and trying to come to terms with my wife's death, but I had Amy. Amy was my world now – my number one priority.

Another difference between us was that I internalized stuff, Pauline expressed everything. She was like my wife; if she had an issue she just blurted it out, believing that getting things out in the open was the way to deal with everything.

Lindsay always used to say that I wandered about inside my own head half the time and kept too much to myself. To a point, that was true, but I didn't see any value in burdening everyone with trivia; if something big went wrong, then I'd talk about it, but I usually rationalized it first, to see if I could find a solution. 'Typical male thing,' she'd say. 'Always trying to fix everything.'

Only I couldn't fix this, my wife was gone and I had to find my own way. I answered the call.

'Do you want me to come early in the morning to help get Amy ready?' Pauline asked, her jarring voice grated in my ear.

I smiled. 'No, it's fine, Pauline, I'm not in the office until about ten, so if you get here about nine that'll be fine.'

I sensed her frustration, and lack of faith in me. 'Have you tidied up?'

I glanced around the untidy living room, strewn with Amy's toys. In addition, an unwashed cereal bowl sat accusingly on the coffee table along with several mugs and a half-eaten banana which had turned mushy and brown. I could detect the faint sweet acetone aroma emanating from it.

'Yeah,' I lied. 'Amy helped me before she had her bath.'

The silence on the other end of the line, microwave

or whatever it was that mobile's worked off, told me she didn't believe me. She knew me too well. Suggesting that Amy was in any way capable of helping rather than hindering me was probably my undoing.

Too tired to argue I eventually had to let her have her way and she promised to be over by eight. Pauline had too much time on her hands. Her partner Simon, with whom she had been for the last ten years, worked as an officer on North Sea ferries. He was away a lot and sometimes only made it back home for a few days a month.

They had great holidays together – usually discounted cruises – but I knew Pauline missed him. I was her project and chief distraction – well, myself and Amy.

After switching off the TV I decided to switch on my iPad and check my work emails in case there were any nasty surprises waiting for me. Since Lindsay's death I'd gone back to work at Perennial Mutual part-time, job sharing with Jenny who was recently back from maternity leave. The arrangement worked reasonably well; I worked two or three days a week on a rota basis and spent the rest of the time with Amy. The life assurance payout on my wife's death hadn't been huge but had been enough to allow me to give up working full-time, at least for the time being. I logged on and scrolled down my work inbox. There was nothing that wouldn't wait, thankfully. I was just about to shut the screen down when I remembered that I hadn't checked my personal account for nearly a week. I was unable to access it from work as the firewall blocked all non-essential Internet sites, including most email accounts.

I glanced at my inbox, which showed forty-seven unread emails. The first was from Nabutti Ingroblu, beseeching me to send her (I assume it was a 'her', it could have been a he) my bank details so she could deposit sixteen million US Dollars into my account. She/he had allegedly been awarded this money as a result of a change in government in Nigeria. (Whenever I experienced a change of government all I was ever awarded was higher taxes). She/he then would meet me in London once she/he obtained a UK visa and we would make mad, passionate love in a Mayfair hotel to celebrate her windfall. Well obviously a 'her' then – hopefully!

The next email was from Donna, a horny housewife from Cardiff, who wanted to meet me and exchange bodily fluids. Wow! My luck was in tonight. Next I had an offer for Viagra from an online pharmacist: '12 little blue pills for 12 little dollars'. Obviously they had been reading my previous two emails.

The next proposal was from Chuck who lived in Detroit. There was a picture of Chuck in the body of the email that showed him sitting in an open-topped powder-blue Rolls Royce, waving a wad of dollar bills – à la Harry Enfield circa 1985.

If I agreed to subscribe to Chuck's monthly wealth programme, I would receive the 'AMAZING SECRET METHOD' – 'amazing secret method' was in huge red letters – of making millions of dollars on the Internet. I suspected that Chuck's 'amazing secret' was simply to send lots of emails to people purporting to have an 'amazing secret' and then sign them up to a monthly payment plan for the privilege. It may also have been a slightly subtler version of Miss/Mr Ingroblu's method of obtaining my bank account details, which he would then promptly empty.

Although I found the whole thing mildly amusing, it saddened me to know that some people would buy into all the hype and end up losing money. Usually those who could least afford to do so. I glanced further down the list and apart from an email from a theatre group I'd once belonged to I didn't see anything I wanted to read and pressed the delete button.

Just as I was about to navigate away from the page, another email popped into my inbox. I was tempted to press delete without even looking at it but decided to have a quick peek. I didn't recognize the sender: LH1975@ blueyonder.co.uk.

Attached to the email was a picture of Lindsay and me on our honeymoon. We were dressed in T-shirts and shorts, standing barefoot on a tropical beach with sand so white it looked like it had just been bleached. When I read the text of the message I decided it had to be some kind of sick joke because it claimed to be from my wife.

CHAPTER THREE

Our honeymoon in St Lucia had been a fortnight of joy and self-indulgence, our once-in-a-lifetime holiday where we denied ourselves nothing. We'd come back invigorated, relaxed, and a good few pounds heavier. Lindsay wanted to try for a baby immediately. I would have preferred to wait and enjoy each other for longer but Lindsay could tempt me to her way of thinking very easily.

'OK, Andy, here's the deal. It takes on average around eleven months to get pregnant,' she explained patiently, talking to me like I was a child.

'OK. So?'

Lindsay sighed and shook her head at my stupidity. 'That's an *average*, and includes all those fertile teenagers that get pregnant at the drop of a hat.'

I didn't think dropping hats had much to do with it – dropping knickers maybe – but I didn't say anything as Lindsay was in full flight.

'So, as we're both a good bit older than the nubile teenagers, logic dictates that it will take us longer than eleven months. I've worked out that we will probably need around fifteen months and that assumes that we have a shag every month when I'm ovulating.'

I smiled at Lindsay's serious face as she delivered her impromptu biology lesson and said, 'Well I was hoping we would have a shag more than once a month.'

Lindsay wrinkled up her nose and frowned at me. 'Yeah, I should have known that out of what I've just said the only word you would hear is "shag".'

I grinned and Lindsay sighed then smiled.

'OK, in your language, Andy Hunter, what this means for you is that over the next fifteen months or so we are going to be shagging constantly and I hope you will be up for it, double meaning intended. Also, I want to make sure your sperm is in tip top condition so we are cutting down on the alcohol and you are not to carry your mobile phone in your trouser pockets. I know there's no proof that mobiles cause any problems, but better safe than sorry.'

Of course, Lindsay became pregnant almost immediately and my promise of 'constant shagging' – which I actually thought sounded like a good name for a rock band – was not fulfilled. The pregnancy went as well as pregnancies could. We oohed and aahed over scan pictures, and despite feeling continuously sick for five months, Lindsay managed to wolf down a huge number of pot noodles, mint choc ices, white chocolate buttons, pickled onions, banana sandwiches and Worcester sauce crisps (no other flavour would do.) This was coupled with an urge to periodically sniff the petrol cap from our car. Not surprisingly she also consumed a fair number of indigestion tablets.

Amy's birth on a sweltering hot May afternoon was the icing on the cake, the fulfilment of Lindsay's dream and a gift from the gods. At least that was how we felt for the first twelve hours. Then Amy screwed up her perfect features and howled and howled, and then howled some more. When she wasn't howling she was screaming, when she wasn't screaming she was bawling. The only time she didn't cry was when she was attached to one of Lindsay's breasts, her preference being the right one. I was the other way around as Lindsay's right breast was marginally smaller than the left, or as Lindsay would say, 'The left is slightly bigger than the right.' In any case, my preferences were no longer important as we tried to figure out what was wrong with our darling baby.

We had been sent home with this small bundle of joy, exhausted and exhilarated. The birth had been a long one – twenty-six hours from start to finish – but Lindsay was proud she had managed a normal birth, and thankfully without any significant tears to her nether regions. The two midwives had been brilliant, a warm girl from the Home Counties and a solid Geordie girl with jet-black hair and a safety pin through her nose. I'd spent nearly twelve hours staring at that safety pin, postulating whether or not snot would leak out of her nostril when she had a cold. I never plucked up the courage to ask her.

The alarming thing for me was that Amy came with no instructions. You can buy anything in the shops, from a washing machine to a flat-pack house, and with it comes a book of detailed plans, instructions, and usually a trouble-shooting section. Years earlier I'd even adopted a cat from a rescue centre and received a huge list of dos and don'ts neatly typed on two A4 sheets.

Yet here we were taking home a brand new human and we received absolutely nothing, except some instructions on how to fit a baby car seat and a vague leaflet about the dangers of female genital mutilation. (The only female genital mutilation I had ever witnessed was that inflicted on my poor wife by Amy.)

When Helen, the health visitor, appeared, the morning following Lindsay's release from the maternity ward, we must have presented a familiar story for her: two bewildered adults trying to get to grips with parenthood.

19

There were no university courses in parenthood, not even a City and Guilds or an NVQ. You can do an NVQ in hairdressing, glass blowing, cloud watching and even train-spotting but *not* in parenthood. The art of being a parent was something you had to learn on the job, gleaning the basics from instructions on the back of various nappy boxes and baby milk.

Helen was exceptionally gifted in platitudes and re-assurances but not much help with our dilemma. Mainly because the minute Helen walked in the front door Amy was happiness and light, no howling, no screaming and no bawling. Even when Helen viciously stuck a pin in her foot to test her reactions Amy only protested mildly.

'What a lovely child, you are so lucky, most babies scream blue murder when I do that.'

Our description and protests of the previous seventeen hours were greeted with doubt and scepticism and Helen left with the firm impression, I believe, that we were serial complainers. Of course the minute Helen closed the front door Amy started up again for the next seventeen hours.

Eventually we discovered that Lindsay wasn't express-ing enough milk and Amy was just hungry. It took nearly a week before a locum community midwife diagnosed the problem. She suggested Lindsay supplement the breast feeds with some formula milk. The first time Amy ingested a bottle of milk, a look of pure contentment spread across her features and for the first time with a full belly, she slipped into a long and peaceful sleep, as did her grateful parents.

As well as instructions on how to deal with a newborn baby, Lindsay and I had come up with a list of things that it would be useful for prospective parents to know before setting out on the journey of parenthood. We'd based this on our own experience and also from what we'd gleaned from friends with older kids.

Travelling by car: In order to simulate the aromas of carting a toddler around in a car seat for a prolonged period of time, take a fresh fish (maybe a herring) and place it somewhere unobtrusive. Under the passenger seat would be ideal. Then leave it in place for around six months to a year.

DVD Players: If you still have a DVD player then you have to squish a soft biscuit into the slot or drawer where the DVD fits, preferably one with jam in the middle to ensure the mechanism completely seizes up.

Televisions: If you own an LCD or plasma TV, take some time to continually bash the bottom right hand corner of the screen until a number of pixels stop working to thus impede your viewing pleasure. (This might not be such a disaster because in order to fully simulate life with toddlers for a period of approximately five years, you would only be allowed to watch: *In the Night Garden*, *Justin's House* and *Nina and the Neurons*.)

Artwork: Take several sheets of paper and thickly smear a variety of coloured paints over each one until you get something resembling congealed vomit. Then allow the artwork to dry, attach some Blu-Tack to the back of each masterpiece and proudly display them on your fridge door for eighteen months.

Tidying Up: Every evening when you get home from work, immediately go into your living room or kitchen and empty a sack of toys all over the floor. Spend the remainder of the evening distributing them randomly around the rest of your house/flat. It is vital to ensure a number of sharp edged toys (Lego bricks are ideal) are placed beside your bed where you are certain to stand on them with your bare feet in the morning, or if you need to get up during the night.

In the end we decided not to publish our list anywhere in case it had a detrimental effect on the UK birth rate.

As our own darling daughter grew, so did our confidence. Eventually we established a routine of sorts, where we would put Amy in her Moses basket beside our bed around 8 p.m. and when she woke up during the night for her first feed, Lindsay would take her into bed and I would stagger bleary-eyed into the spare room and sleep there until morning. Eventually, Amy started to sleep for longer periods and I could snuggle in beside Lindsay for most of the night.

Amy put on weight quickly and became a robust and rotund cherub, with rosy cheeks and a snub nose.

Her first birthday was more of an adult than a baby celebration, with a house and garden bursting with friends and relatives quaffing large amounts of wine and champagne. Lindsay got very drunk for the first time since the birth and had to go to bed early, even before Amy.

It was a week after Amy's birthday celebrations when Lindsay first started to feel unwell. She was chuffed at how quickly she had shed her baby weight, and now weighed less than she had before the pregnancy. She had noticed over the previous few weeks though, a complete loss of appetite and her tummy felt bloated. At first she simply thought it was down to the high fibre diet she had been on to try and lose the weight, but then decided that she was feeling unwell enough to go to the GP. He checked her over and decided it was likely to be a virus: the stock GP diagnosis when they can't think of anything else. He recommended she try to rest, drink plenty of fluids and stop any breastfeeding as it might be contributing to a hormone imbalance. He told her to come back if she didn't feel better in a week or so.

A month went by and Lindsay was still feeling tired and sick. We had even considered the possibility that she might be pregnant – unlikely but not impossible. A pregnancy test proved negative and so she returned to the doctor. He took some blood and urine samples to send away for testing and promised to phone in a day or so with the results. He was still confident it was something minor given Lindsay's age and general good health.

He phoned on the Saturday morning after he'd finished an emergency surgery. He'd noticed her results on his computer system and was surprised to find us at home, expecting to leave a message on an answering machine. The blood test had detected raised levels of a chemical in the blood called alpha-fetoprotein (AFP), which could indicate what he referred to as 'minor liver functionality anomalies'. He still sounded fairly relaxed but the fact that he had phoned on a Saturday and referred us to a specialist the following week meant *we* were worried.

Lindsay's mum looked after Amy while we drove to the hospital on Friday August the fifteenth, a week after our second wedding anniversary.

The first thing they did was an ultrasound. Lindsay had been told not to eat for twenty-four hours before the appointment, which wasn't a hardship as she didn't feel like eating anyway. It was weird because the last time we had seen the result of an ultrasound, it was a picture of Amy in the womb. We didn't get to see the pictures this time and after it was over we were sent home none the wiser. We got a phone call five days later, with the devastating news that it was possible Lindsay had liver cancer and needed to come back in for a biopsy to confirm the diagnosis. What we didn't know at the time was that if they suspected the cancer was confined to the liver, they

23

normally wouldn't perform a biopsy.

We had some sleepless nights waiting for the call to go into the hospital. Eventually, after a week, we were sent a timetable of what Lindsay could expect. It was effectively a full two days of tests and Lindsay would need to stay in overnight. At the end of the second day we were asked to sit in a large room along the corridor from the cancer unit.

The room was unusual for a hospital in that it was decorated tastefully with neutral colours with what looked like original oil paintings dotted around the walls. There were two long cream leather couches and four matching chairs. On the coffee table in the middle of the room were a number of books and magazines. A complimentary coffee machine gurgled in the corner and the coffee aroma partly masked the clinical hospital smell. It was a room made for delivering bad news.

Eventually the oncologist, a sympathetic and kind man called Alan Blythe, came and sat beside us to explain quietly what they had discovered. His face was serious and his lack of a smile told us all we needed to know, but he tried his best to be positive. He spoke almost exclusively to Lindsay. I felt like a bystander as he explained the situation.

'What seems to have happened is that the symptoms you have been having – loss of appetite, tiredness, bloating and nausea – are down to a large growth on your liver. This is inhibiting the organ's normal function and is mainly responsible for all your discomfort.' He paused for a moment and consulted his notes. 'We can treat the tumour in situ, which means we can apply some aggressive therapy which will reduce the size of the growth and that will make you feel a lot better.'

I noted he said 'reduce the size', not 'get rid of'.

He then looked straight into Lindsay's eyes and said,

'The main problem is that the liver tumour is actually a secondary cancer that has metastasized. In other words, it did not form in the liver but has spread from another site in your body. In your case it appears that it began in your pancreas which would also have contributed to your lack of appetite.'

He went on to spell out the options, which were depressingly few. He outlined supportive care options (which meant pain control) and chemotherapy to extend what he referred to as 'lifespan'. By this time Lindsay had completely shut down and wasn't taking anything in. How can you cope with that kind of news when you are twenty-seven years old and have a baby waiting for you at home?

CHAPTER FOUR

A week after the diagnosis and many tearful days and nights, Lindsay started on a course of chemo and what the medical staff insisted on calling 'supportive care'. The chemo made her very sick and after ten days she called a halt to it, deciding that if she had to die, she damn well wasn't going to do it feeling nauseous for the whole of the time she had left. Even the smell of food made her vomit.

It was almost impossible to get a feel for how long we had left. The doctors were non-committal but positive, saying she was a young, healthy woman (apart from dying of cancer of course) and was strong.

We managed eventually to estimate a figure of around six months, tops. What do you do with six months, when in reality we knew that Lindsay would only be well enough for maybe three or four of those months to do anything meaningful?

We discussed travelling, and between us we wrote down a list of places.

My first choice was Australia.

'We could spend a few weeks touring around,' I suggested enthusiastically.

Lindsay sighed. 'No it's too far away and I wouldn't

want to be on a plane that long with Amy. It'd be too much for her.'

Top of Lindsay's list was Egypt. 'I've always wanted to see the pyramids,' she said wistfully, 'but thinking about it, Egypt is very dirty and busy and I think Amy is too young for us to put her through all that. Also the medical system probably isn't very good. What if Amy got ill or I needed something?'

I put our lists to one side. 'What about going back to America? They're reasonably civilized and clean as long as we avoid Detroit.'

Lindsay laughed and knew I was referring to a business trip she'd been on a few years ago to the city; Lindsay had hated the place. She shook her head. 'I'm sick, Andy, and if I was to need some kind of medical care when we were there it'd bankrupt us and I'm probably uninsurable now.'

Lindsay picked up our bits of paper and scrunched them up into a ball. She smiled brightly having reached a decision. 'I reckon the best thing for us to do is just stay home, we live in one of the nicest cities in the world, why bother travelling away and getting everyone stressed and upset when we can just potter about here. I'd be much happier with that. What I really want to do is to spend time with you and Amy – and my mum of course. My days are numbered and I want to make the most of them.' We sat and formulated a plan and we had tears in our eyes as we worked out how we would spend Lindsay's last days on Earth.

Initially I was to carry on working and we would try to have as normal a life as possible. It helped that Lindsay's mother had retired and was there to help, but it was an intense and emotionally charged time, with Lindsay the most composed and bravest of us all.

We had a family portrait taken, spending a wonderful

afternoon in a photographic studio with wind machines and exotic backdrops. Lindsay bought a fabulous strapless dress and had her make-up and hair professionally done. My hair was its usual unruly mane with a floppy fringe and Amy only sported a dark fuzz at that stage. After that day Lindsay refused to allow any more photographs to be taken of her. Even at her best friend Ellie's wedding in late September she refused to pose for pictures. She had also refused to be Ellie's bridesmaid due to her declining health, and on the day of the wedding we went home just after the meal due to her fatigue.

Towards the end of that month Lindsay had her first really bad day. She awoke with a blinding migraine, her first ever, and couldn't get out of bed. We called the doctor who upped her medication, and said she should stay in a dark room until the pain subsided. Bad days began to become more frequent, sometimes it was a migraine, agonizing stomach cramps or occasionally debilitating back pain that left her curled up in agony. The doctors could only administer their 'supportive care'. I cried for her pain, but had to be brave for Amy who couldn't understand why whole days drifted by without seeing her mummy.

Sometimes her skin was so sensitive she couldn't stand being touched and cowered away when either I or Amy went near her. This was particularly hard on Amy who, again, couldn't understand why her mummy wouldn't cuddle her.

Thankfully there were also what Lindsay termed 'remission' days: times when her pain was bearable and we could do normal things like walk in the park or Christmas shop. We started in October, unsure if Lindsay would be around for Christmas, though her goal was to make that landmark.

Given the pain she was suffering her fortitude was

amazing. She would try and smile as much as she could, and once – at Lindsay's behest – we even went on a pub crawl along George Street, making sure we went into the most expensive bars we could find, ordering champagne every time. We even ended up in a nightclub, ridiculously drunk.

I gave up work completely on 5 November, having agreed an extended leave of absence. The day was a particularly memorable one as it was Lindsay's last 'remission' day.

We took Amy halfway up Arthur's seat and watched the fireworks at the castle. We then went to a nearby restaurant and Lindsay watched me and Amy eat. By this time she couldn't face any food at all but between us we managed to drink two bottles of wine. We went home afterwards and after Amy was asleep, made love for what would be the last time.

Her clothes were hanging off her by this time and on the rare occasion I saw her naked or near naked, she was nothing but a series of angles, held together by sinews and ligaments.

One morning, later that week, I was with her when she stood naked in front of the mirror, staring at herself. 'God, even my tits have all but vanished,' she said incredulously.

I put my arms around her and she leaned back into me. I kissed her neck which made her turn her head and smile, then she placed her hands under her breasts and pushed them up slightly. 'I tell you what though,' she laughed. 'At least they're the same size now.'

I loved the fact that she could still make a joke in the face of such adversity. It was her spirit that kept us all going.

A week after watching the fireworks Lindsay decided she needed to move into a hospice. We had talked about this and planned for it, but it was still a wrench as we knew it spelled the beginning of the end. She was no longer able to manage her own medications and needed more care than I or Pauline could give her. Also as heart-breaking as it was, Amy now cried every time she saw her mummy. She was merely expressing how we all felt.

The first week in the hospice was difficult. We'd go to see Lindsay in the afternoon and early evening before Amy's bedtime, but soon this was restricted only to after-noons as Lindsay was usually asleep due to the effect of her medications by 5 p.m.

At least Lindsay achieved her goal of seeing Christmas. She was transported home on Christmas Eve and spent her last ever night there with us. On Christmas morning she watched from a wheelchair as Amy opened pre-sents and shrieked with delight. We had scented candles burning and the lights twinkled on the last Christmas tree Lindsay would ever see. The excitement unfortunately took its toll and she had to go back before we had lunch. It was the last time Lindsay left the hospice. She died at 11 p.m. on 7 January, holding my hand while Amy slept peacefully on my lap.

The funeral took place five days later in the same church where only a few years earlier we'd been married. It was a desolate and gloomy January morning with intermittent sleet. The service passed me by; I can only remember bits of it. I'm told that Andrew Gillan delivered a touching and appropriate eulogy, whatever that meant, and everyone who mattered to Lindsay was there, except maybe her father. He had managed to avoid Lindsay for most of her life and managed to avoid her death as well. It was his loss and it gave Pauline something to moan about but I wasn't bothered. Lindsay had given up on her father by the age of ten and I had never met the man. He lived in North London with Myah, a Vietnamese woman he had met while working in Thailand years earlier. He sent some drooping flowers and a cheap card. Lindsay deserved better: he shouldn't have bothered.

At the end of the service, just as we lifted the coffin, James Blunt's worldwide hit 'Beautiful' started to play. This was at Lindsay's request; she'd planned her funeral in meticulous detail. As the haunting notes of the song floated up into the rafters of the ancient church my despair sank to the floor. I also knew that from that day forward, whenever I heard that song, it would transport me back to that dark moment.

I remembered lowering her coffin gently into the gaping hole that was to become her grave, and the icy wind that whipped around the cemetery. I remembered the dank scent of the freshly dug earth and the tears that were shed. I recalled the sad faces that floated in front of mine, offering hope, sympathy, memories of happy times and shared grief.

I left the gathering after the funeral early, my excuse being that Amy had to go to bed. The truth was: I'd had enough. I declined any help that evening, leaving Pauline to deal with the food and drink bills, and drove home.

Amy was tired; the day had been an exciting one for her. She obviously knew nothing about funerals, and was now used to her mummy not being around. To her the day was just a long one that stretched her bedtime out to eight o'clock. I didn't bother bathing her but simply washed her hands and face before I settled her down in bed. I let her drink her bottle half-lying down. She drifted off to sleep midway through her milk and I had to pull the teat out of her mouth. It made a popping sound as I did so.

Downstairs in the quiet and warm living room, I allowed myself to weep, the sobs racking my body like electric jolts as I poured out my grief.

Grief is a weird thing. At first I was crying for myself,

not for poor Lindsay. I was grieving for the desolate aching her death had left inside me, then for Amy who would never know her mother, and finally for the world which seemed a much poorer and emptier place without my wife in it.

.

CHAPTER FIVE

That had all been around seven months earlier and there I was, staring at an email. From whom? A prankster? If so, who? Maybe one of Lindsay's old work mates or perhaps someone she had pissed off over the years? My wife was a lovely person but she didn't suffer fools gladly (except me for some reason) so I could understand that maybe somebody somewhere might harbour a grudge against her – but if so, why wait until now?

I began to read the text which was headed up in large letters:

Love Byte 1
My gorgeous husband Andy
I'm pretty sure that you will be shocked to receive this from me, what, six months after my death?

Seven and a bit actually, but not a bad guess in the circumstances I suppose, sweetheart, if this *was* from you.

I'm not sure how long I've got, but I'm in an optimistic mood. I will keep this email short, partly because I'm very tired tonight and partly because I know this will be messing with your head, but I hope you like my title. I know you are not as up on techy stuff as me but a 'byte' – as you should know – is the smallest group of information that a computer can process in one go. And that's what I'm gonna do: give you little 'bytes' of information that your brain can handle – and as they come from me, they are loaded with love!

One more thing. I do hope you had me buried as agreed, Mr Hunter. If you changed your mind and had me cremated I WILL come back and haunt you . . . oops I'm doing that anyway. Cool eh?

Anyway – more of that later. Your first thought will probably be, 'Is this real?'. I mean really from me, not unreal as in you're having a mental breakdown and imagining it or anything LOL, but I can assure you it is.

The other thing you will be wondering is why? Ah, babes, that will become clear later, but in this email, I'm going to break you in gently, like the first time we slept together, can you remember that? I can.

We were in town that Saturday night, I think it was our third date, and we were standing outside that horrible little pub in the high street – you remember the one, it burned down the following summer, no loss there – anyway we were outside because I needed a cigarette, and you were leaning on the wall waiting for me to finish. I looked at you and thought, 'Tonight I'm going to shag you, mister.' I was SO horny, and sure enough you came back to my flat and we made love until the sun came up. OK I didn't exactly break you in gently, and I was a bit worried because – let's face it – you are a few years older than me, and I wasn't sure you'd keep up.

34

But you did. I only mention this really so you will be convinced it's actually me writing and not some hoaxer (is that a word, I'm not sure?).

Hopefully the photo helps too, hard to believe I once looked like that, given the state my body will end up in. The rot's already started, but I'm not going to dwell on that, as I'm sure it will only get worse.

I know this is corny but at least it's original – I'm going to mess with your life for a while. I'll give you my reasons later but it will become clear eventually (I hope!) I think it's only fair. I'm dead, you're alive and you can't stop me anyway. I know you can ignore my emails, but I loved you with all my soul, and if you loved me half as much, then you will listen to me. I have only your and Amy's well-being in mind – honest. I also plan to try and right some wrongs that I couldn't get to do while I was well, but I'll tell you more about that later.

Speak soon – well, not actually speak, that would be scary I think – but you'll have to listen soon in any event!

Your gorgeous wife
Linz XX

And that was it. I read it again and again until I'd practically memorized it and yet I still wasn't fully convinced it was real. Lindsay was a systems analyst, so had a much better grasp of IT than me, but could she really set things up so that I received emails months after she died? The only date I could see was the date it was sent, which was today. I would phone my best mate Jamie the next morning when I got to work and ask him if this was possible. Jamie had an honours degree in something bonkers like Applied Physics and Natural Philosophy, but also had a much better understanding of this stuff than me. I needed to be sure I wasn't being scammed or something before I could believe it.

Lindsay probably wouldn't like the fact that I was going to ask Jamie about her emails. She'd never been his biggest fan and tolerated rather than welcomed him. Her over-riding impression was that he was too good to be true. He was very much a political animal and me and Lindsay, well, we just weren't into politics – which frustrated the hell out of him. Jamie would criticize our consumerist lifestyle and Lindsay didn't like that at all. I also made the mistake once of telling her he'd cheated on his long-term girlfriend Molly which further lowered her opinion of him. He'd cheated on her more than once, but I never told Lindsay that after her reaction.

'He's a hypocrite, preaching to us about morality and avarice whilst he shags about behind Molly's back,' she had ranted when I told her. I felt guilty too as it was me who had introduced them. Molly worked in the Human Resources department in my work and they'd got together after Jamie tagged along on one of my work nights out.

Jamie, though, *was* one of the good guys in some ways. He worked hard to try and help those who could not help themselves, and was never judgemental about those in need – unlike his capitalist friends (me) who in his opinion, needed to do lots more to change the world. He was right of course. He was big on saving the planet, recycling, saving the whale, public transport instead of cars and birth control in the Third World. Mine and Lindsay's efforts at recycling consisted of putting our rubbish bags in other people's bins when ours was full.

He had lain off me since Lindsay's death, probably realizing that I was now one of the ones who needed some kind of saving, even though I wouldn't actively go out and seek it.

Jamie Reitano was extremely good-looking with dark eyes and hair from his Italian lineage. He had a boyish face that girls just adored. Whilst I was thirty-two and looked my age, he was thirty-two going on seventeen. He also had the gift of the gab – he could literally have sold sand to the Arabs. If he decided to turn his back on his socialist conscience and sell BMWs instead, he'd make a fortune. I had told him more times than I could count that he was wasting his talent.

He was also the only person I could think of at that point who would be able to tell me if the emails were likely to be real.

I left my iPad lying on the couch and headed off to bed, checking on Amy before sliding under the duvet. The bed still felt empty and cold without my wife in it. We'd only been together a relatively short time, but it was amazing how quickly I'd become used to her sharing my space.

The next morning, after a disturbed sleep peppered with strange dreams, I awoke before Amy and before Pauline turned up. I managed to shower, dress and consume some muesli before Amy started shouting, 'Daddy, Daddy where are you?'

I pretended not to hear her. This was a game we often played in the morning, and eventually she padded through in her bare feet from her bedroom having kicked her socks off again during the night. Her hair was all over the place and she had one of her arms out of her pyjama top. She regarded me accusingly. 'Amy shouting.'

I smiled at her. 'I know.'

'Daddy not come.' I wasn't sure if that was a question or a statement, so I agreed with her, and slipped her arm back in the top. She smelled of innocence and sleep and

I inhaled her scent deeply. I noticed once again that her vocabulary was always present tense.

'Daddy play with dolls' house?' It was definitely a question this time.

'No, sweetheart, Daddy's going to workies. Gran is coming, she'll play with you.'

I could see the wheels going around in her head, as she decided whether to pout and kick up a fuss or wait and exploit Pauline on that front. Amy was at her most intelligent in the mornings, and decided on the latter. I gave her Rice Krispies for breakfast. She ate a few, smeared some over her teddy's nose and the rest found their way onto the floor as usual.

Pauline arrived soon after and shook her head at the mess we'd made.

'Just leave everything and get off to work, I'll tidy up,' she ordered.

I nodded and said guiltily, 'Thanks, Pauline. I'm not at my best in the mornings.'

I grabbed my jacket and left my apartment. I had realized a long time ago that there are two types of people in the world: morning people and everybody else.

My wife was a morning person; I am not. I've always resented having to get up early for work to fit in with their timetable. I'd much rather have started at lunchtime and finished at eight at night. I once moaned about this to Lindsay saying, 'I don't understand why the world is run by morning people.'

My wife answered pragmatically as usual. 'It's simple, sweetie, the world is run by morning people because they get up early and get there first.'

Once out in the fresh air, I glanced up at the sky. It was blue and clear, though the weather forecast had predicted rain. The weather for most of the summer had been unusually bad. People don't live in Scotland for the weather, but we expect a little sunshine in the summer months to make up for the practically perpetual grey skies the country endures for the majority of the year. To make up for it, August – thankfully – had mostly been warm and sunny. Today was no exception and consequently the bus that took me to work was stuffy and airless.

There was the usual mix of people on board, at the front in the easy-to-reach seats were a number of pensioners, up at the crack of dawn and out and about when they really didn't need to be. When I eventually got to retire, the last thing I'd want to do is get up early and go places. I thought the whole point of being a pensioner was to relax and take your time, sleep more and watch crap morning telly, where the ad breaks tried to sell you funeral plans and bus tours to Swansea.

I might change my mind when I get to be that age, I suppose. My mum was a pensioner and she liked getting up early, she always has. It might be something to do with being in the 'end zone' of life, and sleeping at that stage might appear to be a waste of time. But I think it is just a generational thing: my mum grew up on a farm in the fifties and they were all up early feeding livestock and things, so it was expected that you went to bed early and got up early. But then the telly shut down at nine o'clock in those days as well.

As well as a healthy sprinkling of pensioners, the bus also had the usual smattering of mothers – it was always the mothers – taking their kids to school or nursery.

Despite my pass-remarkable attitude I actually liked public transport, I didn't need to find a parking space, or pay through the nose for the privilege. I didn't need to worry about going for a few beers after work, not that I did that very often, but it was always an option. Above all I didn't need to fork out directly for the petrol required to sit in a traffic jam going nowhere for half an hour. Also on the bus I got to people watch. The only thing I would change would be to fit air-conditioning for these occasional hot days, and improve the suspension so that they didn't rattle and bounce so much over the pot-holed streets of Scotland's capital. The trams were due to be introduced any day now, but then the council had been saying that for nearly five years and I wasn't holding my breath.

CHAPTER SIX

Although it was a good place for daydreaming and people watching, I didn't always use the bus. I also owned a three-year-old Audi A4 Quattro. I think to the majority of the female half of the population that won't mean much, and to be honest I'm with them on that. My wife was the car-mad half of our partnership, being weird that way. She loved cars, football and boxing. I could do the football bit, the boxing I never understood the point of, and cars to me were really just about getting from A to B.

When I first met Lindsay I was driving a ten-year-old Honda Civic, in my opinion a perfectly acceptable and very reliable vehicle. (I remember that I said those exact words to her on our second date. I daresay that if we'd had that conversation on our third date, we might not have had our first shag.) Anyway, she had just taken a large mouthful of wine and choked. Some of the wine dribbled out of her nose (attractive or what?) as she coughed and spluttered. That was when I started to learn more about Lindsay and cars. She owned a bright red (every car had to be bright red for her) Mercedes SLK convertible, and the insurance costs at the time for her must have been huge – she was only twenty-four. Soon after, she traded it for a BMW 1 series and just before we got married, that was traded for the Audi. (Note the car lingo, 'traded': Lindsay taught me that.)

The Audi for Lindsay was an acknowledgment of her becoming an adult; it had room for five grown-ups. One night, not long after our wedding when we were out and had, just for a change, drunk too much, she tried to explain her theory about cars with five seats in a sexy slurry voice. I was daft enough to listen – probably because she had a sexy slurry voice. Blokes love sexy slurry voices, especially when they belong to their wives.

'Cars with five seats are either for a mummy, daddy and two kids in child seats, because after the child seats are installed there's no room really for anyone else, or for the catholic family with three kids – but in reality that wouldn't work because if you had three kids the boot wouldn't be big enough for all the stuff, and you would need to move up to an SUV or a weird family car like the Renault Espace. No, what really happens in cars with five seats is that you have space for mummy, daddy and baby. Then if you need help there's room for your mother, or if you are really posh, an au pair, though she would probably demand to sit in the front.'

Lindsay paused and I could see her alcohol-fogged mind whirring. 'When we have our baby, I think we could afford a nanny, or an au pair, especially if I went back to work full-time. What do you reckon?'

I nodded and smiled, agreeing to anything as long as the sexy slurry voice kept talking. 'Yeah, probably.'

She misinterpreted my contented expression, probably because in my inebriated state it resembled a leer.

With an aggressive change to her voice she said, glaring at me, 'Then the cow would want to shag my husband and that would definitely cause some problems, and if she was nice-looking then you'd probably want to shag her back.' Lindsay paused with tears in her eyes. 'I can't believe you want to shag the au pair; we've only been married a few weeks, and you are cheating on me already.'

I remembered, unsuccessfully, trying to work out where the sexy voice had gone and how the hell I'd ended up in this conversation, especially in the middle of a busy bar. Lindsay stomped off out of the pub in a huff. I chased after her, the cool air only accentuating the effect of the wine we had drunk. 'Lindsay, what's the matter?'

She turned to face me. 'You're the matter. Shagging the fucking au pair, and we've not even got a baby yet.' Three youths walked passed jeering at us arguing.

'Lindsay, stop shouting. I haven't shagged the au pair, I wouldn't shag the au pair. We haven't even got an au pair.'

Lindsay considered this new information for a moment. 'I know, but you would, wouldn't you?' She pointed her finger at me accusingly, her eyes blazing. 'She'd be a little blonde thing, twenty-two, over from California or Thailand for work experience and she'd make sure she was alone with you when I was out, and slowly wheedle her way in, seduce you, then before you know it, I'd come home and catch the two of you. She's got her knickers off and your hand's up her skirt. I've seen it before, happens all the time.' She turned and stomped off again.

I couldn't help smiling now. I doubted very much she'd seen it before, and I also doubted it happened all the time, maybe in porn-land it might happen all the time, but not to me, and not in Edinburgh. Also I wasn't sure anyone coming from Thailand would be blonde, and I didn't think 'wheedle' was a word.

Eventually I caught up with my wife and promised that we simply wouldn't employ an au pair and the problem would never happen. We flagged down a taxi and, thankfully, Lindsay fell asleep as soon as the door closed.

43

So that was how a discussion about cars ended up with me shagging an imaginary au pair. The image was not unappealing but a complete fantasy. Every day some memory would find its way to the front of my mind. It might be something I saw, smelt, or heard, like a song, and I would instantly be transported back to some event or incident connected with Lindsay. I had to admit they had become less common over the last few months as time moved on.

I was brought back to reality as it was my stop and time to get off the bus. I squeezed past a double buggy with cute twins, waited for the doors to open and plodded up the hill toward the office. I stopped at a small bakery for a fruit scone and a sandwich for later. The sunny morning had disappeared behind dark clouds and rain looked likely. I hated it when the weather forecasters got it right.

I ran the gauntlet of good mornings – seventeen on that particular day, which must have been a new record – and sat at my desk, switched on the computer and stared at my computer screen waiting for the log-in procedure to finish. My job at Perennial Mutual was Regional Risk Assessor, known internally as RRA. Whenever I said that it sounded incredibly dull, and to be honest it was incredibly dull, but it was a secure job that paid well.

I didn't ever set out to be an RRA. Who does? I was awarded a second class BA in Business, by my third-class university, attended a recruitment day sponsored by Perennial Mutual, and before I knew it I was employed as a Regional Risk Assistant, known internally as RRa, note the small 'a', a very important distinction within the firm. Several years later, my elderly boss dropped dead of a heart attack whilst skiing in Biarritz and Bob's your auntie, I'm promoted.

I'd discovered that huge companies hate the word 'risk'.

It doesn't matter to them that what you do is largely ineffectual and irrelevant, the fact you have the word 'risk' attached to your job title gave you gravitas and credibility. Perennial Mutual, known by staff as PM due to Perennial Mutual being a bit of a mouthful, was no different in that respect. The PM bit had led to some distractions for bored staff and I had heard it referred to as Pre-Menstrual, Pretty Mental, Poor Money and Post-Modernism by a trainee actuary who went to art school.

Most people regretted asking me what I did for a living, because after less than twelve seconds (and I've timed it) their eyes would glaze over and they would rather be sticking needles in their genitals than continuing the conversation. I'd taken to just telling them that I opened envelopes all day long. That way they are never sure whether to believe me or not. The wonderful thing about that is that kids believe me. One of Amy's little friends had an older brother called Kieran, and whenever I saw him he would ask me how many envelopes I'd opened that day. I always told him some astronomical number that he could not, with his ten-year-old brain, possibly comprehend, like three hundred and fourteen thousand twelve hundred and three. I always tried to end in a three for continuity.

In reality I'd always seen my job as a means to an end. It provided me with something to do during the day so I didn't get too bored, I got paid reasonably well and it was a decent environment to make friends and meet new people, hell it was here that I had met Lindsay. If I hadn't have been working here I would never have set eyes on her, and we would never have got together. Lindsay, incidentally, didn't like the envelope story much, as she thought it was demeaning, which made me use it more and more – but I'm a bloke and annoying that way.

These days I had my own office and didn't sit in the

open-plan arrangement anymore. I picked up the phone and dialled Jamie's number. A chirpy female voice answered. The voice belonged to Meredith, whose high-pitched tone sounded like it belonged to a 16-year-old school-leaver. In actual fact, Meredith was seventy-one years old, had more stubble on her chin than me after four days without shaving and wore wire spectacles held together by Sellotape. She had gone to work for the council after retiring from a bank. I was not sure why they hired her as there were scores of young unemployed kids begging for jobs. I believe she benefited from some obscure council policy of positive discrimination for older workers. As always, her first response was that Mr Reitano was in a meeting and couldn't be disturbed. I'd learned over the years from calling Jamie that arguing with Meredith was pointless. I knew three things for sure:

- Jamie never had meetings in his office because there was nowhere to hold a meeting in his 'office'. It consisted of one small room with a tiny toilet cubicle they shared with Madame Gonzo, a spiritualist who rented the shop next door. Jamie worked for Edinburgh District Council and headed up a department called 'Edinburgh Resource Distribution'. The title sounded very grand but in reality he had responsibility for himself and Meredith. His principal role was to find and allocate housing, charity funds or benefit entitlements to those unable to navigate the complex systems for themselves. He always met the people he was trying to help away from his office.
- It was 10 a.m. and Jamie would be in Starbucks catching up on his emails and drinking a crappy frappe latte or something.

- He'd have a hangover from drinking red wine the night before.

I left a message and hung up. Thirty minutes later my mobile rang and Jamie's gruff voice asked, 'Andy, what's happening?'

'Just the usual, Jamie: running after Amy, trying to work and keeping lots of balls in the air.'

'How is Amy?'

I knew Jamie wasn't really interested in how Amy was, he just asked as he thought it was the right thing to do. Jamie and his girlfriend Molly had no kids, well, not yet anyway, so his comprehension of what it meant to be a parent was limited. I didn't hold that against him. It wasn't that long ago that I was as clueless about kids as he was.

'Amy's good, Jamie, a pain in the arse just now, but I understand that's normal.'

'Look, Molly was saying last night that you haven't been over to the flat since. . . .' The pause on the line made me smile. Jamie was not good at dealing with personal issues such as my widowerhood. It was ironic given his skill at manipulating the system for all the underprivileged and lost causes he dealt with on a daily basis.

I bailed him out. '. . . since Lindsay died. I know, Jamie, don't worry about it. I'll get over soon, I promise. I'm actually calling for some advice.'

'Advice?' I could hear Jamie's incredulity on the other end of the phone. 'I thought you were financially OK after Lindsay died. I mean, to be honest, Andy, I'm not sure that the sort of accommodation I can get would suit you, it's all a bit . . . well . . . crap I suppose.'

I laughed out loud on the phone, partly because he'd misunderstood my request and partly because he'd described the accommodation he secured for his waifs and strays as 'crap'. 'I hope you do a better sales job than that when you meet your prospective tenants.'

'Yeah, well. You have different . . . standards.'

I laughed again. 'Oh yeah, I forgot I'm a hopeless capitalist.'

It was Jamie's turn to laugh, 'OK then, I'm assuming from your tone that you aren't looking for access to my office's professional services?'

I smiled at the picture in my head of Jamie and Meredith squeezed into their tiny space. 'No, I need to ask you an IT question.'

'IT? Is there nobody in your office who can handle that stuff?'

Good point. The thought hadn't crossed my mind. That would've been a better option. Never mind, too late now.

'Yeah probably, but I know you are up on this sort of stuff and need to know something – is it possible to send emails from the past?'

'Eh?'

This was going to be difficult, I'd decided at the last minute not to tell Jamie about the emails from Lindsay, he'd probably think I'd lost the plot.

'OK, I've been receiving some emails from a company that no longer exists, it closed down years ago, but the emails appear to be current.'

'Eh?'

For someone with a brain capacity the size of Wales, my friend's vocabulary was surprisingly limited at times.

'All I need to know Jamie is, is it possible for someone, or some company to set something up that means that emails are delayed from being sent by say a week, or a month?'

This time there was no response, no more 'Eh's' thankfully. I took that to be a good sign and that he was actually thinking. He could of course have put the phone down with boredom and wandered off somewhere, to the other side of his expansive office or out for a sandwich I suppose, but I assumed he was thinking. Jamie liked to think.

'Well, if you had someone good, who knew what they were doing, then, yes, you could do that. I'm not sure why you would want to – but, yes, it could be done.' That was all I needed to know, Lindsay was very good at her job.

Jamie continued. 'You just need to build in a delay so that the email is only sent on a pre-determined date in the future. What's this all about?'

'I'm not altogether sure,' I replied, which was the first honest answer I'd given him. 'I'll let you know when I find out,' I lied. 'One more thing, how can I check when the actual email was written?'

'Well that bit's pretty easy, you just go to the file section of the email, click on properties and it should show you when it was modified, and that would give you a date.'

'Thanks, Jamie, I just wanted to make sure that what is happening is technically possible.'

'Well, yeah, it is technically quite easy, but it sounds like it's worrying you, Andy. Maybe you should report it to your IT people and see if they can stop the source, but you need to make sure it isn't being done via different service providers.'

'Eh?' My turn to lose the power of speech.

'We recently dealt with some cyber bullying in one of our case conferences.'

I smiled as two visions flashed into my head: Jamie and Meredith sitting huddled round a manila file in Starbucks discussing one of his clients, and then Meredith being smacked over the head with a miniature plastic Cyberman from 'Doctor Who'. Maybe that was how her glasses kept getting broken.

Jamie was oblivious to my visions and explained with a sigh. 'Basically a service provider is a company that allows you access to email, there are thousands of them, but if we are talking UK only and assuming only the free ones would be used, you are probably looking at a few hundred. That includes your AOL, Yahoo!, Gmail and so on. . . .'

I was silent for a moment thinking it through. 'OK, thanks Jamie, that was very informative. I'll let you get back to your busy day.'

I promised to go over to his flat soon, something that I would put off for as long as possible. Jamie was my best friend, but going over to his flat for dinner with him and his girlfriend Molly felt desperate in some way. I'm not sure why – maybe because they were a couple and it would be a painful reminder of what I had lost.

Lindsay and I had sometimes hung out with Jamie and Molly and maybe it was the reminder of good times I was shying away from, but maybe I was simply over-thinking everything as usual. All I knew was that I wanted to avoid going there, and I didn't try to analyze it any further at that point.

After I hung up the phone I sat back in my seat to ponder on the conversation. Jamie had rightly detected I was worried, but I wasn't worried about cyber bullying – although part of me wondered if what Lindsay was doing could be construed as such? I imagined her smacking me over the head with a plastic Cyberman and smiled. It was comforting to think that my contact with Lindsay wasn't finished. The problem with death is its finality. One minute there is this living, breathing presence and the next you are left with nothing except memories. The fact that there was still going to be some contact from her excited me. It meant it wasn't the end. I knew, of course, that it would be a one-way conversation. But for me, for now, that was enough.

I allowed my memory to drift back to the first time I

ever set eyes on Lindsay. It had been early one morning on 10 February 2009. I knew that because I recorded it on my Outlook calendar. She was working on some IT thing – she called it an 'SS Rebooting Upgrade', which sounds like something Hitler might have done if he was still around. I only remember that because I'd entered it on my calendar as well (must have been a slow day).

It was a quirky way to meet, because after being on holiday for a week I'd sat down at my desk with a large latte from Starbucks, switched on my computer and tried to log on to the company network. Suddenly there was a scuffling noise from under my desk and her head popped up between my knees, dark hair falling over her eyes.

I'd quickly glanced around the open-plan office to see if everyone had a pretty girl under their desk, just in case it was a new company perk which had been introduced while I'd been away, but everybody else seemed to be bereft of such a benefit.

She smiled up at my puzzled face and explained she was doing the SS thing, and I wouldn't be able to log on for at least an hour. And that was it. No lightning bolt, no romantic meeting during a thunderstorm. Just a pretty face staring up at me from between my knees – a wonderful male fantasy moment, except we had our clothes on. She probably sensed this because she soon stood up and asked me to move away so she could work properly on whatever it was she was doing.

Thankfully she was working on the 'Main Hub Node' which just happened to be situated under my desk, and had to come back to that point on a regular basis throughout the week. This meant I had time to work up the courage to ask her out. Thank God for Main Hub Nodes and whoever their inventor was because it took me four days and six hours to do so. She told me later that she didn't actually need to be there on the Friday, but just

51

came back to see me and if I hadn't have asked her out, she would have left the office and never have seen me again, which would have been a shame, especially for Amy who wouldn't exist.

My desk phone rang to rudely pull me back to reality and remind me that I was actually supposed to be working. I spent the rest of the day trying to be productive but my mind kept drifting back to Lindsay and her email.

Then at three o'clock I received another shock. My phone pinged telling me I had a new text and when I read it I could hardly believe what I was seeing.

Hi Andy, Lnzy here – hopefully by now Jamie has assured u that my email is real and that it is possible to contact you from beyond the grave – WHOOOOOOO SPOOKY!!!!!!!!!! Jst in case ur wondering I cd guess that u'd phone him ur so predictable still! Love u sweetie xxx

CHAPTER SEVEN

The shock of receiving both an email and a text from my wife, who was in her grave, made me decide not to tell anyone else for the time being. The main reason was that it sounded really weird. A part of me also wanted to keep the contact secret because it was exciting and sharing it would dilute that excitement for me. My life had been pretty dull since Lindsay died, and this certainly looked like it might shake things up. Who wouldn't find being haunted – which is what it felt like to me – exciting?

I didn't phone Jamie for confirmation that it was possible for Lindsay to do what she was doing via text. I figured that if she could manage to send emails seven months after her funeral then texts would be a piece of cake. However, even after receiving Lindsay's text, I still followed Jamie's instructions and managed to discover Lindsay's original email was created on 12 October. I checked my personal emails at least twice a day for the rest of the week, but it was Thursday evening before I received the next one.

Shortly after settling Amy down to sleep, I closed the blinds on the picture windows of my apartment and switched on the lamps that were strategically positioned around the perimeter of the huge living space. It always made it feel more intimate and cosy. I popped the top off a Corona, plonked myself down on the black leather couch and switched on my iPad. This time Lindsay had helpfully stuck the date on the end of the title. I read it eagerly.

Love Byte 2 – 14th October

Hi my gorgeous husband, at this moment you and Amy are sleeping upstairs, I'm wide awake and needed some paracetamol for my head which is throbbing. I will no doubt need more than that soon, but while I'm waiting for them to kick in I thought I would send you an email.

Tonight I'm going to try and explain what I'm doing. You probably won't like it initially, but I can't change it now.

My grand plan is to find you a new woman, not necessarily a new wife, but a new girlfriend at least. Now I know you are probably shell-shocked by this revelation, but I'm not doing it just for you, but for Amy too. My baby needs a mummy and I know I probably sound just like my mum, who is probably driving you demented by now, but she means well, just like me.

I love you, Andy, but you are pretty hopeless with women, and you probably have this time thing in your head – you know, waiting two years before going out on a date or whatever, but that's too long so I've been doing a little research into the whole dating thing. I once joined an online dating site. I never told you about that, I probably would have one day, had I lived long enough. It was a laugh, and I met a few nice men, one of them was Alexander, the polo player. I told you about him, remember?

I paused my reading to think. When Lindsay and I started dating seriously, we went through our lists of former conquests and relationships. Lindsay outnumbered me three to one, but that wasn't surprising given she was more outgoing than me. I enjoyed jokingly calling her a slut sometimes after that, though I'm not sure *she* enjoyed it that much. Maybe that was why she hadn't told me about the Internet dating. I remembered Alexander though. She had gone out with him for about a year before he cheated on her with his sister's best friend. His loss.

I didn't tell you we'd met online, but I found the whole Internet dating thing exciting in some ways and embarrassing in others. Sometimes you'd meet someone and it would be great, the chemistry would be perfect. Other times it felt like a job interview – weird. Often physical attraction had nothing to do with it, you'd simply sit down with this person and there'd be zero, zilch, no spark, no energy, nothing. Even if we'd had great telephone conversations or emails or MSN chats, sometimes there'd be nothing. It taught me that it's all about chemistry – you either have it or you don't. Like the time we met, as soon as I emerged from under your desk I just knew. So why am I telling you all this? Well you've probably worked it out, but just in case you haven't I want you to go on some Internet dates.

I've already done a lot of the groundwork for you, I've been chatting to women online for a few weeks now, and it's great fun pretending to be a man. Not pretending to be you at this stage obviously, but even without a photo, just about every woman wanted to meet up with me. Some even asked if I was gay, saying I was right into their psyche! I would have made a great lesbian. That's a thought, isn't it? I bet you would've liked that wouldn't you? Well you'd have liked to watch at any rate. I know this is probably freaking you out . . .

She was right it was, especially the lesbian bit.

. . . but please indulge your dead wife. I'm not sure how long I'll be able to keep this up, but to me it feels like I'm doing something positive, so please humour me. ☺ I mean well. Of course, this might all be in vain and you might have already found another woman, in which case I'm sad and hurt ☹. But knowing you as I do, I don't think so. After all, it took you a week to ask me out, and in the end I was practically begging you!

OK. So where do we start? Or, rather, where do you start? I've organized everything via a dating site called Love Bitz. Just in case you miss the inflections, it is meant to read 'love bites' as opposed to 'love bits' – though either pronunciation has interesting connotations, don't you think?

I like that it fits in with my theme as well, though I think calling it 'Love Bytes' would have been smarter.

Anyway, I've chosen this site partly because of the name but mostly because it has a huge number of Scottish girls on it, and with Amy to look after, staying local's important. I've paid for one year's subscription, and your details went live ten days ago, that is in your time obviously not my time. Confusing, isn't it? So from 5 August your profile has been live.

You can look it up if you like, your username is andyh (all lower case) and your password is amy2012.

If I've pitched you right – which I will have because I'm good at this stuff (no sense in false modesty now that I'm dying) – you should get a good number of emails. I've also selected a number of girls that I've sent your details to and an email pretending to be from you. A number of others will get the same in a few weeks' time, so if you don't get on with any of these first girls, you've still got options. You'll know which ones these are because they will reply to you.

As an extra insurance policy I've auto-emailed a few girls from another dating site, suggesting they meet you for a date this Friday and Saturday evening at the Kitch bar in George Street. (It'll make a little more sense in a minute – I promise.) I've set up your profile on that site too, but I'm not telling you which one in case you try and wriggle out of it. Being the gentleman that you are, you will not stand them up I know – they will only have got the email today, so I'm hoping at least one of them will take a chance and meet you each evening. I've made the whole thing appear very cloak and dagger and mysterious like some romantic mystery novel, so I'm hoping at least one of them will be intrigued enough to show up.

The only flaw in my plan is that it will have been some time – six months maybe – since these girls were looking and they may be all loved-up by now. But nothing ventured, nothing gained. And, as I well know, love can sometimes take its time. (Another flaw I've just spotted is that actually more than one or all of them could turn up – that would be a laugh, eh?)

I wasn't even smiling.

The girls that I have asked to meet you (remember they think it was you) are: Jackie, Joan, Ellen and Anne on Friday and Paula, Jane, Caroline & Terry on Saturday. (I assume Terry's a girl; she looked like one, but if she turns up and has a willy I give you permission to leave immediately!)

They all have one thing in common – blonde hair. I know George Street at the weekend is full of blondes, but I have told them you will be in the pub at 7 p.m. sitting at the end of the bar near the toilets.

(I've just thought of another flaw. The pub could have burnt down, or gone out of business, or changed its name, in which case you're fucked – or rather you won't have any chance to be fucked – sorry for the language.)

Well, that's it for now. The deed is done, the stage is set, and the die is cast and all that. It's now up to you, at least for a while. I feel a bit weird setting you up, and really jealous picturing you with some other girl, especially some of the prettier ones. I've even been talking to an au pair – if you can remember that night. It's very difficult for me on one level, but on another, I'm sure it's the right thing to do.

One last thing. In my previous email I said I wanted to right a few wrongs and I've begun the process tonight, well, I've started the ball rolling anyway. You'll find out soon enough what it's all about, and the least you know about it just now the better it'll be for you. I've just re-read that last paragraph and it's not very well worded but trust me, I know what I'm doing. That's one of the things about dying and being in pain; it really focuses the mind.

I will be in touch again soon. In the meantime, please
give it a go. I'll expect an update next time I email you.
LOL. This is what I would have wanted, honest!
Your gorgeous wife
Linz XX

P.S. It's probably NOT a good idea to tell any girls you
meet that your dead wife set all this up. They might think
it's a bit creepy!

Only a *bit* creepy? I re-read the email a few times, and
felt spaced, as if I'd been eating dope cake or something.
The few times I'd ingested drugs had been on a trip to
Amsterdam with Lindsay. It had been cannabis cake and
that was the feeling I had now.

I had been wondering what Lindsay was up to, and
now that I'd found out, it went beyond anything I was
expecting. I wasn't sure what to do.

Was I ready to meet someone else?

It was scary thinking about emails dropping into
strange women's inboxes, emails that I had no hand in
writing.

So what should I do?

It boiled down to two options: I either ignored all
future emails from Lindsay, or I indulged Lindsay's dying
wishes and tried to meet someone new.

It was no contest and I logged on to Love Bitz.

CHAPTER EIGHT

Initially I just read over my profile. The photo Lindsay had selected was one with me and Amy from the photo-shoot we'd done before Lindsay became really ill. It was a flattering photo, which I assumed is why she chose it. I had on an expensive suit, shirt and tie and my dark hair was tidy but still quite long. My blue eyes had been slightly air-brushed to make them stand out more. Putting Amy in the picture also told anyone looking that I had a daughter before they read my byline.

Was that likely to put some women off? Probably, but then there was no point in trying to hide the fact, was there? If someone wanted to be with me, Amy was going to be a huge part of that relationship. I suppose it also told them that my sperm worked.

The blurb that went with the picture was very simple and light-hearted.

My name is Andy Hunter, I am looking for a special and wonderful person to spend time with. I'm not looking for a fling or a one-night stand because I'm not very good at that sort of thing. I have a wonderful young daughter who was entrusted to my care when her mother (my wife) died. Amy is my number one girl, and always will be.

She doesn't need a mother (been there, done that) but a good friend she can be comfortable with and who can teach her girly stuff would be welcome. I don't do girly stuff well because I'm not a girly, but before you can get around to doing any of that you have to be able to like me, which shouldn't be too hard.

I'm a nice guy who is reasonably tidy (having been married I know how important that can be) with a laid-back outlook on life. I can cook, tidy and grow cress seeds in margarine tubs – I actually do that for my daughter, but it is a useful skill nevertheless.

That was the main introduction. The rest of the profile was all about my personality (*easy going*), likes and dislikes (*curry and shellfish*), appearance (*six feet tall, slim, blue eyes and easy smile*), distinguishing marks (*dimple on chin*), annoying traits (*floppy fringe* – well, Mrs Hunter, you got that bit wrong because I've had my hair cut short since you left me alone – *nose slightly too big for face, or maybe face slightly too small for nose, depending on which way you look at it*).

The last section seemed to be trying to put people off me, but what did I know? It also listed 'partner preferences' which was alarmingly vague, and didn't specifically exclude women with warts, dog breath or hairy toes, or God forbid anyone possessing all three in combination. Potential partners with such unfortunate traits I would definitely have removed from my list had I been allowed to do so. I thought about amending the details especially when one of my main interests was listed as cars. (One of Lindsay's little jokes, I assumed.) However I decided to trust my wife's judgement and let it be.

At the top of the page was an inbox in the shape of pouting cherry lips. It was flashing with a tiny number eight in the right hand corner. Being the perceptive chap that I was, I assumed that this meant there were eight messages waiting. I clicked on the icon and it opened up my Love Bitz inbox. The first message was from the site administrator welcoming me to Love Bitz. The second email was from Melody.

> Aw, sweetheart, thank you for your wonderful and perceptive email. . . .

I wondered what Lindsay had said to her. I really should have known because at some point I was going to have to compose another one and it would almost certainly be a disappointment.

> . . . but I'm so sorry I've met the new love of my life now and I am no longer available. We met on another dating site, and have been going out for five months. What a shame because you sound so lovely and so lost. I tell you what, I'll keep your email and if it doesn't work out with Steve – Steve's the new love of my life by the way – I'll maybe email you then.
>
> Love and Kisses
> Mel xxxxxxx

As pleasant as this email was, the fact that Steve was described as the *new* love of her life hinted to me that she had already been through a few *'loves of her life'* and maybe I didn't want to become the next one.

Email number three was from Stacy who had mastered brevity and simply said:

Fuck off, you creepy bastard.

Email number four was also from Stacy.

Oh My God – I am so sorry, I thought you were someone else. Oh My God, I feel terrible I didn't mean to upset you.

I sat back on the couch. Did I feel upset? No. I wasn't upset, a little scared maybe but not upset. Stacy continued.

Oh My God.

Although I'd never met Stacy her stock phrase was already beginning to irritate me.

You see I've been getting really nasty emails from a guy I met on here, and I was sure I'd got one today from him. He's called Andy as well and I assumed when your email popped into my inbox it was from him but. . . . You're not him are you! You're beautiful and sweet and you have a gorgeous daughter and we could maybe have been together forever. Oh My God I've blown it haven't I?

Never mind, you have a nice life now.

Stacy xxxx

After the first few emails I began to question my dead wife's judgement and my own sanity. The fifth email was from Amanda.

Hi Andy, thanks for your email, you sound really lovely, and your daughter is beautiful. I liked your profile, it is refreshingly honest and after reading that and your email I feel like I almost know you. I'd love to chat more but the only problem is I'm packing tonight for a trip tomorrow to Ireland to visit my grandparents for three weeks. I'll email you when I get back yeah?

Take care for now
Amanda xx

PS I've added you to my friends.

PPS I've been thinking – by the time I get back you might have been snapped up and I'd be kicking myself so here is my mobile number, send me a text and we can maybe chat on the phone sometime. Xxx

The sixth email as I expected was also from Amanda.

Yeah I know it would help if I ACTUALLY gave you my mobile number wouldn't it? I am a bit scatty at times, BUT I'm cute – scatty and cute that's not a bad combination.

Text me – 07992 776122.
Amanda xx

Well that was better. I clicked on her profile and because I'd been added to her friends I could see her pictures. The first picture of Amanda (29) showed her sitting on the edge of a desk (I assumed at her work), in a pale skirt ending just above her knees which revealed shapely legs. She was petite with red hair. A pretty face was decorated with a smattering of freckles and an infectious smile. The second picture showed her on a night out with friends, laughing and having a good time. I could like

Amanda. I sent her a quick text so she had my number, seemed only fair. I opened the next email.

Hi Andy

Linda here, thank you for your gentle email, and thank you for the compliment, not many men would appreciate that. Maybe we could chat and see how we get on – let me know.

Linda xx

Unfortunately she gave me no hint about what the compliment was. My wife is/was very annoying.

I clicked on her profile. The first picture showed Linda (32) to be a tall, slender woman. The background of the picture showed her standing outside an impressive-looking detached house wearing a summer dress and flat shoes. She had blonde hair and a round but not unattractive face.

I approved. She looked all right, a nice girl, the sort Pauline might approve of. Maybe the sort of girl I could take home to meet my mum as well. I could see them wandering around Sainsbury's together collecting bits and pieces for dinner.

The second picture I clicked on showed her lying back on a bed supported by a number of coloured pillows and cushions. I noted that the bedroom was pleasantly neutral in its decoration, with the exception of the curtains which were a little too flowery for my taste. Her blonde hair was pinned back from her face by an attractive red butterfly clasp and she had a cheeky smile on her pretty face.

But what really grabbed my attention was the large banana inserted in her vagina and the fresh cream smeared liberally all over her large breasts. Two small strawberries were strategically positioned over each nipple. Linda's photograph certainly changed my opinion of her being a girl Pauline would take to, and the thought of her selecting items for a fruit salad in Sainsbury's with my mum was no longer such an innocent one.

I flipped back to the inbox and opened the last one.

HI Andy, Chloe here, bugger off, I'm married.

That puzzled me: why would a married woman be on a dating site? I opened her profile and her picture showed a slim girl with dark hair and fabulous cheekbones. Nowhere on her profile did it mention she was married. Maybe she only said that to anyone she wasn't interested in or maybe she just said it to everyone and was clinically insane – anything was possible. I wondered if being told to 'bugger off' amounted to cyber bullying – I must remember to ask Jamie.

Apart from Chloe, Lindsay obviously had the knack of chatting in romantic terms to women. I was again left wondering what her technique was. If I could have bottled it and sold it to feckless blokes like me, I'd have made a fortune.

I was still reluctant to do anything about the whole dating thing and Lindsay would have been well aware of that. That was why she had set up the Friday/Saturday night dates. I was unsure and nervous . . . no not nervous, terrified. I hadn't been on a date since . . . well, since I had met Lindsay.

CHAPTER NINE

I spent Friday morning and the early afternoon with Amy. Friday was one of my 'off-work' days this week. First we went to Red Roosters, a huge soft-play arena and then I took her swimming – part of our usual routine. For some weird reason I couldn't help thinking about 'the little red-haired girl' Amanda, then thought that the phrase sounded familiar. I remembered eventually that it was from the Charlie Brown and Peanut books. Charlie Brown had an unrequited love thing going on with a little red-haired girl in a number of the stories. I always thought it was incredibly sad that he never got the girl and never got to kick that damn football. I once read that the whole red-haired girl thing was to do with Charles Schulz, the writer of the Peanuts stories, being spurned by the woman he loved when he was young.

I'm not sure if he suffered a similar traumatic experience on the sports field that led to the whole football issue, but I wouldn't be surprised. I hoped my experience with Amanda, if I ever had one, didn't end up like that. And of course, as soon as I thought about her again I also felt incredibly guilty, as if I was betraying Lindsay, even though she was the one orchestrating the whole thing. No wonder I was confused.

I was still very uncomfortable and reluctant to go along with the whole thing. I didn't feel ready. I'd probably never feel ready and knowing Lindsay she would know that as well. In the end I had arranged for Pauline to come over later and look after Amy, and she had agreed to do the same tomorrow as well. I still wasn't convinced I'd go into town and risk humiliation, but I had given myself the option.

I would have been lost without Pauline. I had made very little demands of her in the way of babysitting at the weekends as I had hardly been out since Lindsay died. Pauline had been encouraging me to get back some kind of social life, so was delighted with this turn of events and had not even questioned what I was doing – in fact if anything she appeared to be a little too eager, and that made me feel even more guilty.

Earlier I had watched Amy clambering over a big soft Tyrannosaurus Rex in the under fours soft-play section, and wondered about the marketing which had led us to transform the most ferocious killing machine that ever walked on land into a happy smiley climbing frame for toddlers.

Later, after we got back to the flat, Amy wanted to watch a Barney DVD, probably inspired by the Tyrannosaurus Rex from soft-play. I switched on the flat-screen TV built into the wall of my open-plan living-dining area. It had become a worry watching Barney ever since Amy overheard me saying to Pauline that in my opinion Barney was very camp. Pauline wasn't sure what I meant so I said, too loudly unfortunately, that I thought Barney was 'a poof'. Ever since then, whenever Amy noticed Barney she said in a very loud voice, 'He's a poof.' However, it made no difference to her liking the DVDs.

After Amy was settled I made myself another coffee

on the fancy coffee machine that came with the rented apartment. This was my fourth already, and I wouldn't sleep that night if I wasn't careful. Somewhere between my fourth and fifth coffee I decided to go to the Kitch bar; I blamed my sudden burst of decisiveness on the caffeine rush.

Before Pauline arrived I tried to tidy up the apartment. If I didn't she would spend the evening cleaning. It was a large apartment and I didn't know where to start. One of the more irrational things I did when Lindsay died was put our house up for sale. I couldn't stand being there; it was the family home we'd bought together and we were no longer a family in my eyes. Obviously I now realized that Amy and I were a family, but at the time I wasn't thinking clearly. Remarkably, I got an offer close to the asking price in the first week of the house being on the market and we moved out three months later. I rented a penthouse apartment in a part of Edinburgh called Newhaven. Most of the windows had wonderful views of the sea – well, I called it the sea, technically it was actually part of the Firth of Forth. To me a river was where you can see the other side, and here the other side was so far away it felt like the sea, so I called it the sea and more importantly Amy called it the sea.

The rent was a bargain at only £800 a month. The developer was unable to sell the apartments and decided to let them out at cheap rates to at least cover some of his costs, while he waited for the housing market to recover.

Since then, however, house prices had plunged even further, so selling up for me had turned out be a great financial decision if not a great emotional one. As well as having wonderful views, the apartment (ex-show apartment) was fully furnished with contemporary fittings and had the benefit of only being a ten-minute walk from Pauline's flat. Pauline had initially moaned the face off me for selling our lovely semi-detached home, but now hardly mentioned it.

One day I would buy a nice house with a garden for Amy but I was in no hurry and for the time being, I had extended the lease for a further six months. Instead of a garden we were one minute from the beach.

Pauline arrived just before 5 p.m. and joined us for dinner. Well, joined was actually an inaccurate description, she arrived and *made* dinner. I didn't know she was coming and my plan was to have beans on toast with Amy – Amy loved beans on toast – with the little sausages. Unfortunately I liked the little sausages too and we usually ended up having a fight over who got the last one.

Pauline decided that we were going to have salmon, new potatoes, broccoli and cauliflower. (I didn't even know we had any salmon – it was buried at the back of the freezer behind a box of Cornettos. I didn't know we had Cornettos either, otherwise I would have scoffed them by now.)

We all sat at the table, and Pauline pulled Amy's high chair close to the table so she would feel part of everything. Pauline remarked, 'Amy's high chair is very clean.'

I nodded innocently. 'Yeah, I washed it all down a couple of days ago.'

Pauline regarded me suspiciously. The idea of me cleaning a high chair obviously didn't sit right in her mind but she let it go.

The real reason the high chair was so clean was that Amy usually sat on the couch next to me and ate her dinner watching TV. She seemed to enjoy sitting in her high chair at the table, so I would need to do that more often.

As we ate, Pauline chatted constantly; she hated silence and her conversation would jump subjects seemingly randomly and was hard to follow at times.

One minute she would be saying, 'So I said to Mrs Collins – she lives across the road from me – that I really should think about getting another car. I know I've got my bus pass and everything, but dragging back all the bags from Asda on the bus is hard work so I usually get a taxi. . . .' The next second she would move seamlessly into, 'I think it's about time the government started doing something about all the unemployed kids that hang around all day doing nothing. . . .'

Amy and I finished eating about the same time and I noticed Pauline studying our plates. We had both eaten the salmon and the new potatoes, but we had both left the broccoli and cauliflower untouched. Pauline didn't say anything as she cleared away the plates. I know she wanted to, but she didn't.

I quickly showered, changed and headed out. Amy was happy when Pauline was there and I managed to sneak out without any drama. Sometimes Amy could be a nightmare when I left to go anywhere, depending on her mood. She used to cry whenever anyone left the flat, she even used to scream when the Tesco Online Shopping delivery man left and he was only in for less than two minutes.

I left them eating Cornettos and watching *Justine's House*. When *Justine's House* normally came on, Amy wanted to throw the cushions on the floor and bounce on the couch. When Pauline was there she was content to simply sit beside her and watch it. I needed to think about that; maybe that was the trick. I usually got bored after two or three minutes and had to go and do something else.

I had spun Pauline a line about going out for a few drinks with work colleagues and although I don't think she was completely convinced (as this was something I hadn't done for ages) she gave me the benefit of the doubt.

As I had also drafted her in again for the Saturday evening I was pushing my luck, especially as I had said that on the Saturday I was meeting Jamie for a few beers. I hadn't met up with Jamie for drinks since Lindsay's death, so this was probably as unlikely a scenario in her head. Again to her credit she didn't question me about it. Pauline was an excellent interrogator when she wanted to be – the Nazis or Spanish Inquisition would have loved her.

I caught a bus into town and by 7 p.m. I had managed to blag the end bar stool in Kitch's bar as per my wife's instructions, and sat nursing a glass of wine.

As I sipped from the glass I became aware that I was nervous. I hadn't expected to be. I was very much a reluctant player in my wife's little tableaux, but the combination of being out in a social environment and waiting to see if anyone showed up had combined to get my adrenaline going.

I had been a touch extravagant and ordered a bottle of wine, which was sitting in a bucket filled with ice perched precariously on the bar. I faced the likely prospect of having to drink the whole bottle myself.

The pub was warm and I could feel the occasional rivulet of sweat trickle down my side. I hadn't expected so many people to be in the pub at this time, but it was probably the Friday after-work regulars. Most of the other stools at the bar were filled and I was perched on the last one at the end of the forty-foot long piece of polished mahogany. I had reserved the remaining black-and-chrome bar chair just in case anyone showed up. If more than one turned up they would have to get their own chair. A number of people had tried to prise it away from me, asking if anyone was sitting there, or if it was taken.

I felt and probably looked uncomfortable situated at the end of a row of platinum blondes who were chatting inanely and loudly about some celebrity who was pregnant with their brother's baby. The nearest of the blondes occasionally glanced my way and smiled sympathetically. I thought initially that she might be one of my 'prospective dates', especially after she smiled at me, but given she appeared part of the platinum party I reckoned not. The overwhelming combination of their perfume and the wine was making my head swim.

I still felt guilty leaving Pauline on babysitting duty, but I couldn't exactly tell her I was sitting in a bar waiting for a troop of ladies to turn up, all pre-arranged by her dead daughter months ago. Hell, it didn't even make sense in my own head let alone trying to explain it to someone else.

I had yet to work out the best way of dealing with that, but knew I would need to tell Pauline something sooner or later; knowing me, it would probably be later.

As I was mulling over the Pauline-Lindsay dilemma in my head, I noticed a girl standing uncertainly at the door. A number of young and not so young ladies had come into the bar and looked around for their friends while I'd been sitting there, and all of them had smiled and walked over to some group or other. This one remained standing uncertainly glancing nervously around the pub. I looked at the torn scrap of paper that I'd written a list of names onto. *Jackie, Joan, Ellen and Anne.* If this was one of them – I appraised her quickly – she looked like a Jackie. Her hair was dirty blonde, and by that I don't mean it was unwashed, well, I didn't know if she'd washed her hair or not, but the colour was dirty blonde. I was babbling nervously inside my own head. I'd end up being committed if that continued. She glanced over my way and I suddenly pretended that the scrap of paper in my hand was the most interesting piece of literature I had ever read.

When I glanced up from my great read, she was walking over towards me. I decided she was a very brave girl coming here based on an email sent to her by my deceased wife. (God! Even that sounded insane.)

She stopped three feet in front of me and smiled uncertainly. 'Andy?' she asked softly.

I nodded and smiled.

She was dressed in a bright-yellow top and had a white cardigan draped over her shoulders. She wore black cropped trousers that ended just above her ankles that were wrapped in matching white sandals. She would not have looked out of place on the stool I had reserved beside the row of 'platinums' at the bar. She was very pretty without being gorgeous and I was amazed that she had shown up. At this point I had a problem with protocol. Should I have kissed her by now, or shaken her hand or simply said hello? Thankfully she noticed my uncertainty and held out her hand. For a brief second I had this ridiculous notion that I should kiss her hand like some stupid English aristocrat. I managed to restrain myself and simply took her hand in mine, it felt cool and soft. Her voice was confident and clear.

'I'm Ellen, I wasn't sure you'd be here, your email was . . . enigmatic.'

That was a big word for a Friday night and I was slightly disappointed that my name guessing was wrong.

I caught a whiff of her perfume, which I reckoned was expensive and tasteful, well, at least compared to the overpowering reek coming from the platinums. I'd forgotten how great women could smell. I mumbled something about being a 'man of mystery' which sounded naff even to me and offered her a glass of wine which she accepted. She placed her bag on the back of the reserved bar stool.

'I think you are very brave turning up out of the blue – thank you,' I said.

Inside my head I heard myself say 'thank you'. 'Thank you' – well, that was my air of mystery gone – plonker.

I gazed at her cropped trousers and thought I'd try and

retrieve the situation with a joke. 'Aw, has your budgie died?'

'I don't have a budgie.'

Ouch. A joke isn't much good if you need to explain it. 'No, I know, well actually I don't know but, well it's only an expression, a joke, you know because you're wearing. . . .' I wasn't exactly sure what to call them – cropped trousers, cargo pants, shallots (aren't they onions?) – so I pointed at her legs instead.

She ignored my pointing finger.

'Why would someone make a joke out of a wee boy's beloved pet dying?'

'What wee boy, I didn't mention a wee boy?'

'Well a wee girl then.'

'I didn't mention a wee girl either.'

This was going well.

'But you might as well have.' Tears welled up in her eyes and she handed me her glass, grabbed her bag and stormed out of the bar. This was a déjà vu moment for me as I remembered Lindsay's reaction to the au pair conversation, but at least Lindsay was drunk. Ellen, as far as I could tell, was stone cold sober. Unlike Lindsay, I didn't chase after her. Maybe that told me something. Or maybe I just didn't want to leave a full bottle of wine behind.

The row of platinums had stopped gossiping for a moment and I could feel their eyes on me; they were probably wondering what I could have said to upset one of their own, especially in a world record time of less than ten seconds. It suddenly occurred to me that I was capable of repelling a woman in less time than it took Usain Bolt to run the hundred metres.

I wondered what would be the best thing to do now. I noticed that the TV volume had been turned up and was drowning out most of the conversation in the bar. A Blue Square Premier football match was due to kick off in two minutes, Cambridge United vs. Woking. I also considered the almost full bottle of Chablis, for which I had paid eighteen pounds thirty-nine pence, and that another of 'Lindsay's lovelies' might show up. I sighed, smiled at the previously sympathetic platinum and ordered some food. Maybe I should have eaten the broccoli and cauliflower after all or at least blagged one of the Cornettos.

I settled in for the ninety minutes. What else could a man do in such a situation?

Later that evening, after I'd sobered up, I returned home and relieved Pauline, who had enjoyed a relaxing evening catching up on a variety of soaps after Amy had fallen asleep. She quizzed me lightly about my evening but didn't employ any of her interrogation techniques. I was reassuringly vague and thankfully she went home none the wiser. I knew she suspected something was going on but had not directly asked me anything, probably because she wanted to make sure of her ground first.

I made myself a cup of tea and switched on my iPad. Out of curiosity I logged on to my email in case Lindsay had emailed me but instead I was surprised to discover a message waiting from Ellen.

Lindsay had never said that she'd made my personal email address available to the mystery dates.

Hi Andy,
Ellen here, I got home and logged on to the dating site and noticed that your email address had appeared. I assume you did this after our disastrous date. Anyway I thought I would send you an email to apologize for this evening.

Obviously Lindsay had built in some kind of planned delay into that dating site – there was no end to her talents. Ellen continued.

I think I was maybe a bit over emotional.

Well, that's one way of putting it.

It's just as soon as I saw you I knew we wouldn't be right for each other. You remind me of my ex-boyfriend. I knew that when I first saw your picture and that was why I turned up really – but it just brought back all the memories, and your stupid joke just pushed me over the edge. I hope you meet a nice girl soon; it just won't be me. So please stop emailing me and please don't ever phone me.

I racked my brain for a moment. From what I could tell Lindsay had emailed her only once and that was to ask her to meet tonight and that was via the mysterious dating site – it hardly amounted to stalking.

Oh, and if you ever see me in the street or in a bar or in John Lewis where I go quite a lot, please don't come up to me or even look at me if you can help it. In fact, if you could maybe avoid John Lewis altogether I would much appreciate it, otherwise I'll always be looking over my shoulder in case you should appear.

Love and kisses
Ellen

I decided that Ellen was a psycho.

CHAPTER TEN

I woke up the next morning with a sore head and a sinking feeling in my stomach. It might have partly been the whole bottle of Chablis I'd consumed but it was probably more likely that my Friday night had made me want to forget all about going out on Saturday. In fact, it made me want to forget about dating altogether; my wife was maybe not so wise after all.

Despite my misgivings, once my hangover had cleared I decided to give it one more go. In reality it was easier to go out than to try and explain to Pauline why I didn't need her child-minding services any more.

After a day spent running after Amy, I dropped her off at Pauline's flat and headed into town. It was overcast and dull, which accurately reflected my mood. I did not expect anyone to show up this time as 'Psycho Ellen' – as I now thought of her – had only made the effort due to the fact I resembled her ex. I decided to wait about half an hour then head home for a quiet evening on my own, Amy was going to stay over at Pauline's and sleep in Lindsay's old room.

This happened occasionally and I knew from Pauline that although she enjoyed having her granddaughter overnight, it was sometimes difficult for her emotionally. It was the only time I ever got to glimpse Pauline's pain. She would perch on the edge of the bed and watch her beautiful granddaughter sleeping, and chastise herself for crying, knowing that little Amy was the only blood connection left to her daughter.

Sitting in Lindsay's old room always wrung out her emotions. It had changed little since Lindsay had left all those years ago. The posters of Will Smith and Savage Garden were long gone of course. Pauline had not kept the room unchanged for any sentimental reason, it was more that, as a spare room, she'd not had the motivation to make any alterations.

Lindsay had occasionally slept in her old bed and even moved back in for a few months after graduating from university. Lindsay and Amy had even slept there for two nights once when I was in London at a conference. That was of course before she became ill.

In my opinion Pauline had not cried enough for her daughter; she kept busy and that was her way of dealing with it. It was probably the only time in her life she had bottled anything up. Once or twice I had sat with her, playing the part of a silent companion, as bittersweet memories floated around the musty old bedroom like dust motes.

I think she now understood why I had decided to sell the house Lindsay and I had bought together – the memories had been too painful to deal with. She had been a little shocked when I'd cleared out all her daughter's clothes and shoes only a week after the funeral, but now realized that had simply been my defence mechanism kicking in.

I know she worried about me; she worried about Amy. Pauline was a champion worrier; she could have worried for Britain. If such an Olympic event existed she would have been in with a shout for the gold.

My mother-in-law wasn't stupid. She knew I was up to something. She would know as well why I wasn't telling her much.

Pauline had welcomed the involvement in our lives. It had definitely given her a sense of purpose and undoubtedly helped her deal with her daughter's death. But could that go on for ever?

If I did eventually meet someone new, what would that mean to her? I wasn't sure, or what her role would be if that happened. They were big questions and I didn't have any big answers. One thing I knew for sure was that parents were not emotionally designed to outlive their children.

I pulled myself from my thoughts and hopped off the bus as it stopped almost outside the door to the pub. I entered with trepidation and discomfort, recalling the previous evening's exploits.

I made my way to the bar and discovered that the bar stool at the end was already occupied by a pretty blonde. The rest of the seats were available and there was no row of platinums tonight.

I decided to take a seat three down from the girl which allowed me a clear view of the entrance. I kept an eye out for anyone who resembled a nutcase, which would signify that my date for the evening had arrived. There was, of course, always the outside chance that multiple nutcases would show up and what I would have done then is anyone's guess.

I ordered a beer and waited. After about twenty minutes I had given up hope that anyone was going to show and I was relieved. I could fall back on my preferred plan B and have a quiet evening to myself at home. I would then have fulfilled Lindsay's request and my conscience would be clear.

I drained my glass and was just about to leave when the girl at the end of the bar jumped down from her stool and walked over.

'I don't suppose you're Andy, are you?'

My heart sank. The nutcase was here waiting for me all the time – it was an ambush.

I had the briefest opportunity to extricate myself and say 'No sorry, I'm Colin, I don't know anyone called Andy. . . .' But I didn't. Instead the nice part of me said, 'Yes, sorry I didn't realize. . . .'

She held out her hand and smiled. 'I'm Terry.'

Of course it had to be her; I wondered if she had a willy. 'Good to meet you, Terry, I'm sorry,' – I was determined to finish my apology – 'I didn't realize that was you sitting there, I just thought you were waiting for someone.'

'I was.'

'Well, yeah, I know that now, but . . . oh never mind, it was a crazy idea. Thank you for coming.' Duh, there it was again, the air of mystery gone.

I ordered myself another pint of lager and Terry surprisingly wanted the same. Maybe she did possess a penis after all.

Our conversation was stilted to say the least. I asked her what she did for a living.

'Hairdresser. What about you?'

Dilemma time, do I tell her the long version or the envelope version? I had quickly gauged that Terry wasn't the sharpest of cookies – which is a saying that doesn't make much sense if you think about it – so would probably believe either. I made the mistake of giving her the long version and I noticed her eyes glaze over after ten seconds – a new record.

It was so obvious that we were in no way compatible but we both persisted, or rather I persisted. I suddenly discovered that I possessed a unique skill of asking stupid questions combined with an uncanny inability to stop.

'What do you do for fun?' I asked, sounding like someone's elderly dad.

'Fun? Mmm . . . I don't know.'

Terry didn't look like she was having much fun so far, so I decided to ensure that would continue and followed up with an equally bizarre clarifying question. 'OK, well, given a choice would you rather, go for a long walk on the beach or for a walk in the countryside?'

'Ehm, well, I don't like the beach much as the sand gets in between my toes and I suffer from hay fever and actually, I don't like walking much. So given a choice, neither.'

I continued the interrogation; I couldn't help myself.

'What about your family? How many brothers and sisters do you have?'

'One sister, Fiona.'

'Is she a hairdresser too?'

'No, she's studying.'

'What's she studying?'

'Beauty therapy.'

'That's nice. Is she beautiful?'

'Eh?'

'Your sister, is she beautiful? Because if she's studying beauty therapy I think it always helps if you are beautiful,' I said, offering an opinion on beauty therapists I never knew I had.

'She's all right I guess.'

'Do you have a picture of her?'

'Eh?' Terry and Jamie would get on well. They could sit and say 'Eh' all night.

'Can I see a picture of your sister?'

'Why?'

I had driven myself down a bizarre one-way street with these questions and I could see that Terry had started to get angry. I was surprised it had taken this long.

82

'Just to see if she is as beautiful as you said she was.'

'I didn't say she was beautiful, I said she was all right.'

'Well, they say beauty is in the eye of the beholder.'

'Who says that?'

That stumped me, 'I don't know, Shakespeare maybe?' (Plato actually, as I discovered on Google later.) 'Look, it's just a saying.'

'I've never heard it.'

'You must have, everybody's heard it.'

'Well, I haven't. Who said it again?'

'I said it.'

'Yeah . . . so you did. But what has that got to do with my sister?'

'Well, if you show me a picture of your sister I can decide if she's beautiful or not.'

'What is it with my sister? Do you want to go out with her or something? How do you know about my sister anyway?'

'I don't know anything about your sister. I only know she's a beauty therapist because you told me.'

'She's not a beauty therapist yet, she's studying to be one.'

'Well, all right, she's a would-be beauty therapist.'

'She will be one.'

'Whatever. Do you have a picture of her or not?'

'Of course. I've got loads on my phone, but why should I show you?'

'So I can see if she's beautiful or not.'

'And then you'll ask her out.'

'Will I?'

'I don't know, probably. You're a fucking weirdo.'

'I'm not a weirdo, I'm just trying to see if your sister would make a good beauty therapist or not.'

'I'm leaving.'

'I don't blame you.'

'Sorry?'

'I don't blame you for leaving.'

'Oh, why? I thought you'd be angry.'

'Not angry, just sad.'

Terry picked up her belongings. 'Sad I'm leaving?'

I nodded. 'A little, but mainly I'm sad that I'm so bad at dating.'

Terry agreed. 'Yeah it wasn't a great date, I've had worse, but it wasn't good.'

I couldn't imagine how anyone could possibly have had a worse date than this. I was dying to ask but was reluctant to reopen the interrogation, or where it might lead to. Terry was about to leave anyway, and I couldn't resist it. I asked one last question.

'Terry?'

She turned back with a glimmer of hope on her face. 'Yeah?'

'Do you have a cock?'

'Fuck off.'

I stayed in the bar for half an hour longer. I told myself it was in case another girl turned up that I could be rude to, but in reality it was in case Terry was waiting for me outside with a baseball bat. Eventually, I cautiously left the bar for my quiet evening at home and reflected on the fact that, if I did go on any more dates, I could expect to be either beaten up, arrested or probably both.

CHAPTER ELEVEN

Pauline was bringing Amy back after lunch so I had the morning to myself. I sat out on the balcony and ate a breakfast of coffee and croissants, then, as the wind turned cooler, I went inside and flipped open my iPad. I couldn't face opening my email in case there was a message from Terry, or worse – her sister.

I was still shocked at how rude I had been to Terry. Despite our lack of chemistry she didn't deserve that and I wasn't sure what had come over me. It was completely out of character. I had never behaved like that before but for some reason she had just annoyed me. All I could think of was that, due to stress, I had subconsciously decided to sabotage the date. I wasn't even drunk and couldn't blame alcohol. I tended to be a happy drunk anyway. I added it to my pile of stuff to feel guilty about, and made a mental note to try and find out where Terry lived and send her some flowers as an apology.

I clicked on to Google and instead searched around the Internet for dating advice to see if I could discover why I was behaving so weirdly. I had made the decision on waking that morning that I was not going to go on another date for a long time, but when I did, I wanted to avoid another Ellen or Terry. I wasn't sure which was worse – probably Terry, as I was mostly to blame for that debacle.

I came across a website called *Men Like Women and Women Like Shoes*. I wasn't exactly sure what the title was all about, but the information was interesting if not particularly useful. It seemed that early on in the dating process women liked their men to be cool and relaxed, keen but not too keen. I obviously needed to avoid being seen as desperate. They also liked them to be engaging but not over-emotional. That part I didn't really understand, but I expect it meant don't go telling them all about the fact that you miss your dead wife and how you'll never get over her, and stuff like that.

The site also advised that both parties should try and keep some air of mystery around themselves for as long as possible and to hold back some secrets, as this helped keep the other person interested. I could do that. I could hold back the part about my dead wife setting me up on dates. That might be a good secret to hold back.

Then it got really confusing as at some point into the relationship, it advised that you need to switch from being 'aloof and independent' to 'partner focused and co-dependent'. In other words: emotional, needy and maybe a little bit desperate.

I began to wonder how I'd ever managed to get married to Lindsay without knowing all this stuff. I must have been incredibly lucky. What would have happened had I become emotionally needy at the wrong time, or displayed desperateness when she was expecting aloofness? God forbid the consequences had I tried to become co-dependent when she was pre-menstrual. What a minefield.

The final piece of useful advice was 'to make sure you pick the right time to display any overt emotion'.

Had I ever displayed overt emotion when I was with Lindsay? I remembered I was first to say 'I love you'. It was just after we'd made love for the first time. In fact I can remember the *exact* moment – it was when I was lying beside her all sweaty and out of breath. It was only partly the exertion of sex that had made me that way, mostly I believed it was the fact that her heating was cranked up full. What is it with women and heating? Why are they always cold and why do they need the heating turned up to Brazilian Rainforest setting? Thankfully I didn't need to enter the moment on to my Outlook calendar. I also remembered that it took another week before Lindsay reciprocated. Cheeky cow.

Maybe that was the secret for me then. I had to sleep with someone and that was the key time to switch over to the emotional needy thing. The three big rules therefore were:

Don't appear too keen.
Don't appear desperate.
Avoid needy and emotional.

So those three, along with not being an axe murderer, were what I needed to remember.

As interesting as the website was, it didn't tell me how to avoid being an arse. I guess that was something I needed to work out for myself.

Pauline turned up just after one o'clock with some bacon rolls, and we munched them while she told me how clever Amy was at picking out her letters.

I knew that Amy was useless at picking out letters. I'd tried with her loads of times and she didn't know the difference between a P and a Q. She knew what an X was as she said it was a kiss, but that was it. Maybe Pauline had asked her to pull out kisses all the time in which case she was probably brilliant at her letters. I wasn't worried. Amy was great at her colours, so I reckoned everything else could wait. She was too young to be worrying about letters.

After Pauline left I took Amy down to Portobello Beach where we spent a busy afternoon building sandcastles.

Later we splashed about in the shallows and tried to avoid getting too wet by avoiding the bigger waves that rolled in. We put some small crabs in Amy's yellow plastic bucket and made them the new residents of Amy's sandcastle. The crabs didn't appear to be very happy with the arrangement and kept trying to escape. Amy squealed and jumped into my arms as Colossal Colin (the biggest of the crabs) took a suicidal leap from the highest part of the sandcastle and landed on Amy's bare foot. He then scampered away back towards the water. Colossal Colin was only about an inch and a half long, but that made him at least twice as big as the rest of the crustaceans we had captured – hence the name.

We let him go as I reckoned he'd earned his freedom with his daring leap. I bought two ice creams and we sat on our waterproof blanket gazing out across the water as we licked them. The summer was drawing to a close and this might be one of the last days warm enough to hang out on the beach and I wanted to make the most of it. The memories would keep me warm when the icy winds of winter whipped in from the North Sea and made the sand a no go area.

Later we had dinner in a small café near Ocean Terminal and afterwards pottered home. I carried Amy on my shoulders for most of the way as she was complaining that her legs were sore. I think she just wanted to go onto my shoulders and she knew how to get me to do that. God help me when she got older and really learned how to manipulate me.

After we got home I bathed Amy and jumped in the shower myself. I'd grown hot and sweaty after carrying her in the late afternoon which had turned dark and humid – perfect storm weather.

I towel dried my hair and pulled on my pyjamas – M&S called them lounge pants, but they looked like PJs to me – I then heard the unmistakable sound of thunder in the distance.

Amy and I rushed over and gazed out through the floor-to-ceiling windows. We saw a storm brewing out over the water.

I was distracted by my phone pinging and left Amy staring out through the window. I was half-expecting it to be another text from Lindsay, but instead it was from Amanda – the 'little red-haired girl' from my previous musings. I'd forgotten all about her, probably because I'd vowed never to go on another date. I regretted sending her my number now. I read her text which started out very like a postcard.

Hi Andy, hope you are well; I'm having a nice time in Ireland, weather wet and cool, but what you would expect here? Went fishing today. Sorry I've just read that back and it reads like a postcard, doesn't it?

Glad she thought so too.

Never mind I can't be bothered changing it. As I've not heard from you, I thought I'd send you a quick text. I'm going to be free later on so if it's OK, I'll phone you tonight – about nine if that's all right. I'll be out at dinner until then. Love Amanda xx

PS If I don't hear from you I will take it that nine is OK. If not I can do later.
PPS Not too much later. I need to be asleep by eleven as we are going shopping tomorrow and I'm tired after fishing all day.

PPPS – That sounds rude doesn't it like I need to go to the toilet lol. No, seriously, I don't think I like fishing much. First time today and had to get up at crack of dawn to fish as fish get up early supposedly! Xx

I might be mistaken, but given Amanda's display of keenness, it was likely that she was not a subscriber to *Men Like Women and Women Like Shoes*. I didn't text back, I wasn't sure I wanted to speak to her, but probably would as being rude to both Terry and Amanda in one twenty-four-hour period would not be good, and maybe I could make up for the Terry incident by being nice to Amanda, but not too nice by following rule number one: don't appear too keen.

I quite liked her text because she didn't shorten her words. She said 'love', not 'lv' and didn't substitute it for a heart shaped thingy, or, the worst I'd ever had – from Lindsay of all people – was a stupid animated pink ostrich waving. Since when were ostriches universally recognized as symbols of affection?

The storm broke just after Amy and I had finished eating the remaining Cornettos. Amy was covered in ice cream and chocolate, and was squirming while I tried to wipe her hands and face to avoid the sticky residue being spread around the room. The plan was to get her to bed early as she was tired, but the thunder and lightning changed that.

Amy, amazingly, was fascinated and not scared by the flashes of light and the huge booming cacophony of thunder. We watched the deluge of rain as it fell like a curtain across the seething waters churned up by the wind and tide. At one point the storm felt like it was directly overhead and the thunder made the whole building shake.

Being on the top floor made the whole spectacle even more impressive and the huge decked balcony beyond the

French doors was streaming with rain water. These doors were never opened when Amy was in the flat as the safety rail around the balcony was too low and flimsy. She often pressed her nose longingly against the glass, eager to get outside, and she did that whilst the lightning flashed and the thunder rolled, fascinated by the deluge. Outside, the wooden patio furniture was being buffeted around in the wind.

The storm passed over quickly, leaving behind a cool drizzle that coated the windows with a film of briny water. Deprived of our spectacular view, I got Amy ready for bed and, after I read our usual selection of books, she drifted off to sleep.

Once Amy was asleep, she stayed asleep. I reckon not even a herd of stampeding horses rampaging through her bedroom would cause her to stir. Thinking about it, were the animals able to negotiate the lift two at a time and wait patiently for the rest of their number to gather before beginning their rampage, they would make quite a racket on the polished wooden floors of the apartment.

The point was that once Amy was asleep I didn't need to worry about creeping around the apartment trying to be quiet. I could watch the TV at normal volume and I was free to drop stuff – being a bit of a klutz that was useful. Some mothers I chatted with at Amy's nursery groups told me they couldn't even sneeze without their kids waking up. Right on cue I sneezed explosively.

Occasionally Amy would wake up during the night – usually due to having a bad dream or because she was cold, having pushed her covers away. (I didn't have the Brazilian Rainforest setting on my thermostat.) Most times, if I spent a few minutes lying with her holding her hand she would drift off back to sleep, but sometimes she would demand, 'Go Daddy's bed'. What happened then is, once she settled to sleep in my bed, I sneaked into hers and we'd both wake up confused in the morning.

The three bedrooms of the apartment were grouped together on the west side of the building. I had the first one nearest the kitchen diner, the spare room was in the middle and Amy had the one nearest the front door. When we moved from the house, I pushed the king-sized bed to one side and reconstructed her little cot-bed. However, once she saw the king-sized bed she never went near her cot-bed again, and that is now dismantled and stored in one of the bedroom closets. Each bedroom had closet space and shoe racks that would have kept Imelda Marcos happy. My feeble clothing and shoe collection barely registered.

Mine and Amy's rooms had their own bathrooms and there was another bathroom near the front door which was hardly used. The spare room contained a fully made-up bed, but was also crammed with the remains of our furniture from the old house and other assorted junk.

All of the main windows in the apartment looked out over the sea in one direction or another, and it was a spectacular place to live. The downside was that many of the other flats in the building were still empty, which made the journey up from the basement car-park eerie at times, and the service fees were a hefty £1200 a year. I negotiated to only pay half of these. Amy and I rattled about in the apartment at times. When we walked with our shoes on or if we dropped anything, the sound would reverberate around the 3000 square foot space. (I wasn't sure what it was in new money.) It wasn't cosy like our old house, but it suited us for now. Lindsay would have hated it, but I wanted a complete change. One day, I'd leave open and opulent and return to cosy and compact – but not yet.

CHAPTER TWELVE

At two minutes past nine my mobile phone vibrated across the coffee table, and I answered it quickly. The voice on the line took me completely by surprise. Amanda had a wonderful gentle Southern Irish accent and I felt like I was talking to one of the Corrs (which one I'm not sure, just not the bloke.)

I remembered not to be rude and asked how her fishing trip went.

'Yeah, it was cold, soggy and very boring. My granddad loves it, sitting there in the early light smoking his pipe and watching the rain, I think he just likes the solitude and getting away from his wife for a few hours. I got fed up after about an hour and took the car into a nearby village to get coffee and sandwiches. How was your day?'

As I described the day myself and Amy had had, it felt natural and easy. I loved listening to her voice, she could have recited names out of the phone book, and with that accent it would have been hypnotic. It was a much better experience than the previous two evenings. Maybe I should just speak to girls on the phone and never actually meet anyone in person; that way I could avoid getting nervous and being an idiot.

The conversation flowed easily and half an hour drifted by. Then I heard a loud rumble in the background from her end. It was either the loudest tummy rumble in history or the start of a storm.

'There's a huge electrical storm starting here,' she explained. 'Looks like it'll be really spectacular.'

'Yeah, that's my storm. Amy and I watched it earlier and we thought it would be nice to send it over to Ireland for you.'

She giggled. 'Thank you very much; it's the most entertaining thing I've seen all day. I'm away to watch. I'll phone you in a few days if that's OK? It was nice talking to you, Andy. Goodnight.'

After I'd placed my phone down onto the coffee table, I suddenly felt a whole lot better. I still wasn't convinced I ever wanted to meet up with Amanda but at least it restored my faith a little. I wasn't tired yet so I flicked on the TV and fetched a beer from the fridge. I couldn't find anything worth watching on TV so, encouraged by my conversation with Amanda, I decided to open up Love Bitz on my iPad. Initially I just wanted to look at Amanda's photo again, but also decided to have a quick look to see if I had any more emails.

I was relieved to see only one new message flashing on the cherry lips. I opened it up and read the contents.

Hi Andy,
Carrie here, thank you for your email, it was very complimentary.

Lindsay obviously liked the look of Carrie and I was again left wondering what her technique was.

I like the idea of meeting up rather than having long chats. I have to be honest with you though – my

94

experience of Internet dates so far has been disappointing but I live in hope.

Well at least we had something in common.

Maybe you will be different. I've got a really busy few weeks coming up though, I've got a wedding the weekend after next, and then I'm on holiday for a fortnight after that, but if you're up for it I could meet up with you this Saturday. If it's too short notice I understand but let me know, otherwise it might be ages.

I don't have a picture on the site anymore, so I presume you just think my profile is completely wonderful but as we're maybe going to meet up I've sent you a link to my Facebook page so you can get an idea. I'm sure you won't be disappointed.

Send me an email if you want to meet on Saturday and include your mobile so I can confirm things with you, because I know how unreliable you men can be.

My first impression was that Carrie was a 'bossy boots', which was not altogether a bad thing – at least she knew what she wanted. I had a quick glance at her profile. I assumed that when Lindsay accessed it months ago it had a picture on it. She described herself as assertive, confident and outgoing. Judging by her email that description seemed to ring true, but physically she described herself as curvy and voluptuous. This set some alarm bells ringing. In my mind those words tended to be euphemisms for 'fat'.

Keeping the faith, I followed the link to her Facebook page and discovered a good-looking blonde. Another blonde. I had nothing against blondes at all but so far my track record with them had not been great.

She was not as petite as Amanda (I couldn't help comparing – it's what blokes do). Her photo showed a tall, well-built girl, but not fat. She shouldn't have used the words curvy and voluptuous. I made a mental note to mention this to her if I ever spoke to her.

I wasn't sure what to do. She was probably another nutcase – or maybe I was the nutcase, at that point in time I really wasn't sure. Could I face another date? Half an hour ago I would have said definitely not, but my chat with Amanda had infused me with some enthusiasm. Knowing I would probably regret it later I sent her an email that confirmed Saturday, and included my mobile number. I would need to check Pauline was OK for babysitting again. Carrie (bossy boots) had suggested we meet in a bar called the Pink Strip. She texted me back almost immediately which was slightly unnerving. Did none of these women read *Men Like Women and Women Like Shoes*?

I sat back, drained my beer and took stock. I decided I was probably a masochist.

The following day I took Amy to the Edinburgh Botanic Gardens again. It was one of my favourite places on a warm day, the seventy or so acres of lush planting felt like an oasis in the city and Amy loved it. I liked the fact there were no cars and roads to worry about and lots of open spaces for her to run about in. Our time limit was about two to three hours as after that Amy's legs got too tired. I did take her trike, but she loved running between the dense foliage and mostly ignored her transport.

We walked up the steep Chinese Hillside which was like a secret path (secret except for the eighty or so loud Americans walking down toward us.) At the top was a café where we bought ice-creams and freshly squeezed mango juice.

I sat on the grass and watched Amy chase her pink ball across the grass. She tried to kick the ball several times but always fell on her bum. Charlie Brown came to mind, and subsequently Amanda, but I quickly pushed her to the back of my thoughts.

If Amy had been a boy, her lack of kicking ability might have worried me, as being able to play football was a pre-requisite survival tool for boys – or it had been when I was at school. Maybe things had changed now. In any event I wouldn't need to worry about that.

Near where we were sitting was a group of youths – well, to be accurate, teenage boys – playing an aggressive game of touch-rugby. They were yelping and yelling and spoiling the peace and quiet for the hundred or so people lazing around enjoying the weather. A few couples were immune to the noise. These were the new couples completely oblivious to anything but each other and the oxytocin pumping through their bodies. They lay entwined and kissing. The end of the world would not have disturbed them. I recalled with a brief feeling of nostalgia that I had been one of them once.

Just then I noticed that Amy had drifted down the hill and was standing still listening to a park patrol woman who was talking to her. The woman had bleached blonde hair pulled back into a pony tail. She was wearing the Botanic Garden standard uniform of brown pre-creased trousers, brown shirt and mustard-yellow tie. The combination would have made even Cameron Diaz look dowdy – perhaps that was the intention.

I was too far away to work out what was being said, so I pulled myself to my feet and walked quickly downhill. I assumed she was making sure her mummy or daddy was nearby and was interested in the safety of my little girl.

When I got closer I noticed that the woman was

pointing to Amy's ball and shaking her head. I couldn't believe it. She was lecturing a 2-year-old about not playing with a ball on the grass.

'Excuse me,' I said, in my most polite voice, 'is there a problem?'

The woman regarded me with her hazel eyes. Her face was hard. Her badge announced she was 'Garden Ranger – Grainger'.

I couldn't help sniggering. It was beyond me not to. You would think when you applied for a job like that someone would take the time to explain what the badge would look like. Maybe she had got married and changed her name in which case, she should have chosen a different husband.

Ms Grainger ignored my outburst. 'Is this your daughter?'

I felt like saying, 'No, I'm just the local paedophile and thought I'd pop over to see what was going on.' But decided the polite Andy might be better than the sarcastic, rude one.

'Yes. What's wrong?'

'She was playing with a ball on the grass and that's against the garden rules.'

'There's no sign that says "no ball games".'

'We don't need signs. That's my job.'

'What, they employ you solely to stop people playing with their balls?' I couldn't resist it, I was expecting Ms Grainger's façade to at least crack into a smile. As it was she completely ignored the double entendre.

'No, I do other things too. I help anyone who is lost and make sure nobody steals plants.'

Given the gardens were spread over seventy acres and had multiple exits, I reckon I could have taken a wheelbarrow full of stuff without being detected by Ms Grainger, but I was more interested at that point about her 'ball minding' role.

'Look Ms Grainger, my wee girl chasing her Barbie ball across the grass is likely to cause zero damage, but assuming you're right and nobody should have a ball here – what about those kids over there playing touch rugby? They're damaging the grass and being noisy. Surely that should be your priority? Amy here hardly understands anything you've said to her anyway.'

Ms Grainger studied the rugby-playing louts for a moment, then said, 'They're too big.'

'Sorry?'

'They'll shout at me.'

'They probably will, but isn't it your job?'

'To get shouted at? No. Do you go to work to get shouted at?'

'No, of course not.'

'Well neither do I.'

With that, she turned on her heel and marched down the hill and was soon out of sight. I decided that Ms Grainger would be a perfect candidate for one of my dates. I probably should have asked her out and reminded her to bring a baseball bat.

Soon after the ball incident we headed home and Amy was almost asleep by the time we stepped out of the lift. Getting her ready for bed was a real chore as she was bad tempered and uncooperative due to her fatigue. Consequently, an hour and a half later I was tucked up asleep as well. Wonderful stuff, fresh air.

CHAPTER THIRTEEN

Tuesday was also a non-work day this week and, although I was of a mind to return to the Botanic Gardens with several footballs to bounce on the grass and a wheel-barrow to fill with illicit plants to test the resolve of Ms Grainger, I resisted the temptation. Instead I took Amy to Athletic-Tots. Amy was unaccustomed to spending so much one-on-one time with me and kept asking where her gran was. (She did this sometimes when we had been together for long periods.) I hoped she wasn't getting bored with my company as it was very likely that given my lack of dating ability, she was stuck with staring at my face for a long time to come.

Athletic-Tots was a group activity held in the main hall of a local sports centre. The play-area was normally cleared of anything dangerous (except for one week when several javelins were left lying out). It allowed the toddlers to run around like headless chickens for an hour or so and blow off steam. There was a small climbing frame with a padded floor underneath and a soft-play area littered with toys, mainly trikes and bikes. It was completely unstruc-tured and I liked it.

Pauline and I often said that if anyone ever had any

doubts that humans were anything but primates, they should go to one of these classes and watch the toddlers climb, jump, clamber and wrestle with each other although I would recommend taking a child with you otherwise you may be suspected of being a paedophile. Also it was worth seeking permission to take said child to avoid a kidnapping rap.

Never more acutely did we resemble monkeys in our behaviour and mannerisms than when we were under the age of three. I wondered why we ever grew out of the jumping and climbing phase. It was probably just as well or we'd have climbing frames instead of coffee machines in our offices – though that might actually be more fun. It would certainly be healthier.

Whilst Amy was bouncing around the athletics hall I felt my phone vibrate in my pocket. (I tended to keep Katy Perry silent when I was out and about. Russell Brand maybe had the same idea which had probably added to their problems.) I pulled it out and peered at the screen. I didn't recognize the number but answered it anyway.

'Hello?'

'Andy?'

'Yeah, who's this?'

'It's Carrie, just thought I'd give you a phone.'

'It's OK, I've already got one.'

'Sorry?'

I really needed to stop making stupid jokes or I would probably remain single forever. I was surprised to hear from Carrie.

'No,' I said, 'I'm the one that should be sorry. It's lovely to hear from you, just my stupid joke about phones. . . .'

'Oh, right yeah. . . . Ha ha. . . !'

Somehow I didn't think her laughter was genuine.

'Anyway, Andy, I just wanted to have a quick chat before we meet up, just to . . . well . . . break the ice, I suppose, and to make sure you are actually going to turn up – I hate being stood up on these things.'

Her reference to 'these things' made it sound like she got stood up on a regular basis.

'Andy, are you still there?'

'Hi, yes, sorry I was just . . . distracted, for a moment. Of course I'll turn up. I'm looking forward to it,' I lied.

'Good. I find men are unreliable most of the time and I just like to know where I stand. Now, I've only a few minutes left as I've got to be in a meeting at half ten. Where are you, it sounds noisy?'

I gazed across the large hall at the numerous toddlers screaming and running in random directions like bad extras in a low-budget horror film. 'I'm at the Leith Athletic Stadium.'

'Oh, I didn't know you were into running and fitness, it doesn't say anything about that in your profile.'

I glanced guiltily down at my latte and large slice of chocolate-smothered shortbread.

'Well, I'm not really. . . . I'm here with my wee girl. She's the one running around like a headless chicken with a million other kids.'

'Oh, OK that sounds like fun.' Again I didn't think she was being genuine. 'As you're busy I'll leave you to it. So I'll see you on Saturday at seven?'

'Yep I'll be there.'

'Are you sure?'

'Sure about what?'

'Sure you'll turn up?'

'Of course I'll turn up.'

'You can tell me if you aren't coming, so I can then organize something else.'

Now I was starting to get confused. 'Do you want to do something else?'

'Eh?'

I sighed. 'Well it sounds like you maybe want to do something else. If you do that's fine.'

'No, Andy, I will definitely be there.'

'Are you sure?'

'Of course I'm sure, that's why I called you, remember?'

At that point I wasn't sure who had phoned who, or even quite why I was having this conversation. I also decided that it was likely to go on for some time if I didn't just agree with her. I'd learned from being married that just agreeing with a woman was usually the path of least resistance.

'No, that's fine, Carrie. I'll see you on Saturday.'

'OK, bye.'

I hung up and wondered if Carrie would turn out to be a nutcase. The signs so far were good for that outcome. Maybe all women (except Lindsay) were nutcases, or maybe she was a nutcase too and I was just blinded by love. That got me to thinking about all the females I came across at the various nursery groups I took Amy to. They varied depending upon my work-share days which changed from month to month. I'd been to most of them now and although I was usually made to feel welcome, occasionally something happened that changed that.

I was normally comfortable in women's company – my work was mostly female and I liked women, otherwise I probably wouldn't have bothered with the whole getting married thing – but in this environment it was different. I was an oddity, a curiosity and, possibly, a threat. Once I was told I was all three by a self-righteous middle-class ex-teacher. I've never got on well with teachers and I can trace that back to my school days.

When I first started going to these groups I was viewed as being unlucky and regarded with pity and sympathy, which was fine – I was getting used to that. However, all that changed one day at Tree-Tots. This was a group run by Marjorie Faulks, a large woman in her mid-fifties. The whole point of TTs, as she called it – her acronym sounded rude to me as she pronounced it 'titties' – was educating the toddlers. Every week Marjorie brought in a four-foot model of a tree, and tried to teach the children all about that particular tree and the effect it had on the environment – quite ambitious for a group of toddlers aged between eighteen months and three. On this one occasion I had made the mistake of chatting to a lovely blonde girl called Janice (yeah, blonde again!) who was a single mother, had a reputation (unknown to me) of being a man-eater and had, according to Marjorie, who told me this later, tried to seduce some of the other mummies' husbands. Why that should affect what they thought of me I don't know, but it seems that after that I was tarnished. My reputation, for what it was worth, had been sullied. Maybe they thought I was out to snare myself another mummy for Amy. Who knows? After that, the reception I received at various toddler groups was frosty for a while – although it had improved recently.

I stopped going to Tree-Tots shortly afterwards anyway as they were running out of interesting trees and the cost of the class was high at £5.50 a session – probably the cost of the materials needed for Marjorie's models. Anyway, I wasn't sure Amy was getting much from Tree-Tots, because at her age she didn't really know the difference between a tree and Simon Cowell.

Besides, on the final week we attended, Marjorie had brought in a large fern tree to the group and used a stuffed dinosaur to explain that fern trees were one of the earliest plants to populate the earth, and had been around when dinosaurs had ruled the world. (As opposed to Take That.) Unfortunately, the dinosaur looked very much like Barney and after Amy had shouted 'He's a poof' for the tenth time, I decided it was time to retreat from Tree-Tots for a while.

The other 'classes' – as Pauline liked to call them – Amy attended on a fairly regular basis were: Little Tots, where they basically played with toys and fought with each other; Lazy Tots, where they did pretty much the same as Little Tots but occasionally did some face painting; Eazy Tots, where they did much the same as Little and Lazy Tots but occasionally baked cakes.

Although the toddler groups had some variation of venue type and activities, they all had one common feature: fighting. No matter where you went there was always, at any one time, two or three toddlers knocking seven bells out of each other. At that age, gender is pretty much irrelevant; boys and girls are equally as strong and aggressive.

I am of sufficient age to have grown up when such playgroups didn't exist. We as kids had to make our own entertainment and, not blessed with any siblings, I could only torment my poor mother as my father worked long hours. Between the ages of two and three I managed to swallow a bottle of coconut imbibed sun-tan lotion, blow up my father's music centre by repeatedly banging the plug and socket with the heel of my hand, and set fire to my 'Pooh' teddy-bear by squishing his head between the bars of the electric fire. (I have to say in my defence that all three of these events could have been prevented with some simple parental prevention measures, but my mother – although very loving and caring – didn't and still doesn't have a great deal of common sense.) At the age of seventy-five, she fell eighteen feet from a tree by managing to saw through the tree branch she was clinging onto at the time. I think this last event illustrates my point well. Firstly she didn't make the connection between the tree branch, her hand and the saw. Secondly, why the hell at the age of seventy-five is she climbing up a tree in the first place?

For my part, only the consumption of the sun-tan lotion posed me any discomfort, producing copious diarrhoea for three days and nights. My father mourned the loss of his music centre until the day he died, and I still have the scorched remains of Pooh Bear somewhere. I believe his remains are interred in the spare bedroom in my apartment.

CHAPTER FOURTEEN

Apart from alternating between spending time with Amy and my colleagues at Perennial Mutual, an uneventful week drifted by. I received no more emails or texts from Lindsay and my profile on Love Bitz didn't pull in any more emails. This was probably just as well given my state of mind.

I had been mentally sparring with myself all week about whether to meet up with Carrie or not. After my telephone conversation with her I wasn't sure it would go well, but despite my reservations I found myself, on Saturday evening, sitting on the top deck of the bus trundling into town.

Weirdly I had a guilt thing going on in my head about Amanda. I had chatted to her on the phone a few times by then and the conversations had been comfortable and easy. I'd discovered she had three brothers and two sisters and was part of a large Irish Catholic family. I did manage to restrain myself from mentioning anything to do with the Irish potato famine, even though that was some 160 years ago. I used to annoy an ex-girlfriend with that particular jibe, probably one of the reasons why she became an ex-girlfriend.

Amanda and I seemed to be getting on well. I would have said we were getting on like a house on fire but that struck me as a silly saying, because if my house was on fire I'd want to run like hell in the other direction, and I didn't think I wanted to run away from Amanda. I had even managed to discuss Lindsay's death and what had happened to her. Amanda sounded sympathetic and interested.

I think one of the reasons I was so reluctant to meet up with Amanda was that I was bound to make a mess of the date. I had wondered if it was possible to keep her interested for another six months or so, by which time I might be ready to meet someone new. Amanda probably wouldn't want to go along with that plan.

The bus arrived at my stop and I jumped off. The evening was pleasantly warm and as I wandered along George Street, the waning sunshine felt good on the back of my neck. A light breeze blew up small dust eddies between the tall buildings, and I watched fascinated as a Walkers crisp packet spun in the air for a few moments before it settled into the gutter where it was promptly flattened by a number 26 bus.

Many of the bars had set up tables outside to take advantage of the late summer weather and they were all packed. The Pink Strip was probably the biggest bar in Edinburgh and as such had more outside space than the others. I was reluctant to take a table on the pavement and preferred the more private setting of a booth inside.

The waitress appeared as soon as I sat down and I ordered a beer. I wasn't sure what Carrie's drinking habits were as her profile didn't go into that level of detail. She arrived just when the waitress returned with my beer and ordered herself a large glass of red wine. She then casually tossed her shoulder bag onto the seat opposite me and slipped into the booth.

She was blonde-haired and blue-eyed which I knew she would be, but her hair had been cut into a short bob, a different hairstyle from her profile photograph where it had been long and luxuriant.

Another feature that had failed to register in her profile photograph was actually how huge her breasts really were. The tight blue top she was wearing did nothing to disguise the size of them, and I noticed a few other men in the bar staring over at us. One poor chap was caught ogling by his girlfriend and got a slap for his trouble. Completing the ensemble were baggy black jeans and lace up Replay trainers.

Our conversation was awkward initially but once we'd both consumed some alcohol we relaxed, and I (mostly) managed to keep my eyes on her face and not her tits. In truth I had two goals, one was to get past the first ten seconds and then to avoid being rude to her. I managed both which already made it a much better date than my previous efforts.

After we'd ordered a bottle of wine to share and some nibbles, Carrie leaned over the table and placed her chin on her hands. She stared straight into my eyes and said, 'So tell me about your Internet dating experiences so far.'

I smiled and told her about Ellen and Terry, intentionally keeping the details vague and that she was my third. 'So I'm not quite an Internet virgin, but close.'

She laughed, her eyes lit up when she smiled and I liked that. 'Well, I'll be gentle with you, I promise.'

That comment broke whatever ice was left and as the wine disappeared we became more comfortable.

Carrie explained she worked for the local environmental health department, mainly in a desk-based role but occasionally she got to go out on inspections and trips to restaurants and bars. Her main role however was to prepare the legal documents connected with any cases they wanted to pursue. She had trained as a lawyer but didn't want to work in a lawyer's office, so started working for the council whilst in her final year at university and transferred over to environmental health after she graduated. I kept my occupation details vague to avoid boring her to death.

After around an hour had ticked pleasantly by there was a natural pause in our conversation and Carrie broke the silence first. 'There's a lovely little place just around the corner – Paddy's Piano bar. Have you ever been?'

'No, I don't think so.'

'Oh you'd remember if you had, come on, let's go.'

She bounced up (literally) which caused a chain reaction in her breasts that rippled on for more than ten seconds. I gulped down the last of my wine whilst trying not to look. We walked briskly to the end of the block and Carrie disappeared down a flight of stairs to a basement entrance. There was no sign over the door and no clue that it was anything but a private address. She knocked loudly on the grey metal door and it was opened by a smartly dressed bouncer who was wearing top hat and tails – something I thought must be uncomfortable on such a warm evening. Carrie just nodded at the man and walked past him. She was obviously a regular. Inside the bar was air-conditioned and chilly and as I followed Carrie through a heavy blue silk curtain, I shivered involuntarily.

The bar was intimate and snug, with tables and chairs arranged against the dark walls. Conversation was muted and the lighting was subdued and soft. A number of long red curtains were draped periodically around the room, giving privacy to some VIP tables but which also made the bar feel silken, soft and hushed.

On a raised platform in the corner was a baby grand piano and the vacant stool in front of it was lit by a single spotlight. Carrie ordered some wine and as the waitress returned with a bottle on ice with glasses, a polite smattering of applause announced the arrival of the pianist. She was dark skinned and exotic. My first impression was a cross between Sade and Halle Berry. She sat and began to play a jazzed up soul song. Her voice was soft, husky and hypnotic and it soared to meet the high notes. I was mesmerized. Three songs later the spell began to wear off and Carrie and I returned to chatting quietly.

Carrie whispered, 'Will you do me a big favour? Will you go and ask her to play "Cry Me a River" by Julie London, I just love that song.'

I agreed and when she finished her next song I carried out her request. A few minutes later she performed possibly the best version of that song I had ever heard in my life and Carrie was ecstatic.

I had to wonder about the singer, how someone so talented ended up playing in a bar in Edinburgh. I thought about the huge number of talentless numpties that auditioned for the TV talent shows, and why someone like this had not been discovered.

I was about to mention this to Carrie when she said, 'I have a theory about dates. I think, no I *know* there has to be the "phwoar" factor. If that's not there you might as well just go home.'

The perceptive part of me noted the nearly empty wine bottle and that Carrie hadn't gone home. 'I assume we've got the "phwoar" factor then?' I was at a loss here, the *Men Like Women and Women Like Shoes* website hadn't mentioned a 'phwoar' factor, so this was unknown territory for me.

Carrie nodded, and gazed into my eyes. 'Well I feel it anyway.'

I felt uncomfortable and squirmed in my seat for a moment before Carrie checked her watch.

'What time is your babysitter leaving?'

'It's Amy's gran actually, so she's not on the clock.' I felt immediately guilty about saying that but the excitement I felt in my loins overrode it.

Carrie waved to the waitress for our bill. 'Excellent, let's get out of here, it's too nice a night to be sitting indoors.'

Outside Carrie hailed a taxi and we jumped in. I was feeling a little nervous and excited by this turn of events.

'Where are we going?' I asked.

'Back to my flat of course, where else would we go?'

Where else indeed? I found myself opening and closing my mouth like a goldfish.

Carrie continued. 'I recently moved into one of the new flats in Fountainbridge overlooking the canal. It's gorgeous. We can sit out on the balcony, have a drink and watch the sun go down.'

I found my voice again and asked good-humouredly, 'What if I'm an axe murderer?'

Carrie took my hands and turned them over examining the palms. 'You're not.'

'How can you tell by looking at my hands?'

'If you were an axe murderer, you would have calloused hands from swinging-the-axe practising.'

'OK you're right, I'm not an axe murderer, but honestly . . . how do you know I'm not some kind of nut-job?'

'You don't look like a nut-job.'

'I didn't know nut-jobs had "a look".'

Carrie nodded. 'Yep they do, I've known loads of them over the years.'

I wasn't sure if that was a good thing or not. She noticed my reticence and leaned closer to me and lowered her voice to a whisper.

'Look, Andy, I'm a very good judge of character, always have been. I trust my instincts completely. Anyway, all I'm suggesting is a few drinks and a beautiful view – and I don't mean me, but I'm pretty good to look at, I think. I know you find me attractive because your pupils are all dilated. I'm not the sort of person to worry about standing on ceremony. If I want something I usually just go and get it. It's just who I am. If you are uncomfortable, you can leave anytime, and if I don't think I want you there any more I'll ask you to go. Fair enough?'

'Yeah, OK.'

I had no idea what I had just agreed to. Was I just going to her flat for a drink? Was she going to tie me up and torture me? Was *she* perhaps an axe murderer herself? I resisted the urge to examine the palms of *her* hands. She might not be a murderer, but I had my suspicions that she might be a nut-job. I had the knack of attracting them at the moment. I also wasn't sure what I was doing in a taxi heading towards a strange girl's flat. I was probably being old-fashioned. Maybe this was how things worked now if you didn't offend your date in the first five minutes of meeting. She was right about one thing: I did find her attractive. She was physically attractive but I also liked her self-confidence. I have always liked strong women.

I noticed the taxi driver glancing at me in his rear-view mirror. He smiled knowingly. What he knew I don't know, but he seemed to know more than I knew – that was for sure. We arrived at her building and after paying the driver, she opened the communal door to her block.

Her flat was on the first floor and her front door opened directly into her living room. It had wooden floors and a small leather couch facing a flat-screen television. The place was filled with light from the floor-to-ceiling French doors that faced onto her private balcony. She opened them and I stepped out while Carrie disappeared back inside. The view was lovely. Her flat overlooked the canal basin, and I noticed there were a number of little coloured barges and house-boats bobbing on the water. It was not as spectacular a view as the one from my penthouse, but there was more to see here, with people coming and going from the boats and flats.

The canal was overlooked on three sides by similar apartment blocks, and on the furthest away block on the eastern corner was a small bar with tables outside. The bar was busy and music drifted across the basin towards us. There was a slight smell of decay in the air which I assumed came from the stagnant water below. That alone would put me off living on a house-boat as the odour must have been much stronger close to the water.

Carrie returned with two large glasses of red wine and we sat and watched the world go by for a while. Carrie was very quiet, compared to earlier and I wondered what was going through her mind. I glanced at her and she smiled.

'What time do you need to be home?'

I checked my watch. It had just gone nine. Amy would be in bed by now and Pauline would be quite happy watching the TV. 'As long as I'm back for midnight I'm probably OK. I don't like to take advantage.'

'Aw, that's a shame. I was hoping you would take advantage of me.'

As Carrie smiled at me, I felt a tingle of excitement slip down my spine into my loins. I hadn't had sex with anyone since Lindsay died, and even then we last made love in early November so it had been nearly a year.

I didn't know what to say so I simply smiled. I was still feeling uncomfortable with the whole scenario but there was no going back now.

'OK then.' Carrie stood up. 'Just stay there for a few minutes and I'll call you through, OK?'

Still mute I nodded.

Carrie leaned over, put her hand on my shoulder and kissed me slowly and sensuously on the lips. I could taste cherry lip gloss and red wine.

A few minutes passed, which seemed like hours, before Carrie called out to me. I put my empty glass down onto the metal table and stepped through the doors into her living room. There were four doors leading out of the room. One was the front door we came in, another was open and revealed a small galley kitchen, and the other two were closed. The first one I opened led into a small bathroom. Amazed with my powers of deduction, I decided that Carrie must be behind the other door which I assumed led to her bedroom. I tried to suppress my growing excitement which was becoming obvious by the bulge in the front of my jeans.

The sight that greeted me when I stepped into her bedroom did nothing to reduce my excitement. The room was dark. Carrie obviously had a blackout blind behind the closed silver curtains. The room was lit by a number of scented candles, the flames of which flickered when I walked in. She asked me to close the door.

Carrie was lying naked on her double bed holding a small silver vibrator. I could also see a number of other instruments of pleasure lined up neatly on her bedside cabinet. Some of them were instantly recognizable from various magazines and porn movies I'd seen such as the 'double intruder' and a pink 'rabbit'. However some of them looked like torture instruments, and one in particular reminded me of a miniature version of a deep mine tunnelling machine that I think I saw once in a documentary on the Discovery channel.

She placed the small silver bullet vibrator on her pillow and then reached over for the 'tunneller'. (I've no idea if that was what it was called, but it was the name I gave it.) She switched it on and gasped as the spinning knobbly multiple-headed device throbbed over her nether regions. Adding to the effect was the multi-coloured lights that were spaced along the edge of the device. The colours changed from red to blue then to green and back to red again. It lit up the room like some kind of weird sexual discotheque. The scent of Carrie's arousal filled the small space and I wondered what my role was to be. Carrie had made no attempt to involve me yet in her reverie and I wondered if I was just supposed to join in. I was aching with the sight of her and watched as her magnificent breasts heaved up and down with the steady rhythm of the 'tunneller'. I began to undo my belt.

Carrie looked up from her ecstasy and frowned. She waved her finger at me, switched the 'tunneller' off and sat up, covering her body with a sheet.

I was taken aback by her sudden display of modesty. Noticing my confusion, Carrie explained. 'You can watch me, Andy, I like being watched, but I don't want you to touch me, and I don't want to touch you. Not yet anyway. I don't know you well enough.'

The whole situation was completely absurd. My life was starting to feel completely absurd. She didn't know me well enough, and yet she was happy enough to invite me back to her flat and let me watch her masturbating.

'Can you sit on the chair in the corner, please,' Carrie instructed. 'That way I can keep an eye on you.' She indicated a small wooden chair opposite her bed.

I followed her instructions while she fired up the 'tunneller' again and the room was once more bathed in multi-coloured lights. Sitting in the corner while Carrie lost herself again I felt like some kind of naughty schoolboy, though quite what sort of school would apply this kind of punishment to one of their pupils I wasn't sure – not one I would want to send my children to anyway. I watched for a moment longer then told her I needed to go to the bathroom – which was true, although I needed an excuse to get out of her room for a few minutes. It took me a while to pee for obvious reasons, but that also gave me time to think. As sexy as it was watching Carrie playing with herself, I didn't feel comfortable with the arrangement. It had been a long time since I'd been in such an erotic situation. Who was I kidding? I'd never been in that kind of situation and I was ill equipped to deal with it. Carrie was not what I was looking for. If I was going to meet somebody I wanted them to be normal, whatever normal was. Maybe there was no such thing as normal any more. Given my recent experiences, I certainly had my doubts.

I flushed the toilet and stepped back into her living room. I could hear the buzzing of her sex toys and gasps of pleasure from her bedroom. Reluctantly I decided to leave, and slipped quietly out of her flat, though I'm not sure why I was being quiet as I doubted very much she was aware of anything other than her own body, and the liquid sounds it was producing.

I headed home, strangely relieved to be out of her flat, and a little sad that yet another date had ended in disappointment, although the image of Carrie on her bed would stay with me for some time, I was sure.

I hailed a cab and phoned Pauline to say I was on my way home. When I arrived she was waiting for me at the front door of the apartment block and jumped into my taxi. I had paid the driver more than enough to cover my fair and Pauline's ride home. Pauline didn't get a chance to ask me how the evening had gone or why I was home early, which was a relief.

Back in my apartment I checked on Amy who was sleeping soundly. I poured a glass of wine and flipped open my iPad. I logged on to Love Bitz. I wasn't expecting any emails from Carrie whom I was sure hadn't even noticed I was gone yet. There was one email waiting for me though from someone called Sandra.

Hi Andy,
I saw your profile and felt really attracted to you. The only thing is I'm actually married.

I sighed. Another odd-ball.

I know my profile says I'm single but you have to say that to get a listing on the site. Anyway my husband and I have . . . mmm what would you call it? An understanding maybe? You see we don't make love any more. We've been married for ten years now and stopped the sex thing about three years ago. We basically just stopped fancying each other so it seemed pointless having sex when neither of us enjoyed it. What we do now is we have an open marriage – at least I think that's what it's called. Basically we can sleep with other people as long as it doesn't get serious. We talked about getting divorced but actually we get on really well, except physically, so neither of us wants to do that. I suppose it is possible we might meet someone else and it might happen, but it hasn't yet.

I guess that's it, so if you want to meet up for a no-strings arrangement then I'd love to see you, but quite understand if you are looking for something different.

Sandra xxx

PS I've added you to my friends so you can see my profile.

Out of curiosity I clicked onto her profile. Sandra (34) had only one visible picture. It showed a petite raven-haired beauty with intense green eyes. I found it hard to believe her husband had stopped fancying her. However, as tempting as her offer was, I didn't need this kind of complication in my life and I reluctantly sent her a quick email telling her that, and sadly shut down my iPad for the night.

CHAPTER FIFTEEN

My rota for the week ahead meant I had to work Wednesday, Thursday and Friday. When I woke up on the Friday morning and got myself dressed I had no inkling at that point what was about to happen. The fact that most of the firm's senior managers had been called down to London for meetings should have alerted me that something was going on. However, as I had been preoccupied with other matters, it was no surprise really that everything had passed me by.

During the week I had received no more contact from Lindsay, which I found surprising. Maybe her 'system' had failed and I would never hear from her again. The thought saddened me but perhaps it was for the best.

I'd had no contact from Carrie either which was a relief. I felt ashamed of myself for running out on her, and likened it to the time at school when Jamie had arranged for a girl who fancied me, Diane Stevenson, to meet me outside the football changing rooms after school. I was aged fourteen and something of a late developer. That particular afternoon I took stage fright and hid in the boys' toilets until she got fed up and left. Jamie had never let me live it down until this day. Now he'd have something else to taunt me with.

I had bitten the bullet with Amanda. I sensed she had become frustrated with me and I had agreed to meet up with her that evening for a drink. I really didn't want to do that, partly because I didn't want to discover she was a nutcase like all the rest, and partly because I would probably do something to mess it all up. She was my back up – my last chance maybe?

As all the senior managers were away, it meant that it would be an unusually busy day for me as I was likely to be the only person left in the building able to make any decisions. The benefit of that would be that it would keep my mind off my impending meeting with Amanda. We'd arranged to meet in a bar called Nine Brothers in the Cowgate at seven o'clock.

All that was for later. In the meantime I'd finished showering and donned a new suit. I had about a dozen new suits in my wardrobe which sounded extravagant, but most were cheap off-the-peg numbers from a retail outlet store near Edinburgh. I had got into the habit of buying a new suit every time I was in the store and, as I tended to wear them into the ground, they did last a long time.

Amy was awake and doing the usual with her breakfast cereal while watching CBeebies. I knew having the TV on so early was probably not good for her brain development, but it kept her occupied whilst I got ready for work. Pauline arrived soon after I'd finished my breakfast and immediately switched off the TV. She explained, 'I can't hear myself think with that racket going on, and Amy's not even watching it.'

That was true. Amy had given up on the TV and was playing with one of her many dolls and a buggy, but I was watching *Gigglebiz*. It was one of the few kids' programmes I actually quite liked and was certainly a lot more cheerful than tuning in to the news.

I thought about protesting but decided her opinion of me would not be improved by knowing I liked a TV programme aimed at children aged seven and under. Maybe that was actually my intellectual level – in which case Amy and I would have some great conversations in about four years' time.

'Andy, remember to take your antibiotics,' Pauline reminded me. I popped one of the tablets on my tongue and washed it down with some of the milk left over from the bottom of my cereal bowl. I'd had a dental abscess in one of my front incisors for most of the week and the dentist had prescribed the pills for me on Tuesday morning. They had certainly helped and I no longer needed any painkillers, but I could still feel the pain as a dull pulse in my gum.

I picked up my mobile and noticed I had seven missed calls, all from Jamie. I wondered what had made him so anxious to speak to me. He couldn't have found out about Carrie already unless she'd put something about my 'fear of sex' all over some social network site. I hardly checked Facebook these days. I'd been too busy with Lindsay's emails and Love Bitz.

I hardly spoke to Jamie these days so the missed phone calls made me wonder what was going on as it was not like him to chase me. Annoyingly, as usual he hadn't left a voicemail, so I decided to put off calling him back until later. I was going to be late for work anyway.

As I dropped my plate into the sink I noticed the calendar beside the cooker said it was Friday 13 September. I was not normally a superstitious person: I tended to avoid walking under ladders, but that was usually because there would be some clown at the top of it likely to drop something onto my head. I saw that more as common sense than superstition.

However, when I arrived at work and plonked myself

behind my desk, I found a sinister looking A4 white envelope marked 'Private and Confidential' sitting on my desk. The words 'private' and 'confidential' usually spelt trouble in an organization like Perennial Mutual.

Inside was a pack with a typed letter attached to the front inviting me to attend a meeting in the main boardroom at eleven o'clock. The information was for senior management eyes only, and it made it clear that the contents must not be revealed to any other staff.

Today was the first time I realized I was classified as 'senior management' but reckoned, by the tone of the writing, it might not be a great time to find myself in such lofty company.

As the RRA I had some insight into the state of the company's finances and knew they had endured a very rocky time recently. For over 250 years Perennial Mutual had ploughed its own furrow through wars, famines, depressions, market crashes and hostile government legislation and, despite everything that had been thrown at them, had prospered. They had spent the last three years trying to do the same thing, all that experience counting against them, and it now appeared they were facing a takeover as the company share price had slumped to an all-time low. (They were mutual in name only!)

I made my way up to the grand boardroom at the allotted time and took my allotted seat around the huge old table. The walls of the oak-panelled room were adorned with the portraits of previous chief executives, dating back nearly 200 years. Sir Daniel Levy had the unenviable task of addressing the meeting knowing full well that his would in all likelihood be the last portrait to hang in this room. Unsurprisingly his voice was solemn and his expression gloomy when he began to speak.

'First of all I would like to thank you all for attending the meeting today.'

123

Not that we had a lot of choice, I thought to myself. I knew that Sir Daniel would now lapse into corporate jargon and I would need to translate for myself what he was actually saying.

He continued. 'As most of you will know, over the last twelve months the directors have encountered some fiscal difficulties . . .' (They'd lost all the company's money.)

'. . . had invested into some bundled commercial property portfolios. . . .' (We bought into some unknown debt from American banks and now own the mortgages on a large number of shacks in Kentucky where people can't afford the payments and keep chickens in their living room.)

'. . . efforts were undertaken to secure the commercial property bundles. . . .' (We lent more money to the Kentucky shack owners who used the funds to buy more chickens.)

The sense of gloom around the room increased as everyone realized the state of the firm's finances. The meeting concluded with the bombshell that all our jobs were at risk – more corporate jargon for 'you are effectively out on your arse'. Suddenly the money I had in the bank seemed inadequate. Sure it was enough to tide me over for a few years – a lot of years if push came to shove (whatever that meant) – but most of that money was earmarked to buy myself and Amy a new home one day, not for buying food, clothes and other stuff. That was what I had a job for.

It was amazing how suddenly you appreciate something only when you are in danger of losing it. I had taken my role at PM for granted. They were a good employer with a benign environment that suited me. They were great when Lindsay was ill, and after her death they went out of their way to help me work part-time. I had a good deal of goodwill towards them and was angry that a very few greedy people at the top had jeopardized my job, and probably the jobs of hundreds of others who didn't even know there was a problem yet – and who had less money in the bank than I did.

As lost in my thoughts as I was I hadn't realized Sir Daniel had stopped speaking and had opened up the meeting to questions. As I had the bad luck to be sitting directly to his right, I was first in line. The whole room was staring at me, waiting for me to ask something intelligent and relevant, neither of which I was particularly adept at, especially under pressure. 'Erm. . . . What about you? Is your job under threat?'

This caused a few stifled giggles around the room and I noticed that Sir Daniel's face had suddenly turned red. He now looked flustered and his answer was delivered in a stutteringtone, 'Well, my position and the other erm . . . directors . . . have yet to . . . well, that is, we have not . . . the overall decision on the organization's future direction has yet to be, well, decided.'

The other disgruntled employees took the opportunity to pin Sir Daniel against the wall with follow up questions.

'Well, are you leaving or not?'

'Negotiations are ongoing—'

'You got us in this mess and you're telling us you're getting to keep your job?'

'Well, I may remain in a reduced capacity—'

'Typical. You and your highly paid cronies bugger everything up and yet it is everyone else who pays the price.'

'Well, it's not quite like that—'

'That's exactly what it's like—'

And so the attacks continued. I'd opened up a whole can of emotional worms and any remote chance I may have had of keeping my job had disappeared in a barrage of aggressive questions and accusatory glances from Sir Daniel for bringing this down upon him. Eventually everyone ran out of steam and we filed quietly out of the room.

Along with everyone else, I was handed a pack by Melanie, the company secretary, and went to the canteen, where I bought a coffee and a stale muffin before reading the contents.

Once I'd digested the information, which was slightly easier than the muffin, I discovered that there would be a thirty-day period during which time the company would prepare my terms of redundancy. After that date I would receive a summary document of my final compensation and benefits. I was due six months' salary and a small sum for the purchase of what the firm called 'ancillary benefits'. I had no idea what ancillary benefits I had, and was quite happy to sell them for the three thousand quid they were offering.

I returned and sat at my desk, feeling shell-shocked and apprehensive. I glanced at my phone and noticed that I had another missed call from Jamie. No texts from my wife. I doubt even *she* would have seen this coming. Jamie, however, was obviously desperate to get hold of me, but I really didn't feel like talking to him right then.

Before I had a chance to wallow in my self-pity I detected a strange aroma in the air which I could have sworn was fish and chips. Having hot food at your desk in Perennial Mutual was strictly forbidden. In fact, when I had my first day induction with the firm it was the first thing they covered. Not where to go in a fire, or what to do if there was a terrorist attack, but the fact that hot food MUST be consumed in the upstairs canteen or in the café area downstairs, and must NEVER be eaten at your desk.

I wandered out of my room and across the open plan office, following my nose. My attention was drawn to a number of skinny waifs who had clearly sensed the mouth-watering aroma too and were practically drooling.

I smiled at Lynne who was particularly skinny and wondered when she last ate a solitary chip, let alone fish and chips plural.

I eventually traced the source of the food emanating from an office pod containing two desks. This was Perennial Mutual's Human Resources department, which consisted of Alan Black, whose speciality was stress counselling – he was off on long-term sick, suffering from stress of all things – and Molly Jenkins, Jamie's much better half.

I sat on the desk beside Molly, who eventually noticed I was there, and acknowledged my presence with a weak smile.

'Hi, Andy, how are things?'

'Not great, Molly, I've just been given my marching orders, but you'll know all about that I suppose.'

She smiled sympathetically and flipped her dark hair out of her eyes. 'Yeah, I know. Big changes afoot.'

Molly had a fantastic figure which she usually kept concealed under baggy clothes and trousers. I knew that Jamie hated her showing off her body which is why she usually dressed so dowdily. (He would have loved the Garden Ranger uniform.) When Lindsay was alive we'd occasionally go out as a foursome and although Lindsay disliked Jamie, she was very fond of Molly. I remembered one evening when we were out together, and Jamie went off on one after noticing Molly staring at a good-looking blond hunk standing at the bar. Lindsay had been staring at him too. He looked like an Australian surfer dude with long blond locks and tanned skin. He had on shorts and a cut off T-shirt and stood out amongst the normal crowd of milk white Scots. The thing was, if Lindsay had a major strop every time I stared at a pretty girl we'd never have been speaking. Window shopping was fine in my book as long as you didn't go in and try anything on. I suppose it should maybe have been a warning sign to Molly back then, but at that point she was still starry-eyed and thought his jealousy was endearing and meant that he cared.

Physically, Molly and Lindsay were very alike. Personality-wise they were miles apart. Lindsay was strong and opinionated. Molly was a gentle soul, with a desire to please and a hater of conflict.

I glanced at the half-eaten fish and chips on her desk.

'Do you want a chip?' she asked.

I laughed, 'No thanks. Are you aware that by flouting company policy so blatantly, you are driving some of our undernourished administrators out of their minds?'

Molly laughed out loud with the dirty laugh I used to love when she got drunk. I laughed along with her and realized how long it had been since I'd actually spoken to her properly. Yes I'd bumped into her in the office occasionally and sometimes said hello if she'd answered Jamie's mobile but it had been too long since I'd spent any time in her and Jamie's company. It made me realize just how deeply my wife's death had affected me. I used to crash at Jamie's place a lot when we were both young, free and single, but since we'd both shacked up with our respective women this had stopped, and since Lindsay's death I had become positively anti-social. I still didn't fully understand why I avoided going to their flat. It probably had something to do with them still having what I'd lost but perhaps it was something deeper than that. Self-analysis wasn't one of my strengths.

I noticed for the first time as Molly looked up that she had been crying. Her eyes were red-rimmed and in confirmation she blew her nose into a paper tissue.

I suddenly realized why Jamie might have been so desperate to speak to me.

'Are you OK, Molly? Anything I can help with?'

She shook her head sadly. 'No, I think me and Jamie are splitting up.'

That came as a bolt out of the blue. I didn't know what I was expecting to hear, but it wasn't that. I hadn't had a clue from Jamie that things had got that bad. Jamie had initially moved into Molly's rented flat, then once they'd bought a place together I'd thought that would be it, despite my misgivings. I remember asking Jamie if that was such a good idea given the way he lived his life and his anti-capitalist views. I wondered what had happened and suddenly wished I'd phoned Jamie back before coming in to Molly's office. I no longer felt close enough to Molly to initiate the conversation so I waited.

Molly sighed and pushed the food away from her. Meeting my gaze she said, 'You know what Jamie's like as well as I do, always away trying to save something from someone or someone from something. He works late pretty much every day and I've never had reason to doubt what he tells me.'

Tears welled up in her eyes and some slipped down her face, tracing a well-worn line through her foundation. She wiped them with her hand and continued. 'Then last night completely out of the blue I get this email, from Anna Stavosky, Polish or Czech or something. Anyway she says that she and Jamie were lovers for a few months while she was volunteering on some project he was running. "Lovers." Doesn't that sound very grown up, very civilized. Except he's *not* a grown up and it's not civilized. It's fucking tragic. Anyway, she says he called it off before it got serious as he was feeling guilty about cheating on his long-term girlfriend, which I assume is me though I'm not so sure anymore. Her final words in this email are that she had been mulling it over for some time and decided to write to me now because I deserved to know what had happened.'

Anger had made her tears dry up and she fixed her dark hazel eyes on me. 'You probably knew about Anna, didn't you? Jamie probably even got you to cover for him or something stupid.'

A look of alarm must have appeared on my face because Molly said, 'Oh don't worry about it, Andy. I don't blame you. I'm the one who should have confronted him. He was at least big enough to admit it when I asked him if it was true.'

I did know about Anna. This was the girl who got Lindsay so mad about Jamie and had made her call him a hypocrite. I remember her being furious that I was party to Jamie's infidelity and that we should tell Molly what was going on. Eventually, when she had calmed down she agreed to wait until I could find out more about Jamie's plans. We never followed up on it because soon after that Lindsay was diagnosed with cancer and that took over our lives.

'The one good thing we did last night when I confronted him was actually have a proper conversation, where we actually talked and I almost forgave him, especially as he swore it was a one off and would never happen again. He spun me the line about how having an affair can make relationships stronger and all that crap, and I almost fell for it until we had *the talk*.'

At this point I am reminded that I do not possess a vagina, and as such have absolutely *no* idea what that meant. She looked at me expectantly. I smiled politely and shrugged my shoulders.

Molly sighed with exasperation as she realized too that I didn't possess the female genes or genitalia to understand what *the talk* is.

'Kids, Andy, we had the talk about kids, starting a family, getting pregnant, fucking without protection, getting up the duff, bun in the oven, being with child or actually . . . you know what? We didn't actually have the talk. I talked and he listened. I'm trying to plan my future.

130

I'm not getting any younger, I'm thirty-one next week, and after three years together you would think he would know me well enough to know that by now, wouldn't you?'

I nodded non-committally, if it was possible to nod in the style of an adjective.

'Yeah you *do* know, because you *are* a grown up. You've been there. You and Lindsay made that commitment. I always envied your relationship because it was everything I wanted, and hoped to have one day. So what do I do? I tell you what I do, I sit down and take both his hands in mine. I look deep into his eyes and I say "Will you marry me, Jamie?" Even after all the shit he's put me through and the pain I'm feeling. I was emotional and I wanted to make everything good again.'

This sounded incredibly romantic, but judging by the binge eating and her indignation, I'm guessing that things didn't go well.

'Can you guess what the moron then says to me?'

I opened and closed my mouth like a goldfish gasping for air a few times and shook my head. I seemed to be doing that a lot lately.

'Bearing in mind we've been pouring our hearts out to each other for about twenty minutes – well, I have anyway, I doubt he even has a heart at times. Well, he does for his waifs and strays but not for me. You know what the bastard says?'

Noting he had changed from moron to bastard and guessing that this was not a good progression, I shook my head again.

'He says . . . he says. . . .' At this point she burst into tears again and mumbles, 'Ask me again next year.' She then repeated it four or five times, getting quieter each time. 'Ask me again next year. How can he say that?' I assumed the question was rhetorical so I stayed silent.

Lindsay had always thought the two of them were not

131

well suited – not just because Jamie was an immature idiot at times, like now, but because she also felt protective of Molly. Lindsay recognized that Molly was a quiet soul who only wanted to be loved, and that Jamie wouldn't be able to do that unconditionally. He had too many causes to fight for and believe in. Lindsay connected with Molly partly because she recognized what a gentle person she was, and partly because they both smoked cigarettes in an age when it was easier to admit to being a syphilitic cross-dresser who enjoyed torturing kittens than a smoker. They used to sneak outside together to have a cigarette, and I am sure they connected during those moments.

Lindsay could never quite put her finger on why she thought they weren't suited outside of her dislike for Jamie. She did say that he tried to flirt with her when Molly and I were out of the room and she also implied that he might be gay. I'm not quite sure how those two things tallied. I also always believed that anyone who lived with a woman in a monogamous relationship was unlikely to be gay, or 'a poof', as Amy would say.

Jamie's natural conversation could easily be mistaken for flirting. When we were growing up he always went out with gorgeous-looking girls and I sometimes envied him his easy way with words, the casual confidence that really good-looking people all seem to have.

I might have been mistaken, but I didn't think bringing up Lindsay's theory about Jamie's sexuality would be appropriate right now and was unlikely to help the situation, so I kept my thoughts to myself.

Molly recovered and dabbed her eyes with the now damp tissue before blowing her nose loudly. As she raised her head I noticed she had a large lump of snot on her left cheek. I didn't feel that pointing that out to her right at that second would help things either, so I tried my best to avoid staring at it as she spoke.

132

'Thanks for listening, Andy, I feel a bit better now that I've actually told someone who understands these things – and Jamie.'

I smiled and reckoned she was giving me way too much credit there, but decided not to contradict her opinion of me. Instead I asked, 'So what happens now?'

It was her turn to shrug her shoulders. 'I don't know. He stayed at his mum's last night, just because I was so furious with him. I think he thinks I will calm down and everything will go back to normal. He even phoned me to discuss getting the cat I've always wanted but he would never let me get because he was allergic to them. '

I searched my memory banks. 'I think he is allergic actually, but is the cat thing not some kind of baby substitute?'

Molly welled up again. 'Shit, I hadn't thought of that. Of course it is. He's such a manipulative bastard.'

I should have kept my mouth shut. I tried to move her on from the cat thoughts. 'So will you forgive him, do you think?'

'Oh I don't know. We've invested so much in each other and everything else. The thought of splitting up fills me with dread for a million reasons. The flat is worth much less than we paid for it, so that would be a nightmare to sort out. The car loan is in joint names and I've no idea what would happen to that. I earn much more than Jamie, you know that, so he couldn't pay for anything if he was on his own renting a flat or whatever. It's such a bloody mess.'

She paused for a moment before carrying on.

'Then there's all that "being single" crap to go through again. I hated being single, it's no fun at all, you sit in on your own all week then spend the weekend fighting off creepy blokes in bars and clubs. That is until you end up snogging one of them at the end of the night because you're drunk and feeling lonely, and the attention of some creep is better than no attention at all. Being single is no fun. . . .'

She suddenly realized she was speaking to probably the most reluctant singleton on the planet.

'Oh I'm sorry Andy, I don't mean you. I know you are single now but that's different.'

I knew that it was actually *not* different at all, but let her off the hook easily. 'I know it is different. I've got Amy so I don't get lonely.' That was a lie obviously but Molly didn't know that.

'Maybe not having kids is a good thing, you know with global warming, melting ice caps, pollution, wars, famines and stuff – all the things that Jamie likes to rave about. It's not a great world to bring a child into. . . .'

Once again she had put her foot in it. 'Oh Andy, ignore me please, I'm talking rubbish. I don't know what to do. I do want to have children, I always have, it looks like I've picked the wrong man and it's a decision I have to deal with, or live with, I suppose. I could always freeze some of my eggs if the worst came to the worst.' At least she could laugh at herself, and she did with that wonderful dirty laugh that made her whole body shake. 'No doubt you'll get Jamie's side of it later and he'll have his own version, I'm sure. Actually, I bet you've had it already, haven't you?'

I shook my head. 'No. He's been trying to get me since last night and we keep missing each other.'

'Well at least you know now why he's calling.' She changed the subject.

'What's happening with you just now? I'm not actually in the loop as a lot of the HR stuff has been outsourced for the top-level redundancies in here.'

I stood up and stretched. 'Well I've got the thirty-day thing then I'm out on my arse.'

She smiled sadly, and said, 'You'll get another job.

It might even do you good to get out of here. You never know, you might even meet a new woman in a new office where everyone doesn't know your history.'

That reminded me that I had a date tonight and I reluctantly left her in her small pod staring at her illicit food and headed home to break the news to Pauline.

CHAPTER SIXTEEN

Back home, Pauline received my news calmly and positively, saying that Amy would benefit from me being around more and a new job – a new beginning – might be a good thing for me too. I changed my reason for going out that night to meeting a few of the condemned souls for some drinks after work. I was of course meeting Amanda, and that distracted me somewhat from the new reality of being nearly unemployed.

Amy was staying at Pauline's. Another 'overnighter' in case I arrived home 'worse for wear', as she described it. I told Pauline that I really appreciated her watching Amy over the last few weeks as I had been going out more than usual. Pauline knew that I'd hardly been out at all since Lindsay's death, but she played along with me.

'It's fine Andy. I understand that you need to get out and about a bit, especially after what happened to you today, just don't overdo it, OK?'

I caught a bus into town and watched the streets get busier as the city centre approached. To say I was nervous was something of an understatement. I had sweaty palms and butterflies in my tummy. Even the pain of the dental abscess had eased completely, probably as a result of the adrenalin coursing through my nervous system. Once I was seated in The Nine Brothers bar, I ordered myself a large glass of Valpolicella in the hope that I would feel less like a cat on a hot tin roof. I was more nervous tonight than on any of the other dates, probably because it felt like there was a lot riding on it. Lindsay had described in her email the lack of chemistry between some men she'd thought she would like, and that you only really knew if there was chemistry when you met them. I wondered what it would feel like to meet Amanda. I wasn't completely comfortable with the whole dating thing and still wished there was an easier way to meet someone.

The bar was busier than I expected but thankfully it wasn't packed. I considered sitting at a table outside again, but the sun was beginning to go down and long shadows were converging on the outside tables, meaning at this time of year it would get chilly quickly. Amanda probably had the Brazilian Rainforest setting on her thermostat too so I would need to stay inside in the warm.

I noticed a few pretty girls distributed throughout the pub. Most of them were seated near the door as if strategically placed there by the management to attract in single or not-so-single males from the street. On the large screen television a snooker match was in session; a young fat chap was trying to manoeuvre his ample belly across one of the pockets without disturbing the green. The audience seemed enraptured, and I wondered about our national psyche that they seemed happy to sit in a stuffy auditorium watching un-athletic men poke at coloured balls with sticks on a warm late-summer evening.

I glanced across the bar and caught my reflection in the mirror. I'd made a real effort tonight, putting on my favourite shirt, shaving again (I can't remember the last time I shaved twice in one day), and applied the expensive aftershave that my wife bought me on our honeymoon. I checked my watch again, she was late.

I carried my drink to a vacant nearby table and took a large gulp of the wine which was delicious, surprising given that it was pub wine. I tried to relax. My mind was naturally drawn back to my previous attempts at Internet dating and I shuddered.

Then I noticed Amanda making her way towards me. She was wearing a light-green summer dress, low-cut at the front with the hem ending just above her knee. Her red hair was long and straight and curled under ever so slightly at the ends. She looked stunning. Most of the guys she passed managed to tear their eyes away from the snooker and watched her walk past, which was always a good sign. I read once, probably on a Google search, that red-hair was caused by some kind of rogue mutated gene. If Amanda was the result, then we should campaign for more rogue genes. Maybe I'd start one.

My stomach churned with nerves when she noticed me and smiled, revealing perfect white teeth. She had a large canvas bag slung over her shoulder and looked relaxed. I felt a sudden grumbling in my bowels and felt an urgent need to fart. I concentrated hard and managed to suppress it. That would not have been the best beginning, especially if she thought it was my aftershave.

There was no uncertainty this time. Amanda leaned over and gave me a wonderful hug and kissed me. Our lips lingered briefly, and she held my hand as she sat on the chair next to me. She smelled of peaches, which I assumed was either her shampoo or soap.

I stared at her for a few seconds before I pulled myself together and offered to buy her a drink. She refused and insisted on getting her own. I watched her lovely bottom wiggle as she walked over to the bar. I took another large sip of wine.

She returned with two glasses of wine, having bought

me another one.

'You didn't need to do that,' I said, embarrassed. 'We probably should have bought a bottle, it would have been cheaper.'

She smiled. 'Maybe, but I've got the car so I can only really have one anyway.'

I loved her accent, so soft, so sensual. I could have listened to her talk forever. I felt like there could be real chemistry this time, as long as I remembered not to ask about her sister and she didn't prove to be a psycho. I had an idea of what Lindsay was talking about.

We talked about unimportant stuff initially then the conversation moved on to her family which was large and extended.

'I think it must be reassuring to be part of something like that,' I said, carefully avoiding any request to see photos of family members.

'It can be,' she explained. 'But there is a lot of pressure too; so many people to remember to include in everything important, and to remember to buy presents for.'

Our conversation flowed freely and after a short time I had finished my first glass of wine, and was working my way nicely through the second one when I noticed Amanda looking at me strangely.

'You're drunk,' she said accusingly. 'How much did you have before I got here?'

'Zis is my slechond glass,' I heard a voice utter. It sounded like mine but I wasn't sure. What was wrong with me?

'I don't believe you, a glass and a half of wine wouldn't do that.' She sighed, I assumed with disappointment. 'I can't stand drunks, there's been enough of that in my family over the years and I really don't want that. I'm sorry Andy, but I'm leaving, it's a real shame as well because I really liked you.'

I tried to think of something to say but my brain was fuzzy. She touched my arm briefly before picking up her bag. As she walked out the bar I felt terrible. The wine must have been bad or something. I staggered out after her, lurched from side to side and almost fell headlong through the open door onto the street in my anxiety to catch up with her. I spotted her walking briskly along the pavement and staggered after her shouting 'Manda' as I went. After that everything was hazy. I could vaguely remember someone helping me into a car and then nothing.

The next thing I was aware of was opening my eyes, but only being able to make out shadows and the outlines of things. I slowly realized I was at home in my bed. My head was thumping and I felt nauseous. As my eyes adjusted to the gloom I decided that the whole thing must have been a bad dream and felt relieved. Perhaps everything had been a dream, the emails from Lindsay, the Internet dating. Maybe Lindsay was still alive. The whole of the last year might have been a very bad dream like that whole series of Dallas in the eighties.

I realized I had only my boxer shorts on. Normally I slept in boxer shorts and a T-shirt, so that wasn't right. Suddenly I was conscious of a presence in the bed beside me. I daren't look. Could it be true, could the whole of the last year have been nothing but a long nightmare? What else would explain the female presence in my bed? I could smell it was female. It must be Lindsay.

I slowly moved my head to the left but it hurt too much to even do that. My brain registered the red hair spread over the pillow and I experienced a tidal wave of emotions: despair that it was not Lindsay, bewilderment, realization and humiliation. Amanda must have brought me home and put me to bed and then climbed in beside me.

I wasn't sure how anything happened. My last recollection was running out of the pub and shouting after her.

Now here I was in my bed and. . . . I tried to look at my watch but it wasn't on my wrist. I gave up. I was too tired to think anymore and I allowed my head to return to its original position and fell back into a dark dreamless sleep.

The next time I woke, the bed beside me was empty. I discovered that I could move my head without the world spinning so I bravely sat up. I could hear the radio playing softly in the kitchen and gingerly climbed out of bed. I slipped my dressing gown on before padding across the hall into the open-plan kitchen. Amanda was there, buttering toast and brewing coffee.

She smiled, which surprised me as I was expecting some kind of chastisement.

'Good morning, Andy. You really shouldn't drink on top of antibiotics you know, especially the ones that say in large bold black letters – DO NOT DRINK ALCOHOL.'

Of course – I'd forgotten all about that, the pills for my abscess.

'God, I forgot all about them. That's why I was so drunk! How did you know?'

'Oh I was all for leaving you lying on the pavement, but thought somebody might rob you or something, so I managed to get you into the back of my car. It took ten minutes but you eventually remembered where you lived, and it was whilst I was looking for your keys that I found the tablets, and the genius that I am worked it all out. You're lucky I'm a Good Samaritan otherwise you might have ended up in a gaol cell or worse.'

'Thank you so much, Amanda. I am so sorry, I just didn't think. Did you sleep all right?'

'Apart from your snoring, yes, I got a few hours.'

'Sorry about that, you should have slept in Amy's room or even the couch, rather than listen to me.'

'I thought about it, but I was concerned in case you threw up and choked so decided to lie beside you until I

141

was sure you'd be OK. I did move through to the couch about one o'clock I think, but once it got light it was hard to sleep. It's so bright in here.'

'We didn't—'

A laugh and snort of derision erupted from her. 'You must be joking. You couldn't even move your head. I've never felt safer sleeping in the same bed as a man in my life.'

She smiled and I laughed briefly, but had to stop as it hurt.

Amanda sipped from her coffee, walked over and gazed out one of the windows overlooking the sea. I picked up a piece of toast and joined her in admiring the view.

'Quite a place you've got here,' she said, without turning to look at me.

'It suits me for the time being.'

'You mean you might move?'

I sighed and explained about losing my job, and the dilemma I had between staying here and ultimately finding a house with a garden for Amy.

Amanda sympathized. 'When I left Ireland to come over here I bought a little flat in Corstorphine, in the West End. My plan was to stay there a few years and move on, but now it's fallen in value and I'm kind of stuck.'

Her situation reminded me of Molly's, but when I thought about it there must be hundreds if not thousands of people in the same situation.

She turned to me. 'Anyway I reckon I'll have to stay put until I meet someone I think is marriage material then maybe make a move.' She smiled as she said the last phrase, and put her coffee cup down on the unit. She moved away from the window. Her body moved so rhythmically, like a panther. I'd never seen anyone who actually seemed to shimmer when they walked. I wondered if that came with the rogue gene. I snapped out of it and noticed she had picked up her bag and coat.

'Are you leaving?' I asked disappointedly.

Amanda nodded and checked her watch. 'Yes, I've got things to do today and need to get a move on.'

She paused and stared at me for a moment, weighing me up I thought. 'OK Andy, I'll probably regret this but let's forget about last night and meet up again properly. This week isn't good – I'm incredibly busy at work and have a conference to organize in London at the weekend – so let's say a week on Saturday. How does that grab you?'

I suddenly realized that I would like to meet up with Amanda again, even if it was only to listen to her voice. I said, 'Two weeks, that's an awfully long time.'

Amanda nodded and some of her auburn hair tumbled in front of her eyes. She pushed it back behind her ear and I was mesmerized. She noticed and smiled. 'Yeah I know. Sorry, but I'm worth the wait.'

Again snapping out of my reverie I asked, 'How about you come up here? I'll cook something for dinner, and we can maybe have a proper chat?'

'OK, Andy, I'll go for that. I think you're a nice guy. I'm not sure you're marriage material, but a few dates will no doubt determine that for me.'

She moved toward me and kissed me on the lips. 'I think you better get some food inside you, and if I were you I'd stay clear of wine until you've finished those pills.'

After she left, I flopped down onto the couch and took stock. I'd had four disastrous dates so far (although the latest one had turned out OK in the end.) I wondered if my wife truly understood how poor I was at dating. If dating was a sport, I would not get onto anyone's team and probably wouldn't even have made the reserves.

CHAPTER SEVENTEEN

I didn't have time to relax for long, as a few moments after I'd parked my arse on the couch and switched on the TV my phone vibrated in my pocket. I flipped it open and glanced at the readout. It was from Lindsay and simply said:

> Hi sweetie, I've sent u another email, so read it when you get a chance.
> Linz xxx

Her system hadn't failed after all, but I still couldn't work out how she had co-ordinated all this texting and emailing. I was excited and at the same time apprehensive about what this one would say. I muted the TV and moved gingerly to get my iPad. I made some more toast while it powered up. In reality I should have set up my email account on my phone, but I didn't know how to do that, and couldn't be arsed reading the one-squillion page instruction booklet to find out.

I logged on to my email account and opened Lindsay's email.

Love Byte 3 - 20th October
My gorgeous husband

I hope you are looking after my little girl, and that you are both well and thriving. It's the middle of the night and I'm up again taking more bloody pain killers. I'm not sure how much longer I can take this, but I put on a brave face for you and Amy – well, mainly for you, thankfully Amy isn't really aware of what I'm going through and long may that continue.

I know this will be difficult for you to read, but I feel I owe it to you to tell you how it is – or was by the time you read this – especially as you and Amy are sleeping and oblivious right at this point in time.

I want you to know that when the time comes for me to go, it will be a relief. I'm only telling you this because I might be so doped up later that I might not make much, if any, sense. Hopefully though I've got a few weeks (fingers crossed months) left in me. By that time I should have finished messing with your life and I can leave you to get on with it, which I am sure will be a relief for you – but I'M NOT FINISHED YET.

OK, so what have I achieved so far? Well by my reckoning I've set you up on a dating site, you've had some emails from potential suitors and you might even have met some of them by now, in fact you might be deeply in love and ignoring my further efforts here! (BUT I DOUBT IT.) You have to kiss a few princesses before you find your frog!

The problem with you, Mr Hunter, is that you will be looking for the perfect person, and probably comparing them all to me – big mistake. By now I'll have been dead for some time and I can do no wrong. I'm perfect because I'm in your memory and cannot blot my copybook in any way. No woman can live up to that.

I'm going to give you another week to sort yourself out. If you haven't found another woman by then I have one more ace up my sleeve. I will play that card anyway, because even if you have found someone else it won't do any harm, but if you haven't then it might just be the perfect last throw of the dice for me.

On another note I guess by now you will have realized that Jamie and Molly have had some problems. I don't feel great about sending that email I have to say. . . .

I hadn't realized that my wife was capable of being so devious. The revelation didn't actually shock me as I should have known Lindsay was behind it. It was a piece of unfinished business from her point of view. She was trying to help Molly. I'm not sure she had but there wasn't much I could do about it now.

. . . but I felt that Molly deserves better than your friend. I hope you don't tell him or her it was me. It will only cause more problems and might make Molly feel so sorry for him that she takes him back. She's a bit soppy like that. She might actually have forgiven him anyway which is very sad but if she has then so be it. I've done my best – or worst – whichever way you want to look at it.

Back to me. I don't know what will happen over the next few weeks. I know we've talked about me going into a hospice. I will try and resist that as long as I can but I reckon it is inevitable at some point. By then I will have finished this project. The good thing about this is that

146

I can play with time. I can spend a few hours planning things here but in your world a week, a fortnight or a month can go by, which is weird and kind of hard to get your head around. It's been a while since I've contacted you (in your time). I was deliberately letting you get on with it (or not, which is more likely!).

Not everything I do will work but hopefully you are at least having some fun with what I've set up for you. No doubt other things will be going on in your life I can know nothing about but I don't worry about that. I'm only concerned with the controllables!

OK that's it for now. I hope that you and my gorgeous wee girl are well and that she's not missing her mamma too much. I'll be in touch soon.

Your gorgeous wife
Lindsay

PS Hope you like the texts, I thought that was really clever of me!!

It was very clever of you Lindsay and, much too clever for me. Of course she couldn't know anything about me losing my job, or that Jamie had been given an ultimatum by Molly and rejected her. The 'ace' up her sleeve worried me somewhat. A week was not a long time, and after the Jamie/Molly situation, anything was possible. Internet dating hadn't really worked for me yet but it was early days and I still had Amanda waiting in the wings. I still hadn't figured out what I wanted from Amanda, if anything, but I hoped whatever Lindsay's 'ace' was ultimately didn't interfere with it. I was more than capable of messing things up on my own.

CHAPTER EIGHTEEN

Pauline brought Amy home later on the Saturday morning and the three of us drove to a family farm park in East Lothian, a few miles south of Edinburgh. It had a narrow gauge railway, farm animals and an adventure playground that Amy loved. It was an exhausting afternoon. We dropped Pauline off at her flat on the way home, and after feeding and bathing Amy she was asleep without me even needing to read a story. I was too tired to log onto my iPad and watched an old movie instead.

After a few minutes I realized I'd seen it before and decided to give Jamie a ring instead. As he was back living with his parents I knew he'd be sitting in his old bedroom sulking. We'd spent countless hours in that room as kids. His mum and dad would be watching TV in the next room and through the wall he'd be able to hear the muffled sounds of some game show or soap opera. The fact his parents could sit and watch so much rubbish did and would annoy him more than anything. He wouldn't have told his parents the whole story yet. All they would know was that he and Molly had fallen out.

Whenever I'd been in Jamie's house when we were younger, I'd always been fascinated by the way his parents and Jamie moved seamlessly between English and Italian when talking. They would start a sentence in English and about halfway through they would switch. If they were excited or stressed then everything came out in Italian.

I wasn't sure what Jamie would tell them about him and Molly splitting up. If he mentioned Anna then I could imagine any discussion after that would be in Italian with over-enthusiastic gesturing.

He answered his phone almost immediately. 'Hi, Andy, I was thinking of phoning you – actually, you're one of the few people left in the world still speaking to me.'

I laughed. 'I take it your mum and dad didn't take the news well then?'

Jamie snorted down the phone. 'Yeah you could say that; you'd think someone had died.'

His parents had accepted Molly as part of the family, and were always pressing him about marriage and grand-children. They were both in their sixties now and had they stayed in Italy, could have expected that both he and his sister Maria would have produced offspring by now. His sister lived in London and worked as a lawyer for Greater London Authority. She was five years younger than Jamie, but as yet she too was unmarried. The news about Molly would frustrate his parents even more.

'How much have you told them?'

I heard Jamie sigh. 'Not that much, I just said that we'd been having problems for a while and decided to split up. . . .'

'So you didn't mention anything about Anna then?'

'You're joking, right? You know what my mum's like. She'd murder me if she found out about that! Molly's a bloody saint in her eyes.'

I felt sorry for my friend and decided to cheer him up a little and told him about my first two Internet dates with Ellen and Terry, I decided to keep the others to myself for the time being. It did the trick and soon he was laughing his head off at my expense, but for once it didn't bother me that much. I felt like I was performing a kind of social service. There hadn't been many occasions in the last year or so where I had felt someone was worse off than me.

We agreed to meet the next morning for brunch and after hanging up I went to bed. Our conversation must have triggered some repressed memories because after I fell asleep I dreamed about the time Jamie and I had investigated how much toilet roll it would take to block up the toilet in his parents' flat. After much experimenting we discovered it took nearly two full rolls shoved down at once to clog up the waste pipe sufficiently for the water to back up. Later Jamie discovered it took a plumber an hour to unblock the same pipe and cost his parents sixty quid. I didn't go around to Jamie's for a while after that.

The next morning, Amy and I donned our coats and ventured out to meet Jamie in the Blue Café in Portobello. The east of Edinburgh was shrouded in haar, which is the Scottish name for the sea fog that rolled in from time to time during the summer and early autumn. Sometimes it burned off after a few hours, other times it lasted all day. The frustrating thing about it was that you could literally drive a few miles to the west and find yourself bathed in warm sunshine.

The Blue Café was a great place to take Amy to as it had a large soft-play area inside if the weather wasn't good and, as it was right on the beach, on a sunny day you could reserve an outdoor table and watch her play in the sand. Today we went for the indoor option. It allowed me to have lunch and some adult conversation with only the occasional toddler interruption. Jamie was the only person there, as far as I could tell, with no kids. It didn't seem to bother him. In fact he was oblivious.

The aroma from the sizzling bacon made my mouth

water. We both ordered a full breakfast and I asked for a small side plate so I was able to share mine with Amy.

'Have you started looking for a new job yet?' Jamie asked.

I swallowed a juicy bit of bacon before answering. 'No, not yet. I've got six months' salary and some redundancy money so I'm not in any great rush. Besides, officially I've still got thirty days while they sort everything out.'

'Hoping for a miracle reprieve?'

I laughed. 'No chance of that, but I'm lucky I can take my time.' Jamie didn't really understand what I did for a living, along with ninety-nine point nine per cent of the rest of the population, so I changed the subject.

'Have you decided what you are going to do about Molly?' I asked, once we had stirred milk into our coffees.

Jamie shook his head. 'The thing that bothers me most is the email Molly received. When me and Anna split last year, I was sure she was cool with it. I don't remember her having any conscience issues with our relationship. She wasn't even Catholic. I was the one who carried the guilt.'

He popped some food into his mouth and stared into his coffee, looking for answers in the steam rising from the mug. He continued. 'Oh, and another thing: I've no idea how she got hold of Molly's email address.'

Obviously, I knew Anna was not responsible for anything but wasn't about to enlighten my friend about the situation. I probably should have let him down gently with a full explanation and given him and Molly the chance to reconcile. The reason I didn't, apart from the fact that I didn't want to explain the whole Lindsay/ Love Bitz thing, was that Jamie *had* cheated on Molly – more than once – and probably deserved to lose her. I felt sorrier for Molly, who was left with the mess to sort out, than him. I therefore suggested a plausible explanation for the email address conundrum.

'Maybe at some point you copied her in on something that had Molly's email address on it.'

Jamie considered the explanation and nodded slowly. 'Yeah, that's possible I suppose. It does suggest that she kept the address and planned to do this at a later date. I didn't think she was that devious.'

'She's a woman,' I offered unreasonably in explanation.

Jamie sighed. 'Yeah you're right. Anyway, as far as Molly goes, I don't think there's anything I can do. I've decided that the best thing for both of us is if I move out permanently and find somewhere new – a clean break.'

'The best thing for both of you? Or the best thing for you?'

Jamie smiled. 'Yeah, well, you'll need to ask her that. I'm doing it for me, of course I am. I can't go on like it's been. We hardly talk about anything important. It's got stale, you know?'

I nodded sympathetically but couldn't empathize. Lindsay and I hadn't been together long enough for that to happen. I doubt it would have anyway. My take on things was that they only got stale if you let them, but I was no expert. I was sure *Men Like Women and Women Like Shoes* would have an opinion, but decided not to refer Jamie to the website for the time being.

Amy came up and ate a lump of sausage before returning to the climbing frame.

'Have you spoken to Molly?' I asked, biting into another rasher of bacon and deciding I couldn't cope with being a vegetarian.

'Yeah, kind of. I phoned her this morning just to arrange things. You know, sort out a time to go and get my stuff. I knew she wasn't happy as she had on that Laser Lights song that she always plays when she's in a bad mood or pre-menstrual. You know the one . . . "Lost In Your Eyes".'

152

I nodded and munched on some toast. Laser Lights were a 90s Scottish pop band who'd had a spectacular first album with four hit singles, the biggest of which – 'Lost In Your Eyes' – was the summer anthem of 1996 and went to number one all across Europe. Their second album was hugely expensive to make and bombed badly, leaving the band bankrupt. I only remembered this so clearly due to an article I'd read in a Sunday newspaper the previous week. The article focused on the lead singer Colin Sparks who, after an unsuccessful attempt at a solo career, occasionally opened fetes and fairs and performed the band's old hits in shopping centres. According to the article he spent most of his off days playing 'Football Manager' and other stuff on his Xbox.

Jamie had finished his breakfast and sat back in his chair. 'Anyway I'm meeting her tomorrow to work out money and who gets what CDs and DVDs. I'm glad we've not got kids, it's hard enough sorting out who gets custody of P!nk, Keane, Coldplay and Total Recall. She can keep Laser Lights.'

I laughed and Jamie smiled which broke his gloomy mood. Changing the subject he asked, 'What about you and this Internet dating thing?'

Jamie couldn't understand why I had suddenly decided to try Internet dating. I hadn't told him about Lindsay's emails and texts, and probably wouldn't unless I had to. To him it must have appeared completely out of character for me. Rather than directly answering his question, I smiled sheepishly and confessed that I hadn't quite told him the whole story the night before and filled him in on my exploits with Carrie. If he didn't know me better he would have thought I was making it up. He knew my imagination was not that good. He almost choked on his coffee when I told him I walked out and left her to her own devices, or rather *with* her own devices.

'You're unbelievable, imagine walking out on that.'

'I was surplus to requirements; she seemed very happy on her own.'

'She obviously liked an audience.'

'Then she should use a webcam.'

'You're a twat. You think the whole world is full of hopeless romantics like you. Sometimes people just want a shag and nothing more. There's nothing wrong with that.'

His words sounded harsh but his eyes were full of mischief.

'Like you and Anna?' I asked with a smile.

'Ouch, that's below the belt.'

'Literally?'

'Now you're being smart. The thing about Anna was that she shared the same thought processes as me.'

'She worked for you, Jamie. You paid her to think like that.'

'She was paid by the council actually, and anyway that's got nothing to do with it. She believed in things, not like you and Molly. No disrespect but, you know, we were passionate about the same stuff: the environment, poverty and helping people who can't help themselves. It's hard being like that all the time on your own – fighting the lost causes. It was nice to have someone in my corner.'

'And in your bed.'

'Well, her bed actually, but it wasn't just the sex, it was the connection. I haven't had that with Molly for a long time, if ever.'

I pondered his last statement before observing, 'I think it must be hard living with you, Jamie. I don't mean that in a bad way, but you are so intense when you get on your high horse.'

Jamie sighed. 'I know I can be a bit like that, but you know most nights with Molly we didn't talk about us or work or anything really. We just sat and watched TV.

Valium for the masses.'

'See, there you go.'

'Yeah I know, but it is.'

I threw up my arms in frustration. 'People like TV. There's nothing wrong with it in moderation. It can be educational if you let it. For example, why did you become so passionate about the environment, homelessness and eventually turn so anti-capitalist and anti-establishment?'

'From reading mostly.'

'Bollocks. I grew up with you, remember? The Discovery channel was *never* off the telly in your bedroom. You learned most of it from that.'

Jamie smiled, defeated. 'Yeah OK, but Molly didn't want to watch anything educational, she was mainly into soaps and reality Big Brother type crap.'

What I said next wouldn't go down well but I knew it was the truth. 'Jamie, most evenings you finish work when?'

'It depends.'

'On an average day, what time do you knock off?'

Jamie knew where this was going, I could tell by his reluctance.

'I get paid from eight until five, with an hour for lunch.'

'That's not what I'm asking.'

'OK, I usually work on a bit beyond that.'

'A bit?'

'Yeah, OK, until seven or eight most evenings.'

'While Molly sits at home alone watching the telly waiting for you?'

Jamie nodded, 'Yeah, OK, I know. Maybe I've not been around as much as I should be.'

I smiled at my friend. 'When Lindsay was alive, we all used to go out sometimes, remember?'

'Yeah.'

'Molly loved going out, but she changed because she

155

wanted to be with you, wanted to try and fit in with who you are, what you are, but that didn't work. By changing, she became something other than herself and lost that spark that made you fall for her in the first place.'

A moment of silence followed, we were both thinking.

Jamie spoke first. 'There might be something in that, Andy, I have to admit. Difficult to see it from the inside right enough. Why didn't you mention it before now?'

I sighed. 'It's only just occurred to me.'

'Well that was bloody helpful.' Jamie laughed. 'Too late now anyway, I can't go back and change things. Anna happened. I can't undo that and I don't think Molly will forgive me.'

'Do you want to be forgiven?'

'Ooh Mr Philosophical today, aren't we? No, Andy, I don't think I do, I just want my own space now. I'll miss Molly, I'll miss that security but I reckon time on my own will do me good.'

'You might be right, but that won't last long. Women throw themselves at you.'

Jamie smiled at the compliment and switched it back to me again. 'Have you any more dates lined up?'

I paused and then told him about the fuck-up with Amanda the night before.

Jamie laughed so loudly that some of the other people in the café turned and stared over at us. 'I can't believe she has agreed to even see you again after that. She might try and get her own back. She might combine the traits of your last few dates – hey that rhymes. She might use vibrators, be abusive and burst into tears at the same time. You know . . . the worst of all worlds!'

I laughed at the picture it created in my mind. 'Yeah, you know what, Jamie? I wouldn't be a bit surprised. In any event I'd appreciate if you keep the details of my personal life to yourself for the time being.'

He nodded thoughtfully. 'I assume you don't want Pauline finding out?'

'No not yet, I think I'd rather find someone I like and who likes me before I cross that bridge.'

Jamie grinned. 'OK, your sordid secrets are safe with me.'

This was a natural break point in our conversation and Jamie yawned and stretched.

'Right,' he said, standing up. 'I've got to find somewhere new to live. I can't stand living back at home. I've got five flats to view today, all hopefully with furniture – otherwise I'm stuffed. All the stuff in our old flat is Molly's.'

Amy had come over and was standing by my chair staring at Jamie. 'Are you going to give Jamie a kiss goodbye?' I asked her.

She smiled and puckered up her lips like a tiny supermodel on a lipstick shoot. Jamie reluctantly bent down and she planted a sloppy kiss on his stubble covered chin. She shook her head and giggled. 'Tickles,' she said.

Jamie laughed and waved goodbye to go flat hunting.

Amy and I finished our food, paid and left. We walked along the beach as far as we could and enjoyed the fresh air and the sense of freedom you get walking by the sea. The haar had cleared a little and a watery sun was trying to warm the air. Eventually we ran out of beach and had to turn back onto the main road to access our apartment. Amy's little legs were tired and I ended up carrying her the last few hundred yards.

In the afternoon we took the bus into town and Amy insisted on sitting upstairs at the back beside a group of teenage girls. One of them was exceptionally pretty and was wearing a green Lycra micro-skirt. Although I was trying not to notice, I occasionally got a flash of her pink panties and had to turn away embarrassed. She looked about seventeen, but I realized this meant she was probably not a day over fourteen. One day Amy would want to go out dressed like jail-bait and I couldn't yet imagine what kind of arguments that would kick off.

Being a mother as well as a father would be doubly hard at that stage and I wasn't looking forward to it. I began to understand some of Lindsay's motivation in trying to get me a new girlfriend. Lindsay would have thought all this through of course, that's what she spent her last few months doing. She told me loads of times that terminal cancer was great for focusing the mind.

As the day wore on the mist disappeared and it tipped down with rain. We spent the remainder of the afternoon in John Lewis. I kept a wary eye out for 'psycho' Ellen and was fully prepared to hide should she make an appearance. There were several false alarms, one of which almost had me ducking behind a display of crystal glasses, but thankfully it appeared that Sunday wasn't one of her John Lewis days.

I found it amazing that even as a bloke who was averse to shopping, I could while away four hours in one store. It helped that Amy loved the toy department, and I found it relatively easy to regress to being a child in such an environment.

I then decided to have dinner in the restaurant as I realized there was very little food in the flat, and I couldn't be bothered going to the supermarket in the rain. Amy was happy with the arrangement, and filled the kid's meal option box to the brim with inappropriate junk that I had to sneakily remove when her attention was elsewhere to avoid a tantrum.

I opted for some pasta and a glass of Diet Coke. Wisely I avoided my preferred option of red wine due to the antibiotics.

I noticed the restaurant was full of families and I was

the only man alone with a child. I received a few sympathetic glances from some mothers, who probably thought I was divorced and trying to grab a few precious hours with my daughter. I'd hate to be divorced with restricted access to my child. How much you must miss.

The bill for dinner came to over fourteen pounds, and it occurred to me that with zero income coming in I would not be able to maintain such extravagances indefinitely.

Later that evening, spurred on by that realization, I decided to take stock of my finances and consulted my iPad after Amy was asleep.

I had a number of different accounts, prudently deciding to spread my funds between banks after the banking crisis. All of my funds were in cash getting next to nothing in interest. I probably should have made some longer-term investments. The banks were always calling me about this, but as I was unsure about how long I was going to stay in the apartment, I wanted the funds handy for buying a house. Cash seemed like the best option and I resisted the sales calls.

I had worked out a great strategy for dealing with those calls, especially the ones that originated from the sub-continent. I simply flipped the phone onto loudspeaker and handed it to Amy.

The conversation usually went like this:

'Hello, is that Mr Andrew?' (For some reason they always thought my first name was my surname which was annoying in itself.)

Amy then said, 'No.'

'Oh, is that Mrs Andrew?'

'No.'

'Can I speak to Mr Andrew please?'

'That's my daddy.'

'This is Robert.' (It wasn't, it was usually more likely to be Zaheer or Ahmed.) Can I speak to your daddy please?'

Amy then usually looked to me and I shook my head.
'No.'

'Robert' was stumped. 'What is your name?'

'Amy.'

'Hello Amy, is your mummy or daddy there?' I'd shake my head again.

'No.'

'There must be someone with you?' At this point, if I had him to hand, I'd hold up Barney the purple dinosaur.

Amy squealed, 'Barney!'

'Oh, can I speak to Barney please?'

'No. He's a poof.'

By this point I was usually doubled up with suppressed laughter with the picture in my head of 'Robert' frantically looking through his procedures manual, in case there was a section relating to homosexual babysitters and why they couldn't talk on the phone.

Eventually either Amy tired of the game or the cold-caller gave up, which was a shame because it would have entertained me all evening.

Back on my iPad, I calculated that with the funds from the house sale, the life assurance money and the payout from Lindsay's pension scheme, I had in total £327,000 in various accounts.

If I added to that total my six months of salary and the £3000 for my 'benefits' that added up to an extra £23,000. It was a relief then that I didn't have to contemplate selling the *Big Issue* just yet.

The money, though nice to have, didn't occupy my thoughts. At first I had felt incredibly guilty as it was only there due to Lindsay's death. As a couple we were spenders not savers, and although we had a good standard of living, neither of us had two beans in the bank, so this situation was new to me. Now I was very glad it was there, especially if I didn't get another job anytime soon.

I was tempted to check my emails but resisted as I was exhausted. It had been a stressful few days so I went to bed. If I had any dreams I didn't remember them.

CHAPTER NINETEEN

I woke up the next morning and realized it was the first Monday in a long time when I didn't have a job to go to. Although I was technically still employed, Perennial Mutual had effectively put me on garden leave which was ironic as I didn't even have as much as a window box. Instead of getting out of bed and heading for the shower I lay and thought for a while. Amy was still asleep so there was no pressing reason to get up.

It occurred to me that I would have to register with recruitment agencies soon. Although I was in no hurry, I knew that securing a part-time role would be much more difficult than if I was available for a full-time job. I also realized that the salary was likely to be depressingly less than I earned at PM. It made me wonder what kind of house I would be able to afford in my new impoverished state. When I last went house-hunting the economy was buoyant and mortgages plentiful, I probably wouldn't need a mortgage this time but running a house was still likely to be more expensive, and my city was one of the most expensive places in the UK to live.

They call Edinburgh The Athens of the North. This, as I understood it, had nothing to do with ruined buildings, (although there are more than a few of them) and certainly nothing to do with the weather which is as un-Athens-like as it is possible to get. I believed it was to do with the city once upon a time being a centre of 'enlightenment'.

Nowadays, in my opinion, it is no more 'enlightened' than any other city, but it is a nice place to live. Edinburgh has a real sense of history and attracts hordes of tourists from April until mid-September, who rush around photographing everything and anyone that don't move. I even once spotted a Japanese lady photographing a dog-turd outside Waverley Station. Maybe they don't have them in Japan.

I was born and grew up in the city, spending my early childhood in a small flat in the West End. It was part of a sixties' development and characterless. Later we moved to a more spacious three-bedroom place in a tenement block three streets away from the previous development, but light-years away in terms of architectural style. The tenement was built in 1853. I know that because above the common entrance door is a huge sandstone block with 1853 carved onto it. The first-floor flat inside had original cornice ceilings and stained-glass windows in the hall and bathroom. It always felt to me like I was peeing in church, but my mum loved it and refused to change it. She still lives there, and although the stairs were beginning to cause her problems, she'd vowed never to leave until she was 'carried out in a box'. I assume she means her coffin and one day I wouldn't suddenly be asked to get a big cardboard carton from Tesco to put her in.

I did leave Edinburgh for a time, moving to Preston to study for my degree, but I had always planned to come 'home' afterwards. Lindsay was originally from Dunfermline, a large town in Fife just across the Forth Road Bridge from Edinburgh. Her mother migrated across

163

the Forth soon after her father left them. Lindsay was only three at the time and she had no memory of anything except the New-Town flat where they lived until she got her job with 'Logical Fix'. She then rented an apartment near Hibernian's football stadium and remained there until she met me. Lindsay wasn't big on change.

We then bought our first – and as it turned out, only – house together.

When we went house-hunting it was an exciting but frustrating time for me. We'd go to see a perfectly nice house and I would think, 'That's a nice house, I could live here', only for Lindsay to say, 'It smells funny'.

I'd look at her incredulously thinking she must be joking, but no she wasn't, so 27 Darnley Drive was knocked on the head because it was offensive to Lindsay's nose. 7 Colquhoun Walk was condemned because the house next-door was yellow and had a very untidy garden. 42 Cherry Tree Gardens was a beautiful old semi-detached house full of character and charm. It had a wonderful kitchen-diner with French doors opening onto a lovely low maintenance garden. I loved the place, but Lindsay reckoned because of its age it would have mice, and she didn't want to share her house with a mouse.

Eventually she fell in love with a stone built semi-detached house: 11 Bridgewater Close. It was almost as old as the house in Cherry Tree Gardens, but for some reason the mouse thing didn't come up and I didn't mention it. I was just glad to find somewhere that didn't smell funny or was the wrong colour. We bought it and it became our family home. The three bedrooms were often fully occupied at weekends before we were married, as friends and relatives (mostly Lindsay's) came to stay. The first year we lived there we had someone staying over every weekend during the Edinburgh Festival which ran for the whole of August.

Even after we were married, and Lindsay was heavily pregnant, we had regular friends over most weekends. It was only after that I found myself alone most of the time. Whether that was because most of our friends were 'couple' friends, and now that I was no longer part of such an arrangement I was off limits, or whether it was simply that they only wanted Lindsay's company, I didn't know.

I still caught up with Jamie of course, but not for drinks anymore, usually just a quick brunch like the previous day. Our idea of a good night out had been a few beers followed by a few more beers whilst we set the world to rights. Then we would get some chips and stagger home, usually sometime after midnight.

It was not so easy waking up with a hangover now, as Amy would be up at the crack of dawn demanding attention and making a huge amount of noise. It was as if she had a sixth sense of when I had a hangover and upped the decibels. As a result I didn't drink much anymore. Jamie of course didn't have any children (or, as he would often say, 'none that he knew about') and with the way current events were shaping up it might be a while before he was in a position to change that. It was likely we would not see as much of each other in any event.

I was distracted from my thoughts by Amy's little voice shouting 'Daddy' and my day had begun.

After breakfast I tried to put on a Barney DVD for Amy. Unfortunately the DVD player wasn't working.

'Amy, why is there a banana in the DVD player?'

Amy ignored me and started playing with her doll. I sighed and realized that 'Why is there a banana in the DVD player?' was up there as one of the sentences I never thought I'd say. When you have a toddler you have quite a few and I'd started to keep a note of them:

'Don't stand on the piano' – when Amy was trying to jump on her electric keyboard.

'Stop swinging on the fridge' – when Amy was hanging off the handle of the American-style fridge-freezer.

'Watch that giraffe doesn't fall on you' – when Amy was trying to pull over a life-size toy giraffe in Hamleys.

'Amy, put your umbrella down. It's not raining in the car' – whilst driving to a country park.

'Amy, why is there a dinosaur in the freezer/toilet/my slipper/my cornflakes?' The plastic dinosaur got around.

After I'd scooped the mashed banana from the DVD player and cleaned it up the best I could, Amy decided she wanted *ET* on instead. Initially I had thought *ET* would be too grown up for Amy but she loved it. It was obviously mentally challenging for her as every time it was on she asked me lots of questions. Usually I could answer them.

'Why is ET sick?' – 'He's eaten too many sweeties.'

'Why does he walk funny?' – 'He needs to go for a poo.'

'Why does he talk like that?' – 'He needs to go for a poo.'

'Why are the bad men chasing him?' – 'They're trying to get him to go for a poo.'

'Why does he want to go home?' – 'He wants to have a poo at home.'

'Where does ET Live?'

The last one stumped me for a while. Whilst bowel movements would satisfy many of Amy's questions, sometimes it wasn't practical. I had thought about trying to explain how ET comes from a different planet a long way from Earth, but that would have raised even more questions from Amy.

Eventually Amy's voice got louder and louder as it tended to do when I didn't answer her. 'Where does ET live?'

Lacking a better answer I said, 'Dundee.'

'Dundee?'

'Yes, Dundee.' Amy's Aunt Millie lived in Dundee.

'Near Auntie Millie?'

'Yes, right next door to Aunt Millie.'

The next time Pauline took Amy to see her sister she would insist on going next door to see ET, but at least it got me off the hook for the time being.

After ET, we headed out. I took the car and we drove to a garden centre several miles outside the city. Amy liked playing in the playhouses and sheds, and inside they had a toy department and garden furniture, including garden swings which were effectively comfy couches that swung back and forth. We sat and played on one of those for ages until a grumpy 'associate' (that's what they called their staff) told us to move.

We didn't buy any plants as I had nowhere to put them. I could have bought some pots I suppose and put them on the deck outside the apartment, but I knew I would forget to feed and water them and they would die. It took me all my time to remember to feed and water myself and Amy. To illustrate the point, as usual there was no food in the apartment so I picked up some fish and chips on the way home. Amy liked fish and chips. They were not particularly nutritious but they were quick and I didn't have to coax her to eat them.

CHAPTER TWENTY

The next few days drifted by quietly – well, perhaps with a 2½-year-old around, quietly was not the best description. I took Amy to a few of her classes and Pauline took her for most of Wednesday, which allowed me to register with some agencies which specialized in financial jobs. None of them were confident in finding me a job anytime soon. They of course didn't use the word 'job', they drifted into jargon, typically saying, 'A suitable position may be difficult to secure in the current economic environment as firms are typically within a contracting phase of their development.'

In other words, like Perennial Mutual, they were booting people out rather than hiring new ones. I spent a depressing morning on the phone, then just as I had finished lunch, my mobile pinged signifying a text. I expected it to be Pauline with an update on either what Amy had eaten for lunch, or confirming that she had undergone a bowel movement. I was never particularly bothered about Amy's toilet habits; only once had she been constipated and simply upping her fruit intake had resolved that. Pauline and my mother, however, were obsessed with how often Amy went to the toilet and what her stools were like. Maybe it was an older generational thing. I had no wish to ponder on the firmness or otherwise of her stools.

When I read the text it was from Lindsay.

Hi sweetie, I've sent u yet another email, so read it when u get a chance. Linz xxx

I still couldn't get used to Lindsay contacting me. It felt like I should be able to pick up my phone and speak to her but I knew her old mobile was still sitting in a box somewhere in the spare room. I had a sudden and aching longing to speak to her, just to hear her voice, to hold her, smell her hair. . . .

I shook my head. I had to stop that thought process. It would only lead to pain and discontentment. I fetched my iPad from under the couch where Amy had left it after playing with some of her Talking Friends apps. She would spend ages shouting at the pussy cat who simply repeated back exactly what she had shouted except in a slightly more shrill tone. It invariably gave me a headache.

Even the thought of reading an email from my wife was weird, especially as her 'latest' email had been written nearly a year ago. The whole thing was bonkers.

Love Byte 4 – 31st October
My gorgeous husband

Hi again,
It's been nearly two weeks now since I last contacted you – well in my world anyway – I think it's only been a few days where you are – I'm beginning to lose track I have to say. You might remember this week (in my time) as I've had a few very bad days but I'm feeling better

169

today – one of my remission days. I notice I'm getting less and less of them now (not a good sign.)

It's Halloween today and it seems appropriate to spook you out a bit!! Whoooo lol.

Anyway I've played my ace today so you should get a response very soon. I hope I'm doing the right thing – but time will tell – well, it will for you, for me I'm afraid time is running out.

I'll be in touch again soon – not sure how much longer I can keep this up. I hope you are taking good care of my little angel. God, I wish I could see her grow up. . . . No, no, I need to stop those thoughts. Nothing I can do to change things.

Your gorgeous wife
Lindsay
Xxxxxxxx

I read the email twice more before I logged off. Her tone was certainly less upbeat and more circumspect, which as time went on (in her world) I could understand. I had tears in my eyes as I closed my iPad. I missed my wife so much, but I felt for her too. During her illness the focus had been on spending time together, trying to control her pain, especially at the end, and any talk about our feelings was put on the back-burner. I guessed that Lindsay was using her emails as some kind of release valve to vent her emotions, as well as a way of messing with me. I didn't have such a luxury.

I wondered what the ace was and how I'd ever find out about it, she could have told me a bit more about what she was up to. I was completely in the dark and that was obviously her intention.

In the end I didn't have to wait long. The ace turned out to be completely unexpected at first but logically, again, I should have been able to figure it out.

At quarter past four, around two hours after I'd read Lindsay's email, my phone rang. The volume was at maximum so Amy must have been playing with it again. 'Firework' belted out so loud that it filled the whole penthouse. I didn't recognize the number on the readout so I answered it cautiously.

'Hello?'

'Andy?'

I recognized the female voice but couldn't quite place it.

'Yeah, who is this?'

'Hi Andy, it's Molly.'

I didn't even know she had my number, though there were a hundred ways she could have got it, I suppose. 'Hi Molly.' I assumed she was calling me to talk either about Jamie or work.

'It's nice to hear from you. How's PM getting along without me?'

'It's quieter, not so much because you're no longer here, but mainly because they've laid off about another eighty or so since you left.'

I hadn't realized the axe was going to fall quite so soon or affect so many. 'Is your job OK?' I asked.

I heard her sigh. 'Oh yes, I'm fine for the time being, they need me to deal with the ones losing their jobs, and for the next wave after this one. The new bosses are sweeping the place clean.'

'You mean there's even more to come?'

'Yes, another three hundred or so.' I whistled down the phone.

Molly sounded anxious. 'Listen Andy, I don't have a lot of time to chat – I just wanted you to know I got your

171

email and I don't really know what to think, to be honest.'

Neither did I. What email? Then it dawned on me – God, I could be so dense at times – Lindsay had sent her an email pretending to be me. What the hell had she said? What should I say?

This is where Lindsay's strategy was seriously flawed. I was left swinging in the wind. My mind was spinning – Molly! Was my wife trying to set me up with Molly? The girlfriend of my best friend – or rather the recent, very recent, *ex*-girlfriend of my best friend.

'Andy, are you still there?'

I suddenly felt like hanging up and pretending I had just got cut off, but decided that would be very rude and I didn't want to do that again. Molly had enough problems without me adding to them.

'I'm still here, Molly. Sorry, I was thinking. . . .' I didn't know what else to say so I didn't say anything.

'I'm not surprised you are thinking. God, it was so unexpected. I don't know what you want me to say.'

Neither did I.

Molly continued, 'I've got a lot on in here today, so I haven't really had time to think things through, so let me take a bit of time OK and I'll text you this evening.'

'OK, Molly, that sounds like a reasonable approach.' I couldn't believe I had just said that. *'A reasonable approach?'* How very business-like – what a dick I could be at times. I tried to gain back some ground. 'It was nice to hear from you Molly.'

I could hear Molly chuckle. 'Oh Andy, I think you expected to hear from me all right, so don't act all surprised. Later, OK?'

'OK, Molly.'

The line went dead and I was left sitting on my couch in shock. Lindsay had certainly done it this time. I couldn't wait to read her next email. I wondered when it would arrive and if she had any more surprises in store. I hoped not, I didn't think my nerves would stand it.

I wasn't even sure what she had said to Molly, or rather what *I had* supposedly said to Molly. My life had suddenly got even more complicated.

That evening it got more complicated still when Molly texted me.

Hi Andy. Molly here. I've spent the day thinking about ur email – it put me off my work I have 2 tell u – but I've decided we should meet up as u suggest.

I wondered where we were to meet – hopefully she would give me a hint or she'd end up there on her own.

I started 2 think of all the downsides 2 u and me getting together and then decided 'fuck it' nothing might come of it anyway and it spares me sitting in all weekend on my own. So C U Friday at 7. I think of all the venues u suggested that Pizza Express in Leith is best – I like pizza.

Love Molly
Xxx

I couldn't help smiling at the 'I like pizza' comment. It also hinted that she was playing down the meeting which was good. We could maybe just keep it along the lines of friends or work colleagues – nice, safe and not any kind of date. Definitely not a date I told myself, that way I was less likely to do anything daft. Before I could think too much about it my phone pinged again and I read the text.

Hi sweetie. I hope u liked my ace. Of course Molly and Jamie might still be together and all I've done is stir up a hornet's nest but either way you are better off without Jamie Reitano as a friend anyway. . . .

Your gorgeous wife
Linz xxx

I had two texts sent within seconds of each other. The timing was uncanny, scary even. Lindsay was definitely playing me – I genuinely believed she was well-meaning with her meddling, but I wondered if she was really trying to set me up with Molly, or trying to get rid of Jamie whom I knew she disliked intensely.

The way she had organized it was probably a win-win from her point of view. I'm not sure what it was for me.

CHAPTER TWENTY-ONE

September was nearing its end, but the evening was unseasonably warm when I arrived at the Pizza Express in Leith. The sun had been smiling all day and a few of the locals appeared to have over-indulged in both sun and beer. I arrived before Molly. I always seemed to turn up early for these things. Maybe I should have altered my strategy and left the girl waiting, but I was too nice to do that and also scared in case she thought she'd been stood up and buggered off. Besides, this wasn't a date, it was me simply meeting an old friend for pizza. I hadn't told Pauline I was meeting Molly when I had dropped Amy off earlier that evening, but I had told myself that didn't mean anything.

The waitress showed me to a quiet table outside overlooking the water, and asked what I wanted to drink. I smiled and ordered a Diet Coke. I decided to avoid any alcohol until I found out what Molly wanted to do. I had finished my course of antibiotics – that was at least one good thing. I had a little time to think while I waited for the waitress to return. The previous evening I had consulted *Men Like Women and Women Like Shoes* to see what they had to say about meeting up with your best friend's ex-girlfriend.

First of all they quoted the Bible about 'coveting thy neighbour's wife'. Molly wasn't my neighbour (neither was Jamie) so I decided that didn't apply and ignored that section. Then they came slightly more up-to-date and discussed the Chelsea footballer John Terry and his clandestine affair with Wayne Bridge's ex-girlfriend. As I was not a professional footballer I disregarded that too. Finally they quoted an incident with an obscure South American gangster whose ex-girlfriend had gone on to date his brother. It didn't end well for the brother who was kidnapped, drugged and then had his penis surgically removed and re-attached to his left hand, between his forefinger and thumb. It gave a whole new perspective on having a 'hand-job' but wasn't terribly helpful for me in my predicament.

Overall I took from the website that they did not recommend my current situation. However, I doubted Jamie would go to the same lengths as the South American gangster, at least I hoped not. Besides, it wasn't a date anyway.

Despite the useless advice from the website, I was relaxed about meeting up with Molly. After all, I knew her reasonably well so it would be different from my previous dates (even though it wasn't a date) which had that air of mystery about them. Also in the plus column, I didn't think she was likely to run off crying after ten seconds, she didn't have a sister and I didn't expect her to want to whisk me back to her apartment to demonstrate her masturbation technique. So for those reasons I was calmer this time and hopefully there would be little I could do to offend Molly. However, knowing me, I would find something.

The waitress returned with my Diet Coke and a small plate of crusty bread and olive oil. I absent-mindedly dipped the bread into the oil a few times before popping small pieces into my mouth. I watched some wading birds as they searched for insects and small fishes amongst the rocks and mud of the harbour.

Molly caught me by surprise and sat down at the table whilst I was bird-watching. I jumped visibly and she laughed out loud. She looked stunning – an over-used term I know, but in this case I couldn't think of a better description. She was clad in a red dress with a swooping neck line that revealed the pale globes of her breasts. (Helped I think by a push-up bra.) Her long dark hair was pinned up and this accentuated her neck. Her sparkling brown eyes caught the sunlight as it bounced off the water. Her lipstick matched the red of her dress exactly. She looked marvellous and reminiscent of a glammed-up version of a Special K advert. Jamie would not have been pleased.

What a contrast to the last time I'd seen her sitting in her tiny work pod, sobbing and snivelling on her chips. I'd obviously known Molly for years but it suddenly struck me that she was a real hottie.

She waved at the waitress who sauntered over. Without even looking at the menu she said, 'A bottle of Hermitage Shiraz please.' She eyed my Diet Coke and shook her head disapprovingly. 'And two glasses. Oh, and can you bring some ice as well.' She turned to me. 'I know I'm a philistine but I like my red wine chilled.'

She broke off some bread, stuffed it into her mouth and mumbled, 'I'm starving. I've hardly eaten anything all day.'

The wine arrived and Molly poured two large glasses and dumped some ice in both glasses. Some of it spilled onto her fingers and she provocatively licked it off, running her tongue slowly and sensuously over her lips. She enjoyed my rapt attention, laughed her dirty laugh and kicked me under the table. I burst out laughing too and any tension instantly evaporated.

We opted to have pepperoni pizzas with a side salad and garlic bread to share. We talked shop for a while, and once that was out of the way I asked about Jamie.

Her face turned serious and she poured the remains of the wine into our glasses, and ordered another bottle while she thought about what to say.

She casually touched my hand before drawing back. 'Jamie seems to be doing fine, he's got himself a one-bedroom flat in Gorgie, near the Hearts football ground. I bumped into his mate Alan in the Snuggle Bar last Saturday and he said he and Jamie had been out on the pull on the Friday.'

I reached out and held her hand. She didn't pull it away. 'He's probably only saying that to get you going. You know what guys are like.'

She smiled. 'Oh I know what blokes are like. I actually don't care about what he's up to – well that's not true, I do a bit because we were together for years and I still have feelings for him. But it's not that he's out looking for a new woman that bothers me so much. It's more that I'm stuck with all the debt and, just as I predicted, he's just wandered off and doesn't care. I'm stuck with the mortgage, the car loan, all the bills and so on. I'm lucky if I can afford to go out once or twice a month.'

'Has he signed everything over to you?'

She shook her head. 'Not yet. He will do, I just have to organize it. There was a bit of an issue about the car, he said he wanted to use it when I didn't need it and said he would pay me some money monthly, but I didn't see how that could work so I'm just going to take that on as well. Besides, I'd never see any of the money, I know him too well.'

I squeezed her hand gently. 'How are you feeling now?

Are you still bingeing on fish and chips?'

She laughed. 'Nah, I've moved onto chocolate Häagen-Dazs. No really I'm OK. It's always sad when you split up. It feels like I've failed, you know? Like somewhere down the line I fucked up. I know ultimately it's for the best. He doesn't want what I want, he's not ready and maybe never will be – everyone's different.'

'So did you end up snogging some creep on Saturday night?'

She almost choked on her wine. 'God, you've got some memory, haven't you? No I went home alone, and to be honest I really didn't want to go out in the first place. Jen, my friend – I don't think you know Jen, I have her on Facebook so you can have a look at her, she's very pretty but a bit of a tart – she insisted we go out. As usual she ended up disappearing with someone about midnight and I was left alone. Which was OK, I wasn't great company anyway so I can't blame her. I went home and watched *Dirty Dancing* until I fell asleep, what a cliché eh?'

I shrugged, not sure what to say. We both gazed out over the water for a few moments. It was a pleasant silence, not uncomfortable.

The waitress returned with another bottle and Molly topped up our glasses. I didn't need to worry about getting drunk this time as Molly would be there long before me at this rate.

Molly played with a loose curl of hair that had escaped from her clip. 'So what about this email you sent me? What's that all about?'

I obviously hadn't a clue what it was all about because I hadn't written a word of it. I bit my lip trying to think of an answer. 'Which part of it specifically?'

She shook her head and smiled. 'OK, I know you've always quite liked me – I've seen you looking at me sometimes, back in the days when we all used to go out

179

together – but I never thought anything of it as you were with Lindsay and you were just another bloke who stared at me. This email though, that took me by surprise, especially as you've been talking to me at work and stuff. I didn't really get the vibe from you.'

'Vibe?'

'Yeah, you know, that you were interested.'

I shrugged and decided to be open with her. 'I don't know what I want, to be honest, Molly, but I have to say that you look absolutely gorgeous tonight.'

She blushed and laughed. 'No more wine for you, Mr Hunter. No seriously, Andy, stop trying to change the subject. That email was lovely, right from the heart. You made it sound like I was your last chance at happiness, which obviously isn't true. There are thousands of single girls out there looking for someone just like you.'

I decided to come clean – well sort of. 'I've actually been on an Internet dating site, Love Bitz, and it hasn't been great I have to admit.'

'Andy Hunter, I am shocked.'

I could tell by her broad smile that she wasn't shocked at all.

'So maybe I am your last chance after all,' she said laughing at my discomfort.

I told her about some of my dates, including 'vibrator girl'. I intentionally avoided any mention of Amanda as she was still kind of in the picture. She absolutely loved my stories and was practically falling about laughing by the end.

'God, no wonder you sent me an email, you must think I am the only normal single girl left in the universe after that experience. Very lucky for you that I split up with Jamie then, and very clever of you to wait a little before asking me out . . . you did ask me out on a date, didn't you?'

That was the problem of not knowing what Lindsay had said, it had left me in the dark. I would say that if she was ever to do that again she should copy me in on the emails.

'Well. . . .' it was decision time. Was this a date? If I decided it was a date would I suddenly turn into an arse? Would Molly become a nutcase? 'I think I'd like it to be a date,' I decided, probably because I had half a bottle of wine sloshing about inside of me.

'OK. It's just that your language was vague, you know, "meet up", "have a drink", "chat". It was very non-committal.'

Damn, I could have got away without it being a date. Never mind. 'Well I wanted to keep it low key, just in case you were . . . well, not that keen. You know, having just broken up with Jamie and that.' That was a nice manoeuvre.

'Yeah, that's another thing. You never mentioned Jamie once.'

'Yes, well I didn't want to in case it upset you. Besides, this has nothing to do with him, he's away out looking for someone else. I think he's completely bonkers for that. He'll never find anyone as nice as you.'

I hoped she wouldn't see through my compliments. She shouldn't as I meant every word, which surprised me.

She blushed again. 'I like you, Andy, I always have.'

This was news to me, but nice news, like 'you've won the lottery' or 'here, have an extra two weeks' holiday'.

'But, I am not exactly sure what I'm doing at the moment. You know, with Jamie and stuff. I've only been away from him for a few weeks and I need to sort out my head.'

'Your head looks great to me.'

'Yeah, stop it. That's too much now.'

I knew I would do something wrong.

181

'Can't we just have a nice time and not look too far ahead?'

I wasn't looking anywhere beyond the next glass of wine, so that worked for me.

We watched a family of ducks paddling around in the shallows. There was another silence but not as comfortable as the previous one, now that we'd moved to 'date' mode.

Molly broke the silence. 'You said one thing in your email that bothered me slightly.'

'What was that?'

'Can't you guess?'

Never in a month of Sundays I thought, and again wondered why not being able to guess something would bring about such a weird saying. 'Nope,' I said.

'That's odd. I thought you would know straight off.'

I would if I'd written the bloody thing.

'It's that bit about me reminding you of Lindsay, I found that' – she was obviously struggling for a suitable word – 'disturbing.'

I nodded, 'Yes I can see that, but it was a compliment.'

'Yeah, stop it, too much again.'

'It's the wine talking.'

'No, Andy, it's you talking. I know you. Remember, I'm not one of your Internet bimbos.'

'No, you're one of my work bimbos.'

She laughed and kicked me under the table again, and once more topped up our glasses. I was suddenly very glad Amy was staying with Pauline tonight because tomorrow looked like being a hangover morning.

Molly looked serious again. 'Listen though, it's not just me that's getting over something. You are as well, it's still early days.'

Which is exactly what I had thought. Lindsay, though, had other ideas.

'I know, Molly, but I feel ready to go back out there

again.' It sounded like I was fighting in a war or something. Given my experiences over the last few weeks the analogy wasn't too far off the mark. 'I think it's what Lindsay would have wanted.'

'You can't know that, Andy, that's a silly thing to say.'

If only she knew; I was almost ready to tell her everything right there and then but resisted. Another glass of wine and I probably would have.

'OK, sorry, it was maybe a bit silly, but Lindsay wouldn't have wanted me to be alone for the rest of my life, so that's why I did the Internet thing, it seemed like a good idea at the time.'

Molly took both my hands in hers. The last time she'd done that was with Jamie the night she found out about his affair. I hoped she wasn't about to propose again, like she had with him. Instead she said, 'Tell me about Lindsay.'

'You know Lindsay, you knew Lindsay.' There was that tense thing again, and I was feeling tense as well.

'I knew her as someone to stand outside and smoke fags with, and occasionally eye up other men with when you and Jamie weren't watching, not as a life partner. What was she like? What do you miss? And what don't you miss about her?'

She let go of my hands and sat back waiting expectantly.

Now there was something I hadn't been asked before. What *didn't* I miss about her? I gazed into Molly's beautiful eyes and tried to think clearly.

'Are you sure you want to know all this?'

Molly smiled encouragingly and I sighed. I took some time to frame my thoughts as I felt this was an important moment, probably for both of us.

'I miss her smile. That sounds weird, but I miss her ever so slightly crooked smile which greeted me whenever

I came home from work or woke up in the morning. In the middle of the night I used to love reaching out and touching her warm body, just to know she was there.'

'What else?'

'I also miss the fact that we were on the same wavelength. You know when somebody said or did something odd or funny, I could glance at Lindsay and know that she was thinking exactly the same as me. So I reckon that's the kind of stuff I miss more than anything.'

I also desperately missed her body, the physical side of loving and living with someone and the ongoing physical intimacy, the occasional grope of her lovely bottom, nuzzling the back of her neck when she was loading the dishwasher or talking on the phone. I decided to spare Molly that for now.

'OK, what *don't* you miss?'

Hmm, that was trickier and I had to think hard for a few moments.

'I never liked that Lindsay was never wrong. No matter what happened it was never her fault, even when it was. She loved it when I messed something up and would go on and on about it for ages. I messed up a lot so she got lots of opportunities. And if I'm being honest, I suppose, it was that the bed had to be immaculately made up every morning before we left for work. It didn't matter if we were late, it had to be done. I guess the main reason that annoyed me was because I could never do it properly or at least properly in Lindsay's eyes.'

'Is that it?'

I considered for a moment and remembered one more thing. 'If we ever had an argument about something she'd always say, "If you don't believe me, Google it", which of course I never did because if I took up that challenge and Googled it I wouldn't be able to win anyway.'

'How come?'

I sighed and smiled while answering. 'Because if I Googled whatever disputed fact we were arguing about and it wasn't there, she would just say "Well it was there when *I* looked", which implied either that I was lying or that I was somehow technically incompetent. If it *was* there then it just vindicated her, and either way I lost.'

Molly laughed, 'I must remember that if we ever have an argument. Seriously, is that all you've got?'

I nodded. Molly rolled her eyes. 'God, she must have been a saint, your wife.'

I laughed. 'Well, maybe I am wearing some rose-tinted spectacles, but I can't think of anything else just now.'

I leant forward and took her hands in mine, partly copying what she had done to me, and partly because I felt like I wanted some physical contact with this beautiful girl sitting opposite me, who had told me not five minutes ago that she liked me.

'What about Jamie, what *don't* you miss about him?'

She pulled her hands away. 'Aw that's not fair, we've just broken up and I don't have a very positive view of our life together at the moment.'

'I know but maybe just the small stuff, you know, the kind of thing that makes you think, "God, why did I put up with that?"'

I was getting good at this.

She ran her hand through her hair and took a big slug of wine. 'OK the small stuff, like him being a slob and leaving things lying everywhere, was annoying but not a deal breaker. I think the main thing was that he was very controlling and manipulative.'

'Like the cat thing?'

Molly nodded sadly. 'Yeah, I didn't notice it at first because he was very subtle. He'd compliment me when I wore some really dowdy clothes, and would be very hostile and critical if I wore a short skirt or a revealing top.

185

You know, saying I looked like a tart, or one of his favourites was, "Molly, nobody wants to see your thunder thighs, put them away." He said it kind of jokingly but he meant it, and it hurt.'

'So he usually got his way.'

'I guess.'

'What else?'

'Oh the usual. It was all right for him to go out with his mates and get pissed, but if I ever wanted to do anything like that it was a battle, a struggle to get his blessing. I was in love with him so I was blinkered to it for a long time. Don't get me wrong, there were things I loved about him. He was very gentle and could make me laugh. He was incredibly organized and always remembered anniversaries and birthdays – he even knew when it was my mum's wedding anniversary.'

I knew Jamie had to be organized to get away with all the cheating and sneaking. Instead I said, 'Maybe he just used his Outlook calendar a lot.'

Molly ignored my comment.

'So we had some good times, but when it came to the big thing, the crunch, he just wasn't up for it.'

We sat mulling over our memories for a few moments whilst finishing off the second bottle of wine.

'What shall we do now, Molly?' I asked as I stretched.

'I'm in no rush to go home, but what about Amy?'

'Amy's staying at her gran's tonight so I've got a free pass.'

'Oh, OK that's good. Why don't we walk along Leith and we can maybe stop for a drink somewhere, hopefully a place with a bit more life about it.'

We paid the bill, going Dutch at Molly's insistence, and slowly pottered along the waterfront. We passed Ocean Terminal where the Royal Yacht was now moored as a floating tourist attraction, and eventually stopped in at a small bar which sat on the harbour and had a fabulous wooden deck protruding out over the water. We both had enough wine and instead opted for a couple of bottled European beers with the exotic sounding name 'Slake'.

We sat at a table on the deck, and Molly – who was obviously feeling the effect of the wine – started giggling.

Smiling, I asked, 'What?'

'Nothing.'

'What is it?'

'Oh I was just thinking about that girl with the vibrators. What was her name again?'

'Carrie.'

'Yeah, Carrie. I can just imagine your face, I always thought you were a bit if a prude.'

'I'm not a prude.'

She booted me under the table again which made me think I would be better sitting beside her.

'You are so.'

'What's prudish about not wanting to spend my evening watching a girl using vibrators on herself?'

Molly screeched with laughter, drawing attention from other tables. 'Just listen to yourself. Most men and some women probably, would spend a fortune to see that.'

She booted me under the table again so I got up and sat beside her. She laughed and leaned her head onto my shoulder.

She went quiet, tilted her head and fixed her eyes on mine. I leaned forward slightly and kissed her gently on the lips. I lingered for a moment. It felt strange that it wasn't Lindsay, but it was a nice kind of strange. I placed my arm around the shoulder of this gorgeous warm woman and it felt . . . comfortable. She leaned into me and we sat in silence enjoying the moment.

We finished our beer and Molly said, 'I've had enough to drink I think, can we go and get a coffee?'

'We can get coffee here?'

'Is there not a Starbucks nearby?'

'Yeah, a few minutes' walk.'

'Let's go.'

Once we were out of the bar and on the main road, I took Molly's hand. It had been a long time since I'd held a woman's hand. Not since Lindsay had become ill. I began to feel guilty again and wondered if the feelings of guilt ever stop.

As if reading my mind Molly asked, 'Do you miss her all the time? You know, is it constant or does it come and go?'

I sighed. 'It comes and goes, certain things can bring back memories, you know – like music, places, sensations. . . .'

'. . . And holding a strange girl's hand?'

I marvelled at her perception. 'Yeah I guess, except you're not strange, Molly.'

'I wonder what Lindsay would say if she could see us now.'

It wasn't really a question so I let it go unanswered but of course, this was all Lindsay's doing. One day I might have to explain that, and it would be tricky. We arrived at Starbucks and sat at a table near the door. My apartment was now only a five-minute walk away.

Almost on cue, Molly said, 'Once we've finished these you need to show me this fabulous apartment of yours. I'll be so jealous now that I'm stuck with my dump for ever and ever.'

I felt a tingle of excitement. I was not expecting to have Molly back at my place. I also felt a little uncomfortable. Maybe nothing would happen, maybe a little snog. Maybe that would be OK.

'Aw Molly, that's not right. Your flat is lovely. I've been there, remember?'

'Yeah I know, but I don't have warm feelings about it just now. Maybe that'll fade.'

As we walked the short distance to my apartment, I began to feel nervous for the first time that evening, but it was a 'nice' nervous. We didn't say much on the way probably because there was a certain tension between us. Dare I call it sexual tension? I wasn't sure.

As I opened the door and stepped into my penthouse Molly gasped in surprise.

'This place is awesome!'

She ran across the floor of the living room and pressed her nose against the glass of the doors that opened out onto the deck. She reminded me of Amy, except her nose was obviously higher up. Her warm breath steamed up the cold glass. 'Can we go outside?'

Her excitement made me smile and I got the key from on top of the microwave in the kitchen and opened the doors. She rushed out onto the balcony and I returned to the kitchen and fetched two glasses of Prosecco. Once outside I handed her one, and she sipped it breathlessly.

'What a view! What an incredible place to live. I knew it would be spectacular.'

Her childish excitement made me smile. It was dusk. The sun had gone and darkness was approaching, spreading out like a dark fluffy blanket in the late summer evening.

We stood in silence, leaning on the balcony, and watched the lights flicker on across the bay. It felt romantic. It felt right somehow. I was at peace. It was one of those moments I would always cherish, always remember, even if nothing more ever happened with Molly.

Molly, however, obviously had other ideas. She took my glass from me and placed it with hers on the table. She put her arms around my neck and kissed me. This time it was urgent and passionate, her tongue snaked around mine and it felt erotic and wonderful. This beautiful girl wanted me, wanted me to love her and I didn't feel worthy or ready. I remembered Jamie telling me that some people just wanted a shag and there was nothing wrong with that. Maybe he was right, maybe I should just go with the flow. The fact it was Molly did make me reluctant, it would be another item to add to my pile of things to feel guilty about. I gave in to the moment.

I held her tightly and pushed myself instinctively against her, and she gasped into my mouth. I could feel her curves, her tight wonderful body and knew that tonight would be a night I would remember for many reasons.

I took her hand and led her inside, she kicked her shoes off and we headed to my bedroom. Once there I left the lights off and threw open the door that led out onto the deck that wrapped around the whole penthouse. The breeze made the curtains billow in the doorway and Molly shivered deliciously as I pulled her close to me. The lights of the bay and the moon were enough to illuminate the room. Molly's silhouette was like a dark version of her and I watched transfixed as she unzipped her dress and let it slip to the floor. She was standing in her bra and panties watching me expectantly. I clambered clumsily out of my jeans which made her laugh and I unbuttoned my shirt.

I moved to her and pulled her into my arms and I could feel her cool skin luxuriously against mine, and it sent an erotic charge through my body. Our lips were pressed together and we fell onto the bed in a tangled heap of arms and legs and impatient thrusting.

I gasped and pulled away for a moment and gazed down at this picture of loveliness beneath me and didn't feel worthy. Molly gazed back at me, seriously and expectantly. Her skin was pure silk and the muted moonlight danced in her eyes as I slowly kissed her mouth before nuzzling into her neck. She moaned and I was instantly transported to another level of arousal. There was no way back now. I slipped off her panties as she undid her bra. I kicked of my boxers and lost the shirt. Apart from our breathing, the only sound was the breeze and the distant lapping of the waters against the sea wall seventy feet below.

I dipped my head to taste her. She was wet, pungent and intoxicating. After a few moments she moaned and pulled me on top of her. She gasped impatiently. 'I want you inside me now.'

I slipped into her easily and urgently and as we became rhythmic, our breathing got faster and faster. She was getting close and my mouth was pressed to hers. Gently she bit my tongue, and then erotically broke the kiss and took two of my fingers into her mouth and sucked them seductively. This pushed me over the edge and I exploded inside her, nearly a years' worth of sexual frustration and deprivation literally draining out of me. I collapsed beside her.

Molly leaned onto her elbow and smiled down at me.

'Andy, that was wonderful, you have no idea how much I needed that.'

'Not as much as me.'

It dawned on me – rather late it has to be said – that we hadn't used any protection.

Reading my worried expression (she was good at that) Molly said, 'I'm on the pill still – so you needn't worry on that score – and I'm a clean-living girl so you won't catch anything from me.'

She forgot, though, that I knew her boyfriend better than she did in that respect, and God only knew what he could be harbouring. The thought of catching a second-hand venereal disease worried me for a moment before I decided it was too late to worry about that, for the moment anyway. I decided to do what Scarlett O'Hara would do: 'I won't think about it today, I'll think about it tomorrow.'

Molly noticed my continuing worried expression in the half-darkness and giggled as her breasts bounced deliciously against my chest. 'You're such a worrier, Andy, although this is going to make our lives very complicated.'

'I know.'

Only she had no idea how complicated it was going to be for me. Things had gone from being very simple and very lonely to incredibly complicated and busy. I decided to Scarlett O'Hara that thought as well.

Molly wouldn't let it go however. 'I don't want to come between you and Jamie.'

Bit late for that I think.

'You do want to see me again?' she asked anxiously.

'Of course.'

I hadn't actually thought about it. Having Molly in my bed just felt good, which surprised me. I felt guilty, for a number of reasons, but I decided that I did want to see her again.

'I can see you just now.' I smiled, kissed her gently and nuzzled down into her breasts. 'I hope you are staying the night?'

'If you want me to?'

'Yes please.'

We made love again, slower this time, and then we both slipped into an exhausted sleep. I got up during the night to pee and noticed rain was slanting in through the open door. I closed it and shivered, then pulled the duvet over Molly. I gazed down at her sleeping form which was turned slightly away from me. She was so lovely, and so vulnerable and I suddenly realized my feelings were stronger for her than I had imagined. I wasn't sure why I felt like that. Maybe I'd always felt that way but somehow had buried them somewhere whilst I was with Lindsay and Molly was with Jamie. Had Lindsay lived, I would probably never have allowed any feelings for Molly to emerge. The human psyche was a very weird place.

I wasn't in love with Molly. I couldn't be yet. I wanted to protect her from more hurt, the kind of pain that Jamie had inflicted upon her over the years. And yet I was conscious that the way things were going, I may end up treating her worse than Jamie had.

What I should have done was phone Amanda and cancel the date we had planned. I didn't though. I didn't want to. I wanted to see her again to find out how I felt about her. Maybe if I could spend some time with Molly the following week, before my date with Amanda, I might change my mind.

I slipped back into bed and spooned in behind Mollie's naked back. She sighed softly and continued sleeping as I draped my arm over her and closed my eyes.

In the morning, breakfast was leisurely and sensual: heated croissants, orange juice and coffee, eaten in bed between lingering kisses and love-making.

Later we showered together and finally got dressed. Molly was meeting her mum for lunch and soon Pauline would be back with Amy.

Molly tried her best to remove the creases from her lovely red dress, but it still looked a little crushed when she was finally ready to leave.

I offered to drive her home but she insisted on getting a taxi, so I ordered one for her. It soon arrived and we had one last lingering kiss at the lift before she left. I went back into my apartment and closed the door. Both the penthouse and I felt empty. I didn't have time to linger on my thoughts however, as only a moment later there was a knock on the door. Initially I thought Molly must have forgotten something and I rushed over hoping for another kiss. I opened it and was met with the excited face of my daughter, held aloft by my mother-in-law.

I took Amy into my arms and she gave me her super-model kiss.

Pauline smiled knowingly at me. 'Was that Molly Jenkins I saw getting into a taxi downstairs?' I nodded sheepishly. 'The same Molly Jenkins who has recently broken up with your best friend?' I repeated the gesture. Pauline sighed and shook her head. 'You are playing with fire there, are you not?'

I nodded for the third time.

'Well, it's your life.'

CHAPTER TWENTY-TWO

Most of the following week was guilt-ridden. I talked with Molly on the phone and I talked with Amanda on the phone. I even managed to avoid mixing them up. The guilt I felt about everything did not help me make a decision which I was clearly very bad at doing. I had tried to meet up with Molly again during the week, but she'd cried off saying she wanted some time and space to think things over. She told me that she did want to see me again, but wanted to get Jamie out of her life before that happened.

On the Thursday evening she'd phoned and explained how she was feeling. I could tell from her voice she'd been crying.

'Jamie was here this evening picking up more of his stuff. He's not making it easy on me and you've obviously not told him about us yet.'

I had not been able to bring myself to do it – it was unfair I know – but it was all tied in with my indecisiveness. I was being unreasonably selfish and would no doubt come to regret it later.

'I know, I'm sorry, Molly, I just haven't found the right time.'

'Well you'll need to find the right time soon, I'd hate him to find out any other way.'

'Can't you put an announcement on Facebook or something?' I suggested flippantly.

'I bloody well will do that if you don't tell him.' Molly sighed. 'Look Andy, I don't really care, he's going to be out of my life soon anyway – hopefully by the weekend when he picks up the last of his stuff and gives me the flat keys – but if you want to retain some kind of friendship with him, you'd better tell him about us.'

I changed the subject. 'What's happening with the flat and things?'

'He's seeing the lawyer tomorrow – one that I'm paying for, of course – to sign everything over to me. It feels like all I'm gaining is heartache and a load of debt, but I suppose it will be my debt.'

'Well at least it allows you to move on.'

I could hear raw emotion in Molly's voice. 'Yeah, I suppose. I could really do with a hug right now.'

'I wish I could come over, Molly, but Amy is sleeping, why don't you come here?'

'Tempting, but no I still want to wait a few days. After tomorrow things will feel clearer for me I reckon.'

'Do you want to meet up tomorrow?'

'No, I promised my mum we'd go to the cinema tomorrow and Saturday I've got to take her to my gran's in Aberdeen.'

'Sunday evening then?'

'Meeting up on a school night, Mr Hunter? That's brave.'

I laughed. 'It's not a school night for me anymore – no job, remember?'

'Oh yes, I almost forgot about that – OK let's go for Sunday evening – I will still need a hug.'

'I'm sure I can manage that.'

After she'd hung up I was glad she had not suggested Saturday as that was the night Amanda was coming to my flat for dinner. I had yet to decide what to cook but something simple, like spaghetti bolognaise, that even I couldn't balls up was probably a good idea.

I had changed into my PJs and was contemplating one more cup of Earl Grey before bed when my phone pinged. I read the text and knew that I wouldn't be going to sleep anytime soon.

Hi gorgeous. Your dutiful wife Lindsay here. Just typed u another email – so read it when u get a moment – as it's < 10 at night where u are Amy should be sleeping and u will be thinking about going 2 bed – ur so predictable! Do u still love Earl Grey? ☺

PS if u have proved me wrong and are right now sweating between the sheets with a hot bitch I don't want 2 know! Sometimes ignorance is bliss. Linz xxxx

I logged on to the iPad and wondered what she had in store for me this time. I noted whilst logging on that I was not looking forward to reading her emails as much as I used to. This was probably because they complicated my life, but then had that not been her intention all along?

Love Byte 5 – 5th November
My gorgeous husband

What a wonderful night we had! Fireworks, drinks and sex – what more can you ask for? Well I'd maybe liked to have eaten something but never mind you can't have everything and I don't want to get fat do I?? LOL

You and Amy are both sleeping soundly and I'm in the

kitchen drinking your Earl Grey tea and typing (obviously!). I keep waiting for you to get up one of these nights and ask me what I'm up to – but it's not happened yet.

I feel pretty good tonight. I'm still glowing from our love-making which we need to do more of (as long as I'm up for it – or you are able to get up for it – I know I'm not a pretty sight these days).

OK down to business. As Stan Laurel said to Oliver Hardy after he'd burned his house down, 'I don't think there is much more I can do for you here'. I've played all my cards and you are in the hands of the gods.

I do hope that you and Molly get together. I know she looks very like me and that might feel a bit weird but she has a completely different personality. (Also her skin is much nicer than mine – that always annoyed me – maybe you can tell her that one day.)

If you have already found someone via Love Bitz then that's great too. If neither of these options has worked then hopefully – if nothing else comes out of this – you will have stopped moping around thinking about me as much.

I wish I could scoot forward in time just for an hour or two to see what has happened – that would be so much fun and would set my mind at rest.

OK I'm away for now, I'm going back to our warm bed to spoon into your back. Hopefully I'll still be horny in the morning and we can have another shag – bliss!

PS I wonder how many more times we will make love before I die – hey that's a good title for a song –'making love before I die' – the sort of thing Girls Aloud would do – I wonder if they're still together.

Your gorgeous wife
Lindsay
Xxxxxxxx

I logged off sadly. Poor Lindsay. That was the last time we made love. I remembered looking at her in the morning after I'd woken up and thinking how peaceful and contented she looked. That's why I had tiptoed through to the bathroom to shower and get ready for work. I think I had even left the house before she woke up. If I'd known she wanted to make love again I would have stayed in bed with her, or at least woken her up.

We didn't know at the time but that was her last week at home, and from then on the pain got worse and the drugs stronger. I went to bed with a heavy heart and shed a few more tears for my poor dead wife. Perhaps they were for myself and Amy – it was hard to tell at times.

CHAPTER TWENTY-THREE

I had finalized details with Amanda for Saturday and Amy was spending the night at her gran's again. Pauline thought I had Molly coming over for dinner and I hadn't dissuaded her from that assumption. I didn't want to explain anything to her at that point. I'm not sure I could have anyway.

I had showered and changed into an old pair of jeans and put on a clean shirt. I was careful with the aftershave and rubbed a small amount of gel into my hair to muss it up a bit.

Having previously visited Morrisons for supplies, I started dinner. I soon had the chopped onions and mushrooms simmering with the meat and garlic in a large pan on the range cooker. The apartment filled with the aroma of garlic and oregano, and I had just set the pot of water to boil the pasta when the buzzer sounded. I glanced up at the clock: right on time.

Amanda breezed into the apartment and planted a kiss on my lips while simultaneously handing me a bottle of Chianti. She filled me in on her week as she watched me put pasta into boiling water. I loved her soft Irish accent and could have listened to her all day. (I really needed to get beyond that.)

Amanda worked as an events coordinator for a Scottish brewery and spent much of her time rushing around the country organizing sponsored events and promotions. The previous two weeks she had been in London overseeing her employer's huge stand for an exhibition at Earls Court. It sounded glamorous and cool but as she also pointed out, it was hard work, especially this last week when she had been part of the exhibiting team which meant smiling all day and fending off semi-drunk businessmen who decided that all the brewery girls were fair game for a grope.

Amanda plonked herself down on the couch with a glass of the Chianti and picked up a framed photograph from the coffee table.

'I take it this is Lindsay and Amy?'

Amanda was studying the family portrait we'd had done just after Lindsay's cancer diagnosis. I sat down beside her and Amanda handed the photograph to me.

'Yeah, Lindsay wanted a family photo done before she got too sick. I think that was the last time she ever posed for a photo of any kind.'

Amanda put her hand on my arm. 'She was very beautiful. You must miss her?'

I didn't think the question was a rhetorical one so I smiled sadly and just put the photo back down on the coffee table. I then walked over to the cooker and turned down the gas under the pot of pasta which was threatening to boil over.

The room was filled with steam so I opened one of the doors that opened onto the decked balcony. Amanda wandered outside with her wine. I made sure neither the pasta nor the sauce were likely to burn and joined her.

We both leaned on the wooden rail and gazed out over the coastline. The breeze was heavy with the salty tang of the sea, and the air was filled with the cries of gulls and the crashing of the waves on the rocks below. The sun was setting in the west, but was obscured by dark clouds that threatened rain later.

'It's pretty spectacular living here; I don't think I'd ever want to leave,' Amanda said wistfully.

I took a sip of wine. 'I only rent the place, so I don't really think of it as mine.'

'You could buy it. Would the owner not sell?'

I shook my head. 'I wouldn't want to buy it. Half the apartments are empty and there is some talk about the council taking over some of the flats to rent out to over-spill tenants.'

'What are over-spill tenants?'

The breeze was getting stronger and, being late September, it was cooler now the sun had gone. I noticed Amanda shivering, so I ushered her inside and closed the door before I answered her.

'I'm not one hundred per cent sure. I went to a recent residents' meeting, and a number of the owners and tenants think it will be the problem families from some of the poorer estates around Edinburgh who get shipped in.'

Amanda looked puzzled. 'You mean they'd move some of their worst cases into a luxurious place like this?'

I smiled. 'Maybe. I suppose if you work for the council it makes some kind of sense as they can pick the flats up pretty cheaply, and in an apartment like mine you could accommodate a family of five or six quite easily.'

I noticed Amanda putting two and two together. 'So you will be leaving before that happens.'

'Yeah,' I said, sitting down beside her on the couch. 'It isn't likely to happen until the middle of next year and I was planning on being gone by then anyway. I'm not a snob, but I reckon the reason this place is so peaceful is because most of the flats around me in this block are empty. Regardless of who would be moving in it would become a lot more crowded and noisy, but I imagine the type of families we are talking about here are likely to bring a lot of baggage with them.'

Amanda smiled. 'Emotional baggage?'

'Yeah, and physical baggage. Bikes, dogs, cats, budgies, snakes, lizards, tarantulas, God knows what else. Whilst I like animals, these flats aren't really designed for them. I also feel sorry for the residents who have bought a place here as suddenly they are likely to find the lifts full of feral children and their friends.'

I stood up and walked over to the kitchen area. 'Dinner is served, m'lady.'

Amanda smiled and sat herself down at the table.

The food was good (even if I do say so myself) and as the wine kicked in, I found myself relaxing. Amanda was good company and had a wicked sense of humour. I couldn't help comparing her to Molly. Amanda was more widely travelled than Molly and her cultural background was completely different. She talked about her time growing up in Ireland. Her father was coming to stay with her for a few days the following week, as he hadn't been to see her in Edinburgh since he helped her move all her stuff over when she bought the flat. After that he was on his way to the USA for business.

'I eventually introduce all my long term boyfriends to my dad. He's a good judge of character,' she explained. 'My mum's OK, but she's a bit of an air-head. That sounds unkind, as she's got a degree in Art History or something, but she made the decision early on to become a baby machine. My dad's always busy. He sells machine tools to the gas and oil industry, so he's away a lot – especially now the economy is in the toilet. He travels to the US and the Middle East nearly every month. He had to do an international relations course recently. Did you know that in Qatar, if you shake someone's hand for more than twelve seconds you have to give them a fish?'

I didn't know that. I must remember to take a fish with me if I ever go to Qatar. 'They are hosting the football World Cup soon: how many English fans will take fish with them?' I wondered aloud.

Amanda punched my arm playfully and told me more about her clan. Most of her family still lived in their home town Gorey in County Wexford. I'd never heard of it, but it was south of Dublin and was full of tourists during the summer. No wonder she felt so at home in Edinburgh then.

Amanda also revealed she was dyslexic. Thankfully, this had been diagnosed early on in primary school and she'd been taught ways to cope with the condition using phonics and coloured overlays. Her particular type of dyslexia was helped by this.

One of the things I'd always wondered about dyslexia is why they need to use such a complicated word to describe the condition. Once, at Perennial Mutual, I had to complete an assessment for a placement student who was dyslexic, and had eleven attempts at spelling 'dyslexic' before resorting to spell check and even then it didn't look right.

Amanda managed to cope with the condition most of the time and explained that it was only when she was under stress that she had problems. She was also slightly colour blind which she had been told was quite common with dyslexic people. She had issues with green and red and often mixed them up.

One thing I did notice about Amanda during our dinner was that she was much more opinionated than Molly, though I wasn't sure that was a good thing. She was also much more outgoing and gregarious than Molly. As the evening drew on and we drank more wine, our conversation became more intimate. Amanda knew I found her attractive, I couldn't hide that in the way I looked at her – and the fact that when we sat close together on the couch the bulge in my jeans was obvious.

When she kissed me I stopped comparing notes with Molly and just enjoyed the moment. I slipped my fingers around to the back of her head and ran them delicately along her neck. She shivered and pushed her body against me and we lay down on the couch, her on top. She slipped out of her top and skilfully removed my shirt, and ran her tongue across my nipples.

'I didn't expect a good Catholic girl to be so forward.'

Amanda kissed me and said mischievously, 'I'm not a good Catholic girl, I'm a very bad Catholic girl.' She giggled and added, 'Thinking about it, I'm actually a very bad Catholic.'

She took my lip between her teeth and nibbled on it gently. 'Do you want to talk about religion, Andy, or do you want to take me to your bed and fuck me?'

Another question I didn't need to answer and soon we were nakedly entwined between my bed sheets. This time I had put condoms on my shopping list and didn't have that anxiety to add to my growing pile. During the night the rain hammered so hard on the windows it woke both of us up, which was a good excuse to make love again.

Later I lay and listened to Amanda breathing and the rain tapping on the windows, and took stock of things. I needed some time and space over the next day or two to think things over. I had gone from being the worst date in the world to having two lovely women on the go. It was a situation I'd never experienced and it felt strange, alien even.

If I was ever going to move on from Lindsay, I would have been lucky to have either of these pretty girls to help me, to have both of them was beyond belief. It did occur to me of course, that maybe neither of them would work out long term, but I knew I would need to give it a go with one of them. Lindsay had manipulated things to try and make it Molly, and that put me off a little. I think one of the issues was that my male ego said that I had found Amanda by myself.

Also Molly was part of my past. Did I want a part of my past to be a part of my future? Maybe a clean break and a new start would be much healthier. Molly also bore a strong resemblance to my wife and I wasn't sure that was healthy either. Eventually it dawned on me that the 'clean break' thing wasn't right anyway as Lindsay had set up my profile on Love Bitz, so she was indirectly responsible for Amanda being in my bed as well. I knew I should follow my heart which whispered Molly's name into my brain. Unfortunately my heart was not the part of my anatomy in charge at that point in time.

CHAPTER TWENTY-FOUR

In the morning the rain clouds had cleared and sunlight slanted into the room between a small gap in the curtains. I awoke and nuzzled into the back of Amanda's neck. She moaned softly and pushed her buttocks against my growing erection. I ran my fingers gently down her back. Her skin was soft, silky and the colour of delicate porcelain. We made love again, slowly this time compared with the previous evening's exertions and then we both dozed for a while. Little did I know it but that was to be my last lazy morning for a while.

We eventually got up and showered before meeting in the kitchen for breakfast. I leaned over the table and gave Amanda a lingering kiss on the lips. She stood up and pulled me towards her, thrust her tongue in my mouth and giggled. She then sat back down, finished her croissant and orange juice and said 'I need to go soon, Andy, I've got stuff to do today. I've hardly been home and have a suitcase full of dirty clothes to wash, and as I said I've got my dad turning up this week and the flat is a pigsty.'

I wondered what Pauline would think if she knew about Amanda. Would she think I was some kind of serial shagger? I didn't think I was – I wasn't even sure how many people you need to be sleeping with at the same time to qualify for such a title. I remembered asking Google once how many people you needed to kill in order to qualify as a serial killer. I wasn't planning on becoming one or anything – though it would have been useful knowledge for a would-be slayer. It came about because I was watching a programme on Harold Shipman, the murderous GP (who looked a bit like Santa but didn't have any nice surprises inside his sack) and wanted to know.

I wondered what we used to do about life's imponderables before the Internet. Now we just ask Google and get an answer to everything. It might not be the right answer but it's an answer all the same.

In the case of serial killers, it seemed to be generally accepted amongst the Internet community that you needed to have murdered at least three people at different times to be considered a serial killer. There was huge debate about the space required between the killings – killing three people at once (the members of your family for example) made you a mass murderer but not a serial killer. I did wonder about the mental stability of the large numbers of discussion groups on a variety of forums who had opinions on such stuff. (I'm sure a few of my previous dates would now be paid up members – either of their own volition or after meeting me.)

I then considered that, as I had been online reading it too, I maybe shouldn't take that line of thought any further. In any event I reckoned that I needed to be sleeping with three people at the same time to qualify. I was one short, but given the complexity of my life with two on the go I was in no hurry to fulfil the criteria.

I became aware that Amanda was staring at me curiously. 'Penny for them?' she asked, smiling.

I shook my head. No way would a penny be enough

to betray that particular thought process. Before I was forced to concoct some kind of answer to satisfy her question, there was a loud knock on the front door. I assumed that it would be Pauline bringing Amy back early. She was apt to forget her door key but knew the entry number for the keypad downstairs. I can't say I was happy about her showing up early, as now the serial shagger test might need to be applied.

I wondered if there was some way of maybe gently persuading Amanda to hide in the large hall cupboard, or maybe amongst the junk piled up in the spare bedroom. The problem was finding a good reason or explanation for her to comply with such a request.

Simply asking, 'Amanda, can you go hide in the cupboard, please, as my mother-in-law is at the door, and the last time she was here I was with another woman and I don't want her to think badly of me?' probably wouldn't cut it. Neither would, 'Amanda, I think this is a good time to show you how much junk can be piled into a spare bedroom' or 'Amanda can I show you the inside of the hall cupboard? It has some very interesting old porn & Star Trek Next Generation DVDs that you might like.' Truth be told, I was more worried about what she might think of me hoarding Star Trek DVDs than the porn collection – a sign of the times.

As I was standing frozen to the spot thinking through the above useless options, there was another even louder rap on the door.

From the corner of my eye I noticed Amanda looking curiously at me. 'Aren't you going to answer the door?' she asked, quite reasonably.

'I think so,' I answered. Unsure of what else I could do, I sighed and walked over to the front door and opened the lock to admit Pauline and my hyper daughter. I was shocked then to find Molly and Jamie on the other side.

Both of them pushed me aside and marched into the penthouse.

My thought process took some time to catch up with events. I had been expecting my daughter and her grand-mother, not my worst nightmare. I even peered out into the hallway to see if Pauline was there.

When I came back into the apartment my first thought, probably inappropriate, was that Molly was dressed to kill in a low-cut top, tight jeans and black high-heeled boots. She spotted Amanda who jumped up from her chair in surprise and knocked over the jug of orange juice. I watched as it flowed across the table and dripped slowly onto the floor.

Angrily, Molly shouted, 'So this is Amanda the bimbo.' Turning to me she asked, 'What is she doing in your flat? In fact don't answer that, I can see for myself.'

Amanda's eyes flared. 'Who are you calling a bimbo, dressed like some cheap hooker!'

There was me thinking she looked classy as well. Amanda glared at me accusingly. 'Did you tell her I was a bimbo?'

I hadn't mentioned Amanda to Molly, or Molly to Amanda. Why would I? How could I?

If I had, then neither of them would have slept with me again, or probably even have spoken to me again. I then realized the reality of the situation, that both of these scenarios had now come to pass. I was spared answering by Jamie who admitted, 'Actually, it might have been me.' He smiled sheepishly and appeared to be enjoying himself. I think he was the only one. At that point I was still confused as to why they were there and what his involvement was.

I was obviously not cut out to be a serial shagger. Completely ill-equipped to deal with the situation, I got angry and turned on Jamie, probably the only one in the room I could have at least some kind of moral anger with, given the things he'd told me over the years that I had never passed on to Molly. 'How do you know if she's a bimbo or not, I never said that to you. I hardly said anything about her.'

Amanda shouted at both of us, 'Stop calling me a bimbo.'

'Fucking tart then,' Molly hissed.

'Takes one to know one,' Amanda hissed back.

Molly then turned on Jamie, 'You've known he was seeing this tart for ages and yet only decided to tell me this morning?'

Jamie held up his hands in defence. 'Whoa there. I only told you about the tart because you decided to confess to me about your affair with him. Fair's fair. You were cheating on me with him, I was just getting even. Besides he told me not to tell anyone, so I didn't. Anyway I've hardly seen you recently to tell you anything, Molls.'

'That's because we've split up, Jamie, that's what you wanted, remember?' Molly shouted.

'No, Molly, that's what you wanted because I didn't want to have kids with you yet.'

'You walked out, and started seeing other girls.'

'I would never cheat on you, Molly.'

I couldn't stand it and joined in the shouting. 'Molly, Jamie cheated on with you the Polish tart, remember?' I lowered my voice. 'He's probably been cheating on you from the day you met, I can't keep track of the number of women he's had during the time you've been together. Dozens probably.'

Jamie's face turned red. I'm not sure if it was with anger or shame. 'The Polish girl wasn't a tart, and I haven't been with a dozen women, Molly, that's not true. Anyway that was all in the past, you're the only one I want now.'

Molly's face was a similar hue and Amanda and I

briefly became spectators. 'You only want me now, Jamie, because someone else wants me. If I was sitting at home oblivious in front of the telly you wouldn't be interested. I'm just someone you like having around because you're scared of being alone. I'm just a trophy to you now and you're angry because someone else actually respects me and treats me well.'

Jamie angrily waved his hand around the apartment and fixed his gaze on Amanda. He laughed and spat out his words. 'Respect! You call two-timing you with this bimbo respect? Is this treating you well, fucking her while you think he's at home with his daughter playing happy families?'

'At least he knows how to play happy families, Jamie. You don't ever want to grow up or take responsibility for yourself.'

Jamie shook his head. 'I can't believe you're defending him. He's standing here with the bimbo, and you're defending him.'

'Stop calling me a fucking bimbo,' Amanda shouted. Her soft Irish accent sounded strange when she shouted and not at all threatening. Molly and Jamie ignored her but she continued anyway. 'I've got a degree in applied physics from Dublin University.'

I glanced over at her. 'I didn't know that.'

Amanda shook her head at me. 'Well, if we'd talked more and shagged less I'm sure you would've found out.'

She was probably right, but I also wondered how you end up being an events coordinator with a physics degree. Maybe it had something to do with her dyslexia, though now probably wasn't the best time to ask about that.

On the other side of the room a realization dawned on Jamie. He turned away from me and asked Molly, 'You're in love with him, aren't you?'

She sighed but didn't deny it.

I couldn't believe she was in love with me. How *could* she be after today? Jamie obviously thought the same thing and stated the obvious.

'How can you be in love with him? He's shagging someone else, right in your face, you silly cow. And, anyway, he only likes you because you look like his dead wife. He's playing out some kind of sick version of Stepford Wives. Besides, look at him. Compare him to me! He's not as handsome, not as fit and nowhere near as dynamic. Andy's a plodder, Molly. Why would you want to be with a plodder?'

I had suddenly discovered what my friend really thought of me and it wasn't a pleasant way or time to find out. It occurred to me that I might be a plodder, but one who earned twice what he did. (Or had until recently anyway.) Again, I decided this was probably not the time to bring that up. I gazed at Molly and wondered what she was thinking. She returned my stare and shook her head sadly.

'You know the main thing I liked about you, Andy, was that you were *nothing* like him. Well at least I *thought* you weren't. But maybe over the years you've learned a thing or two. If so, he's taught you well. You're certainly following his example. "Aw poor Molly, she's a soft touch. She's a doll you can twist and bend and make into any shape you want. She'll fit right into your life, you can screw her, dump her, treat her like shit and she'll still be there waiting for you when you come home." Except I won't – at least, not any more I won't.'

I didn't know what to say. Her words had cut through me. Molly deserved to be treated so much better than this. I felt ashamed. I'd let Molly down. I'd let myself down and I'd let Lindsay down, I think . . . though I was confused about the last part.

If my dead wife was looking down on this scene she'd

213

be enjoying herself immensely. I had just got carried away. I'd never had two women who wanted to be with me at the same time and it had been intoxicating and exciting. Deep down I probably knew it would turn out badly, but hadn't thought it through. I was now getting my just deserts.

As Molly's exercise in self-analysis came to an end, the apartment was silent for a moment.

Predictably Jamie was first to break it and asked, 'So Amanda, besides spoiling your breakfast, this must be an enlightening morning for you? You're having a nice morning with your boyfriend, a leisurely breakfast following some slow comfortable sleepy sex, then, whilst you are lying in the glow of your passion, Andy here is figuring how to get you out of his bed before Molly comes around later. I bet he doesn't even bother to change the sheets, enjoying the thought of all his women's juices and perfume mingling together.'

Amanda smiled calmly at Jamie and her Irish accent filled the air. 'Sounds like your fantasy, Jamie, as you are the one getting off on all this. You're the only one enjoying it. You were supposed to be his friend, and yet you have brought this all out in the open. Not that I'm sorry, you understand. I would rather Andy had done it himself but we are where we are. The one thing I don't get, why the betrayal?'

Indignation filled Jamie's voice as he whined, 'Betrayal? I'm the one who's been betrayed.'

'How's that work?'

'He was sleeping with my girlfriend, that's how that works.'

Molly shouted at Jamie, 'We'd split up! You wanted out.'

Jamie turned to her but lowered his head. He had tears in his eyes. I was unsure whether he was capable of faking it but I wouldn't have put it past him – I wouldn't have put anything past him at this stage. His voice was soft and low.

'I didn't want out, I wanted to stay with you but you wanted kids, I didn't. Not yet anyway.'

'Why, Jamie? Tell me why.' Now Molly was crying. I noticed tears in Amanda's eyes too. It seemed that only I had not succumbed. It occurred to me that maybe I had no tears left. Perhaps I'd used them all up when Lindsay died.

Jamie whined again. 'Oh, Molly, I don't want what we had to be over. If we had kids where would that leave us? We would have no time for each other, or rather you would have no time for me, I'd always take second place to any baby, I just couldn't stand that.'

'Jamie, that's crazy, of course a baby would come first, but if you truly loved me and wanted me to be happy then you would accept that, and any baby would be our baby and should be just as important to you. That's your problem, you can't imagine anything being more important than you, you can't take second place to anything. You are so incredibly selfish, you don't even realize it.'

The room grew quiet again as the three of them gradually realized that they were still in my apartment, and that I was responsible for all their current angst. They all turned their gaze toward me just as my iPhone started to blast out 'Firework' (saved by the Perry.) The tune seemed very appropriate given the current explosive atmosphere inside the room. It was Pauline and I answered it nervously in case she was downstairs. If she had been, I think I would have locked myself in the spare room with all the junk until everybody left. In any event, that option was starting to look more and more attractive. In reality I expected that she was phoning to arrange to drop off Amy, but her voice was urgent and breathless.

'Amy is sick, Andy.'

I experienced a sinking feeling in my stomach. 'What's wrong, what's happened?'

'I don't know, she woke up late up this morning and was very drowsy. At first I thought she was just coming down with a cold or something, but since then she's got steadily worse. She's burning up now. I think we should call the doctor.'

Pauline had been an advocate of not even giving Amy Calpol unless she felt it was absolutely necessary, and even endured a few nights of Amy's restless moaning when she was teething. So, if Pauline thought we needed a doctor, I wasn't going to argue.

'Never mind the doctor, let's just take her up to the sick kids' hospital. Can you get her stuff ready and I'll be right there?' I hung up and grabbed my wallet and car keys from the kitchen unit. I picked up a spare set of house keys and paused. I realized that Amanda and Molly would probably never speak to me again, so I reluctantly tossed the keys to Jamie. He would probably never speak to me again either but my options were limited. 'I need to run. Amy's not well. Can you lock up when you leave?'

Jamie and Molly looked mildly concerned but Amanda was furious. I could see the anger burning in her eyes. She moved to try and block my exit.

'You're not leaving now, are you?' Her tone was sarcastic and hard. This was a side of her I hadn't seen, but then after spending only two evenings with her, during one of which I was only partially conscious, maybe I shouldn't have been surprised.

'My daughter's ill, Amanda, I need to go.'

She shook her head but refused to move and I had to push past her. She tried to grab my arm, but I shrugged her off. I was aware that I was leaving one awful mess behind, but suddenly none of it really mattered to me and I realized that nothing was more important than Amy. I felt guilty that I'd neglected her somewhat over the last few weeks whilst pursuing my own selfish agenda, and vowed to change that.

I slammed the door and pressed for the lift. The indicator told me it was on the ground floor so not wanting to delay my departure I ran down the stairs two at a time. Once in the basement I unlocked my car, started the engine and gunned it out of the car-park. I ran the red light at the end of my road after checking to make sure the road was clear, and a few minutes later I was pounding on the door to Pauline's flat.

CHAPTER TWENTY-FIVE

Amy was worse than I imagined and Pauline had phoned an ambulance. My baby girl was feverish and dopey and I couldn't rouse her at all.

I paced up and down the floor, asking, 'Where's the fucking ambulance?'

Pauline shook her head, all the colour had drained from her face.

I heard Katy Perry again as my phone rang. Irrationally for some reason I thought it might be the ambulance phoning to say they were outside, even though I knew I hadn't made the call. I fished the phone out of my pocket. It was Jamie.

I thought that perhaps he was phoning for an update on Amy and I answered it. I should really have known him better than that.

'Listen, Andy, I've got two really pissed off women here, I think you should come back and sort it out.'

I was furious. I was more than furious. I didn't lose my rag very often – I am pretty laid-back in nature, placid even, but when I'm pushed I have a terrifying, uncontrollable temper. I managed to keep myself in check, for Amy's sake as I needed a clear head to deal with the next few hours.

'Jamie, just fuck off. Just fuck off and never ever call me again, you insensitive bastard.'

Pauline managed a brief smile as I hung up. At that point she was probably assuming that Jamie was furious after finding out about Molly, but she didn't know the half of it and I wasn't about to tell her anything more at that stage. Thankfully, the buzzer of the flat sounded; the cavalry had arrived.

The next few minutes passed like hours. Time seemed to slow down as the paramedics did tests and examinations, which to me looked like a lot of poking and prodding of poor Amy who was even less responsive than before. I just wanted them to get her into the ambulance and off to hospital, but they told me they needed to try and stabilize her before moving. I didn't really know what that meant but they inserted a drip into her arm.

My poor baby didn't even notice as they shoved the needle into her skin. This worried me more than anything else that had happened. The fact she didn't react to that at all couldn't be a good sign.

Eventually, after what seemed like an age – but which in reality was only minutes – we were on our way to the hospital. With the IV in place, Amy seemed to wake up a little and then started screaming. It appeared to be the siren that caused the upset because when the ambulance slowed down for a moment and the siren stopped, Amy went quiet. We drove the rest of the route with flashing lights only. With the siren off, Amy was calm. Her eyelids flickered and she appeared to be slipping in and out of consciousness.

I felt completely useless as I held her hand and cried. I did have some tears left after all. I wished I could take her place, I wished I could be the one in pain and hurting, not my poor baby. I was so scared for her and myself and I hated not being able to do anything. The paramedic sitting with us was not forthcoming with what was wrong, which meant he probably suspected something but wouldn't tell me. I recognized some of the symptoms as being common for meningitis (bloody Internet again).

After Lindsay died, I was paranoid and tried to isolate the worst illnesses that my baby could catch. After a few days of this torture I gave up looking as I was in danger of developing Münchausen's syndrome by proxy if I carried on. In my memory, meningitis, along with ebola, was up there near the top of my list of illnesses to avoid. I could remember the symptoms of ebola and was pretty sure Amy was free of that. However her sensitivity to the ambulance siren and the fact that we had to dim the interior lights rang alarm bells with me.

The paramedic refused to speculate and told me it could be a hundred things, and that was why he needed to get her to the hospital to run tests. He had inserted another IV line into my baby's other tiny arm. I tried to read what the bag said but it made no sense to me.

Then Amy wet herself. The ambulance was immediately filled with the pungent smell of urine. She raised her head and said 'pee pees.' I smiled and told her it was OK, it didn't matter. Her pink leggings were soaked and she appeared to be more distressed about wetting herself than anything else. She had been so good at potty training and rarely had accidents anymore. Her distress made me even more distraught but I realized that this would probably not help anyone, least of all Amy. I would need a clear head to get through the next few hours, so I tried to restrain my emotions and hold myself in check. I glanced across at my mother-in-law who was ashen grey with fear and worry. I looked away – that didn't help.

The paramedic radioed ahead to arrange for a receiving team to meet us on arrival. This meant we dispensed with the normal checking in processes. I listened to this news with relief and anguish, relief that my baby would be helped immediately and alarmed that such precautions were necessary. The paramedic, Tom, tried to explain the situation to us.

'I'm not sure what's wrong with your daughter. As I said it could be a number of things, but what is worrying me more than anything is her temperature. It's too high and we need to get it down, which is why I want her seen immediately.'

The ambulance screeched to a halt under the Accident & Emergency loading bay, and we were all hustled inside. Amy was given a quick examination by a consultant. The name on her badge said Miss Linda Patel. She was dark, small and serious and whisked Amy straight into intensive care. A team of medics were waiting for us and they quickly changed Amy into a small gown that still looked ridiculously large on my delicate daughter. The team spent half an hour running tests, taking blood and trying to reduce her temperature. Both of the IVs the paramedic inserted were removed and replaced with a new line that Miss Patel told me was a combination of saline and strong antibiotics.

After a while, Pauline and I were asked to step outside. We were told we could come back once Amy had been stabilized and moved to her own bay. We were shunted along a corridor by a fussy nurse and parked in a small waiting room. I noted that the number on the door as we entered was 101. I assumed this was just an insensitive bureaucratic blunder, and not an intentional reference to George Orwell's 1984. One thing was for sure, I would be facing up to my worst fears in that room. As it was, I'd grown to fear sitting in small hospital rooms. The experience had not been a positive one for me and my little family.

Eventually, after possibly the longest two hours of my

life, Miss Patel walked into room 101 and sat beside us at the small table.

'Is Amy all right?' The fear must have been obvious in my voice.

Miss Patel appeared to choose her words carefully. 'We've got her temperature down. She had what is called a febrile fit, which is one of the reasons why we asked you to leave the ICU. Normally it's not serious, but can be very distressing for loved ones. The underlying cause is more worrying. I believe Amy has bacterial meningitis. If she hasn't, then the treatment we are currently giving her will do no lasting harm.'

She paused and fixed her gaze on me, her dark eyes pools of medical intelligence. 'Meningitis is basically a brain disease. It causes the tissues that line the brain to swell. Amy is very poorly, Mr Hunter. I need to be open with you. Just after you left the room we performed a lumbar puncture. You know what that is?'

I nodded, holding back a sob. 'Needle in the spine.'

She pushed a small curl of dark hair behind her ear. 'Yes, we withdrew a small amount of fluid and sent it to the labs for testing. The problem is we don't really have time to wait for the test results, which is why I assumed the worst and started the treatment.'

Pauline took a hold of my hand and we leaned into each other for support.

The doctor moved over to the water cooler and poured some water into a cone shaped cup which she then handed to me. As I took it from her, some water spilled onto her hand and I realized I was shaking.

'What do you both know about meningitis, assuming that's what it is?'

'It can be fatal,' I said, my voice quivering.

'It can be, yes. If I had to guess – which I'm not normally in the business of doing – but if I had to, I would say this is neisseria meningitis or more commonly known as meningococcal. The fatality rate is around 10%. Usually though it is because the patient gets help too late, or the subject is weak.'

Pauline jumped in and said. 'You mean sick, underlying health problems? The news was full of stuff about swine flu and how it hit the ill and sick most. Amy has always been—'

'—no, this isn't like swine flu,' the doctor interrupted. 'Amy is classed as weak because her immune system is immature, so fighting the illness is much harder. Most fatalities that *do* occur, happen in this age group. I'm not saying Amy will die, I just want you to know the facts. I believe, based on cases I've seen, that she has this variant which is not good news, but so far there are no signs of septicaemia – blood poisoning – which *is* good news. You also appear to have got her here early. Often a child becomes ill during the night and parents wait until the morning to come in.'

'How do you know if she has septicaemia, and what happens if she does?' Pauline asked anxiously. I was glad she was there as I was not thinking clearly enough to ask intelligent questions.

Miss Patel nodded to acknowledge the question. 'Normally the septicaemia is identified by the appearance of the rash that everyone associates with meningitis, but we have sent blood away for testing as well, so we will know shortly in any event. The rash doesn't always appear if septicaemia is present. Even if Amy does develop the condition, the treatment we are administering is appropriate.'

Miss Patel was silent for a moment, probably giving us time to digest what she had just told us.

'What happens next?' I asked, wondering when we could go and see my daughter.

'Well, what we do now is monitor her. In terms of immediate treatment, we have done all we can. The next few hours are crucial for Amy and it's really down to her what happens next.'

The look of horror on my face must have been obvious. They were leaving the future of my toddler's life in her own hands. She was two and a half years old and did not know the difference between lunchtime and a week next Tuesday, and they were leaving it up to her to decide her own fate.

Miss Patel tried to clarify her statement. 'What I meant is that she'll either fight it or her condition will deteriorate. If she doesn't improve then we could try a different type of combination of antibiotic, but at that stage it may be too late. . . .'

Pauline's eyes were wide in terror, 'You mean she could die?'

Miss Patel rubbed her tired eyes, and nodded, 'It's possible. I think we caught it early, so I'm hopeful, but it is an unpredictable disease.'

At that point I couldn't stand to hear anymore. I couldn't afford to lose Amy as well. 'Can I see her?'

Miss Patel smiled. 'Of course, but I need to prepare you, she is in intensive care and has a lot of monitoring equipment and intravenous lines in her at the moment, all very routine to us, but I know it can be very upsetting for parents.'

Pauline rose to follow us but the doctor said, 'Only one at a time, if that's all right, we try and keep everything calm and quiet for obvious reasons.' Pauline nodded and sat back down.

I followed the doctor out of room 101 and into my own personal hell.

CHAPTER TWENTY-SIX

Nothing could have adequately prepared me for the first time I walked into that room and saw my deathly pale child wired to multiple machines. The sight of Amy lying on a hospital bed with tubes emerging from everywhere was a memory I would take to the grave, and relive in countless nightmares for the rest of my life.

When I entered, a nurse, whose name badge said Angela Coyle, brought over a chair and made me sit down beside the bed. Despite Nurse Coyle's best efforts, I sat in silent shock for what seemed like hours. When I held Amy's hand, it felt cold and lifeless. Angela explained that Amy had been sedated so they could treat her condition properly. It was easier that way. It wasn't easier on me, but I accepted the explanation. The nurse fussed over a machine for a moment or two then left me and my baby alone. I watched the machine's readout after she left. It was connected to Amy by six separate cables taped to different parts of her body. I knew it was there to monitor her condition, her vital signs, but mostly all it did was flash intermittently, first red, then yellow, then green. Occasionally it would bleep, usually on the green light, sometimes on the red but never on the yellow. As time ticked by, I became increasingly convinced that my little girl's well-being was in the hands of a demented set of traffic lights.

A little later Staff Nurse Coyle returned and told me I had a visitor, and that my mother-in-law was anxious to see her granddaughter. The second part I grasped immediately and cursed myself for being so selfish, of course Pauline wanted to see Amy. The bit about a visitor didn't register. I nodded to the nurse and followed her out of the ICU.

Pauline met me at the door. 'How's Amy?'

I shook my head, 'No idea – she's unconscious and wired up to some traffic lights.'

Pauline regarded me strangely but simply said, 'I'll go and sit with her for a bit. There's someone to see you. I told her to go home, but she seemed genuinely upset when I explained the situation. She's in there.' Pauline tilted her head towards room 101. Before I could ask anymore the nurse led Pauline away to see Amy. I shrugged and trudged down the hall.

When I stepped inside, Molly Jenkins jumped up and walked over to me. I couldn't have been more surprised had Coco the clown appeared with some coloured balls and started to juggle. She put her arms around me and I immediately started crying. I had no idea I would do that, but I couldn't help it. Having someone hold you was obviously some kind of fundamental human need and I let the grief pour out of me. After a few moments I felt much better and a little embarrassed.

'Sorry, Molly, I didn't know that was going to happen.'

Molly smiled and wiped some tears from her own eyes. 'It's OK, Andy, I can't imagine what you've been going through. How is she?'

I shrugged. 'Unconscious and wired up to traffic lights.'

Molly looked puzzled, 'Sorry?'

'Doesn't matter – I didn't expect to see you here, in fact I didn't expect to see you ever again.'

Molly smiled once more, this time it was a sad smile and didn't reach her gorgeous brown eyes. 'I'm not sure why I'm here, Andy, but I was concerned about you. Jamie told me you lost your rag with him, so I figured it was serious and came to see. I'm not sure what I think about everything at the moment and to be honest, this isn't the time to deal with it.'

She was right, of course. I couldn't think about anything at that moment beyond my little girl. At some point I would have to deal with everything but not just then, for the time being I just accepted Molly was there to help if she could, and I sat beside her on a hard orange plastic chair. The chairs were uncomfortable and I'm not sure why they had to be orange. We sat in silence for a few minutes before Molly reached over and took my hand in hers. Then we sat in silence again, but strangely now that she was holding my hand the seat no longer felt so uncomfortable.

After half an hour Pauline returned and I left Molly to go back and sit with Amy. Later when I returned to room 101, Molly had gone. I thought that I might never see her again and that saddened me.

Time drifted and I lost all track of it. Shifts changed, nurses and doctors came and went, while I remained constant. At some point Pauline managed to persuade someone to provide me with a large padded chair which was placed adjacent to where Amy slept. I slumped into it and dozed fitfully. My dreams were scrambled and chaotic. Often I woke up wondering where I was and my spirits always slumped when I remembered. Pauline was more sensible than me, and went home occasionally to freshen up and grab a few hours of quality sleep. She knew better, however, than to try and prise me away from the ward. After what seemed like forever, but was in fact only twenty-four hours, Miss Patel came and took me back to room 101.

She smiled at me, which was the first time anyone had smiled since I'd arrived in Hell. Miss Patel glanced at some notes she had resting on her lap, then spoke.

'Amy has responded well to treatment and although she's still sedated we are now scaling down the antibiotic cocktail she's been receiving. Your daughter is going to be fine.'

I was speechless. I felt like going down onto my knees and worshipping this woman in front of me. I could have kissed her hands or feet. A broad grin crossed my face and I managed to utter the immortal line, 'Oh thank you, Doctor.'

After I'd said it I realized it sounded more like a line out of a *Carry On* film, but I didn't care, my precious baby was going to be fine and nothing else mattered.

My spirits had lifted but I continued my bedside vigil as Amy was still sedated. Sometime during the following twenty-four hours I slipped into a deep sleep, fell out of my chair and bruised my knee. The noise I made doing this persuaded the nursing staff to insist I moved myself to room 101 and slept there. I pushed my padded chair down the hospital corridor and sulked.

CHAPTER TWENTY-SEVEN

Finally, on the third morning, I reluctantly left Amy sleeping peacefully in her hospital bed. Most of the wires and tubes had now been removed and she looked more like my daughter, and less like a teenager's science experiment gone wrong.

She had been moved into a quiet side room and although the doctors all reassured me she would now be fine, I still had to be practically dragged from the building by Pauline, who promised to stay with her until I went home, showered and changed the clothes I had been wearing for three days. I was definitely starting to whiff a bit. She also suggested I slept for a few hours before coming back to relieve her. As I drove home I noticed, when I glanced into the rear view mirror, that my eyes were bloodshot. They felt gritty and sore, so maybe a few hours' sleep would be a good idea. I had also been suffering from an aching shoulder for most of the morning which I attributed to sleeping uncomfortably in the padded wooden chair the previous few days.

I drove into my designated parking space in the basement of my building, clambered wearily from the car and took the lift up to my flat. I didn't have the energy to walk up the stairs. I was beat. However, when I opened the door to my apartment, thoughts of sleep immediately vanished from my mind. Someone had been into my home. My iPad was lying smashed to pieces on the floor. There was a dent in the wall where it had obviously been flung with some force. The glass shelves that had held a few ornaments (none of them mine) had been trashed and numerous plates, cups, saucers and most of my drinking glasses had been thrown around the living room and kitchen. A few dents were evident here and there in the plaster indicating where they had been flung, again with force. A few of the cups hadn't broken and were scattered around the room like someone had lost the plot at a chimps' tea-party. Worst of all, however, was that the picture of me, Lindsay and Amy had been ripped from its frame and torn in half. The frame and glass had then been smashed.

I was tired, angry and wasn't thinking straight. I had endured a horrible few days and couldn't cope with much more. I Googled the local police station number on my iPhone. Although I had been burgled and violated – was that the right word? – it didn't feel like a 999 job. Given the recent emergency situation I had experienced with Amy, I was awake enough to realize I shouldn't misuse the emergency services.

A bored sounding voice answered the phone on the third ring and I explained my predicament. The bored voice perked up considerably and, after taking my address and mobile number, promised to send someone round within the hour.

I had been hoping maybe they could come over in a few days as I was anxious to get back to the hospital, I needed time to clean myself up so maybe an hour would be OK. I thanked the voice and hung up.

While I was waiting I removed my rancid clothes and socks and dumped them into the washing basket. If the police arrived and saw me in my current state, they would have assumed I was the burglar and arrested me. I shaved the stubble from my face and then stood under the shower for a long time, letting the hot water and steam cleanse me. I washed my greasy hair and made sure every inch of my body was soaped and rinsed clean before stepping out of the shower cubicle.

I padded through to my bedroom and lay down on my bed for a few moments, enjoying the feeling of being naked, warm and clean.

It would have been so easy to slip into a deep sleep. Instead I got off the bed, slipped into a clean pair of boxer shorts and wriggled into a clean shirt. I was towel drying my hair when the intercom buzzed. That was quick, I thought. Much less than an hour – the police must have been having a slow day! I dropped my damp towel onto my bed and padded over to answer the door. Two male officers came into my apartment. One was tall and dark with Mediterranean features which reminded me of Jamie. That made me a little uneasy as it suddenly occurred to me that maybe he had something to do with this; he did have a fiery temper. The other policeman was smaller with a pinched nose and watery eyes.

Initially I was uncomfortable with the way they both stared at me, then suddenly realized that I hadn't put my jeans on yet and was standing in my shirt and boxers. I smiled an apology and ran back into my bedroom, and pulled on my strides and a pair of slippers.

When I returned I apologized and explained I'd just come out of the shower.

I offered them a drink which they both accepted. I started to gingerly make my way across the debris to the kitchen area when Mediterranean policeman said, 'Try not to touch anything.'

I stopped in my tracks between a broken dinner plate

and a rectangular glass vase which was missing one of its sides. I didn't even know there was a glass vase in the apartment. Maybe the burglar brought it with them to add to the general mayhem. It was more than likely though that – like the salmon and the Cornettos – it had been just pushed to the back of something somewhere.

'How am I supposed to get you a drink without touching anything?' I asked quite reasonably without turning round.

They both looked at each other; policeman number two said, 'Well it's just for fingerprints, you see. Have you got a towel you could use to open the fridge?'

I nodded and wrapped a tea-towel around my hand. I fetched three diet cokes from the fridge, then looked around for glasses. I studied the floor and realized none of them had survived the carnage.

'Sorry, I seem to be fresh out of glasses,' I observed drily and carefully made my way back across the room, handing them a can each. I opened mine and drank deeply, glad of the caffeine hit.

The police introduced themselves and gave me their cards. The watery-eyed officer was called Detective Sergeant Geoff Mokes and the other one Detective Constable Giovanni MacDonald.

I was surprised to learn that it was the watery-eyed Mokes who was the senior officer. It was his colleague who had an air of authority about him. I wondered about the name too – Giovanni MacDonald – a real cultural mix there. They were very pleasant and took it in turns to ask questions. They were also very sympathetic when I explained where I'd been for the last few days.

'Must have been a very upsetting experience for you then to come back here and find everything smashed up?' asked Mokes.

I shrugged. After the few days I'd had, the fact that

Amy was going to be OK made everything else feel irrelevant. If the apartment building had been burned to the ground I probably wouldn't have cared. They might not have let me back into the hospital due to being too stinky, but that didn't matter so long as my baby was all right. As far as I was concerned, this was simply a minor annoyance that was keeping me from her.

Mokes took my shrug to mean I was tired.

'We can come back later if you want but as I'm sure you'd rather be focused on your daughter I'll try and hurry along, OK?'

I nodded gratefully. 'Thanks.'

'Have you any idea how the intruder got into your apartment, the door appears sound and no windows are broken. . . ?'

He left the question hanging and I realized that of course there was no sign of a forced entry.

'I don't know . . .' I offered lamely.

Mokes continued. 'Does anyone else besides your daughter and partner live here. . . ?

'My wife's dead, so it's just me and Amy.'

The revelation of my wife's death changed the officer's attitude slightly, and they took another look around the apartment as if to size up the possibility that maybe I hadn't been burgled at all and this was how I normally lived. Even in my exhausted state I picked up on it. It was something I had grown used to over the previous few months.

They evidently decided that nobody could live in such a wasteland and DS Mokes mumbled some apology and carried on.

'What has been taken from the apartment? Have you managed to look yet?'

I sighed, 'I don't think anything has been taken, I only rent the place so not much in here is actually mine. A lot's broken but nothing seems to be missing.'

MacDonald added a pennyworth. 'So we are looking at malicious damage rather than burglary then?'

'Is there a difference?' I asked.

Both of the officers looked at each other and smiled, I could see the police joke coming but couldn't get out of the way.

'About eighteen months,' they said almost together and laughed.

I couldn't help smiling. It was infectious.

Moke closed his notebook. 'Do you mind if we have a look around before we decide what to do next?'

'Be my guest,' I said. 'Try not to break anything.' I'm not sure they appreciated my tired joke but they got up and walked across the apartment, broken glass and crockery crunched under their feet.

A few minutes later I was almost dozing on the couch when Officer MacDonald shouted, 'Mr Hunter, could you come through here please?'

Both officers were in Amy's room.

I walked slowly, avoiding the detritus. When I entered the room I immediately saw what had made them so excited. It pulled me from my stupor. Huge red letters were scrawled on Amy's wall (in lipstick I discovered later) that said:

Fuck Of and Die

'Have you upset anyone recently?' DC MacDonald asked me.

I nodded my head sadly. 'Yeah, I've upset *everyone* recently.'

The light went on in DS Mokes's eyes.

'Do any of them have a key?'

'Maybe,' I volunteered reluctantly.

As soon as I saw the words I knew who it was, unless I'd upset some demented hairdresser (which I remembered I had). A quick mental calculation told me that this wouldn't be from Terry (or her sister). The message was clearly from Amanda who had no doubt been stressed when she'd scrawled the letters onto the wall, causing the spelling mistake.

I reluctantly admitted to the officers that I knew who had done the damage and that I wouldn't be pressing any charges. I apologized for wasting their time. They were sympathetic and suggested I changed the locks.

I let them out the door, grabbed the sweeping brush from the hall cupboard and started to clean up the worst of the mess. I was not going to get any rest but, in any event, I was too wired now to sleep.

CHAPTER TWENTY-EIGHT

I drove back to the hospital leisurely in marked contrast to my last emotionally charged trip. As I walked through the entrance, the clinical smell reminded me of my sense of panic from a few days earlier when I had wondered if my little angel, the most precious thing in the world to me, would ever make it out of there again.

Amy was still snoozing when I got back up to her room. The consultant, Miss Patel, warned me that she was likely to sleep a lot over the next few days as her body recovered.

'The healing process has less to do with drugs and more to do with the body taking back control of things,' had been the paediatrician's parting wisdom when she had placed her hand reassuringly on my shoulder, and left to tend to what she described as 'more urgent cases'. The fact that Amy was no longer on her priority list gave me more confidence than anything else she did or said, and I at last accepted that my precious baby would be home with me soon.

One more night (not a cue for a Phil Collins song) was how much longer they wanted Amy to stay in hospital. I wondered, if I had been a single mother rather than a single father, they would have reacted differently. Did they suspect that Amy was being neglected? That I, a single (or rather, widowed) man was in some way less capable of caring for his child than a woman would have been? Maybe I was just being paranoid but suspected that this was how the world worked. I was able to understand their doubts. I had them myself. I also fully expected some kind of referral to the social work department in the months ahead – sooner if they ever found out about my apartment being trashed.

I realized that over the previous weeks I had become self-absorbed and obsessed with sex and women, behaving like some animal in musk. I had to shoulder most of the blame for that, but Lindsay had started it all and was continuing it. During the long hours of sitting by Amy's bed, as I watched and listened to the machines blink and bleep, I had realized that those few weeks of bad behaviour (which is how I'd labelled it in my head) had nothing to do with Amy's illness. It had just been a coincidence, but the guilt and fear I had experienced made everything seem scarier than it should have been. I likened it to waking from a nightmare bathed in cold sweat, where the memory gradually melts away as the sun comes up.

As soon as I returned to Amy's room, Pauline left for home, anxious to recharge her batteries. She wouldn't return that day as I'd assured her that the worst was over and I'd stay with Amy until I could take her home. I'd not mentioned the trashed apartment. That would wait until later – she'd had enough worry for the time being. Besides, I wasn't sure how or where I could even begin an explanation.

Amy's small room was cluttered with equipment, most of which thankfully was not in use. When I gently touched Amy's face she murmured quietly but remained asleep. Her skin was surprisingly cool even though the hospital room was uncomfortably warm. She'd had no nourishment for three days and was probably burning fat reserves. Her slim frame would not have much of that and I decided to make sure she ate some food when she awoke later.

A nurse appeared and smiled a greeting in recognition. I had become a semi-permanent fixture lately, and would be glad to get home despite the wonderful work and unselfish devotion of the medical staff.

I slumped into the uncomfortable chair beside her bed. My padded one was probably still in room 101. I considered fetching it but I had received some strange looks previously when I had wheeled it along the hospital corridor, and to be honest I was too tired to repeat the exercise. Despite the hardness of the seat I almost immediately slipped into a deep, dreamless sleep. When I was awoken later by plates clattering as the catering staff delivered food, the sun had slipped from the sky and the room was dark. The room was lit by a small lamp beside Amy's bed. Amy was awake.

'Daddy', she cried and beamed at me. My heart broke and I buried my face into her hair, breathing in her scent. I let the tears pour down my face which made her hair damp. The nurse wandered into the room, noticed my tears and wandered back out again with a smile on her face. My show of emotion might have just staved off a visit from a social worker for the time being.

Amy was allowed to leave the next morning, and as I strapped her into her car seat she asked 'Is Mummy home?'

I had absolutely no idea where that had come from. She had never referred to Lindsay in any form that made sense in any way – except when she had seen her in photographs or the wedding DVD, and even then she had no point of reference as she could not remember Lindsay. I planned on telling her all about her mother and what had happened when she was old enough to understand, I was sure that would have been when she was about five, not two and a half.

I finished strapping her in and gave her a hug. 'No, sweetie, Mummy isn't at home, Mummy is in Heaven.'

That seemed to satisfy her for the moment and her attention was distracted by her favourite teddy which I had brought with me in the car. Then she asked, 'Daddy, when I go to Heaven, will you come with me?'

I stared at her in the rear view mirror until the vision misted over as tears filled my eyes and poured down my face. That was probably one of the most heart-breaking things I had ever heard in my life. I sniffed and tried not to let her see me crying and I answered in a broken voice, 'Of course, baby, but that won't be for a very, very long time.'

Amy seemed to think that over, then asked, 'Will teddy go to Heaven?'

I wasn't sure where all this stuff was coming from, it was as if her illness had opened up a part of her brain that had been dormant before, or maybe this was what happened at her age. It was all a bit of a mystery to me. I would need to Google it later. Parenting via the Internet! Maybe I should have phoned social services and reported myself.

CHAPTER TWENTY-NINE

I spent the rest of the day in the apartment trying to cater to Amy's every whim and desire, and I let her eat anything she wanted, which wasn't much apart from sweets and crisps as I had very little proper food in the flat. She seemed to have shrugged off her illness pretty well. I just assumed that the recovery rate of children at her age was very fast.

As the day wore on I noticed she was more tired than usual and, I thought, painfully thin. Pauline arrived later and brought lunch for everyone, guessing correctly that I would have no food in the flat. Pauline cuddled Amy and said she looked fine and would soon regain any weight she'd lost.

After lunch Pauline left to go shopping, as her boyfriend was due home the following day and they had booked into a romantic country house hotel for a few days.

I had managed to clear up all the mess and, apart from a bizarre lack of glasses and the odd strange dent in the plasterwork here and there, it was hard to tell anything had happened. Only one cupboard full of crockery had been smashed. Another identical sized cupboard still had a full complement of plates and bowls. I wondered who the landlord had in mind when he had purchased all this stuff. My iPad was inoperable and I would need to get another one, but apart from that I tried to put the whole incident to the back of my mind.

I hadn't said anything to Pauline about the break-in, and if I managed to buy some new glasses over the next day or two, I might not mention anything. The knowledge might have made her a little uneasy if I needed her to babysit Amy in the apartment for me.

After Pauline left I got my daughter settled down for her afternoon nap on the couch. She was still clutching her precious teddy tightly to her chest. She'd not let go of it since we'd got out of the car earlier that morning. We had made the bear at the Bear Factory the week Lindsay died. The bear's birth certificate said it was a female bear called Joy. Amy called her Teddy. I couldn't help staring at her face – Amy not the bear, though that had a pleasant face too. It was peaceful with slumber and I was so thankful to have Amy back home with me. I had been so sure that she was going to die. . . . The thought made tears spring into my eyes again. Thankfully, to spare me any more painful recollections, my mobile vibrated on the kitchen table. I didn't recognize the number, but answered it anyway.

'Mr Hunter, this is Detective Sergeant Mokes, from the other day?'

'Oh hi. Yes of course, I'm sorry once again for wasting your time.' I was apologizing a lot lately.

'Don't worry about it, I was just giving you a quick call, as I'm about to close the file on your case and I wanted to make sure you didn't want to press any charges. I realize you weren't at your best yesterday.'

I didn't want to press anything. I just wanted to forget about it all. 'Thanks for your call, Detective, but I'm just trying to put it all behind me – so no, I don't want to take it any further.'

'OK Mr Hunter, that's fine, I just had to check. One more thing before I go. I know you probably haven't had a chance yet, but I would definitely recommend you get your locks changed.'

'Thanks, yes I will.' I meant it as well, but on my list of things to do it was around number seventeen or something.

Later that evening, once Amy was sound asleep in bed I muted the TV, sat on the couch with my phone and tried to psyche myself up to make some calls. I was going to try and fix some of the mess I'd got myself into. I hadn't always been a confident but incompetent womanizer. My first serious girlfriend at school looked like Eric Bristow in drag – for those who can remember the famous dart player in his pomp. For those who can't: Google him circa 1983 and imagine the addition of a flowery dress and a black wig and you are somewhere near Diane, my first love. Maybe she was still single and available. . . . On reflection I'd probably be better off single.

Firstly I tried to get hold of Amanda. Her phone rang out and after four rings went to voicemail. I was relieved and left a message apologizing and followed up with a text. I had no illusions about resurrecting our relationship, nor did I want to.

Next I tried to phone Molly. When she had visited me at the hospital I wasn't in any position to judge or deal with her mood, or take on how things were between us. Given she came to me in my darkest hours I assumed that all was not lost between us, but I was well aware of how I had betrayed her and didn't deserve any second chances. I only got through to her voicemail too. I left a message for her to call me and was secretly relieved she didn't pick up as I had no idea what to say to her. For the same reason, I didn't text her.

Lastly, I pulled up Jamie's number from my contact list

and hit 'call'. It rang for a moment before I heard his voice. 'Well Andy, you are the last person I thought I'd hear from. How's Amy?'

At least he had the decency to ask.

'Much better, thank God. She only came home this morning.'

There was silence for a moment. I was first to speak.

'Listen Jamie, I don't expect you to understand – I'm not sure myself what's been going on in my life for the last few weeks – but if it makes you feel any better nobody is speaking to me. . . .'

'Serves you right.' I could hear the bitterness in his voice. I couldn't blame him, but I wasn't about to let him have all the moral high ground.

'Look, Jamie, I'm sorry about what happened but—'

'You mean you're sorry you got caught.'

Was that what I meant? I wasn't sure. I had wanted time to decide who I liked best between Amanda and Molly and with hindsight it was obvious who was suited to me, who was the natural choice. At the time I'd got caught up in it all. My ego had carried me away.

'Maybe you're right, Jamie, I was in a situation I was not equipped to deal with. Shagging about is more your style than mine.' Jamie didn't respond but I knew the barb had hit home. 'Anyway, I'm just phoning to let you know that nobody is speaking to me and I can't say I blame them, but I can't change what happened and to be honest, the last few days with what has happened with Amy has given me a whole new perspective on things.'

I chose my next few words carefully. 'I didn't plan what happened with Molly, we just went for a chat and hit it off. I guess if you'd never cheated on her then none of this would have happened.'

I wasn't trying to deflect my guilt in any way, but I wanted him to know that he was partly responsible.

There was anger in his voice. 'I know that, Andy, I've tried to tell myself things would have been OK if that stupid Polish bitch hadn't sent that email to Molly in the first place. I still don't know why she did that.'

I knew the stupid Polish bitch was oblivious and I hoped Jamie never found out otherwise. He sighed and there was resignation in his voice. 'I think that Molly and me were just about finished anyway. Maybe we could have fixed things but I doubt it. What made me really mad was when she told me about the two of you. You should have told me, not her.'

'I know that, Jamie, I just couldn't find the words or anything. I was going to eventually.'

The word 'eventually' hung in the air for a moment.

Once again I broke the silence. 'One more thing, Jamie, have you still got the spare set of keys to my apartment?'

'No, I didn't take them. I left with Molly a short time after you rushed out. I gave the keys to Amanda. She said she had to get her stuff together and would lock up when she left.'

I thought that was what had happened but I just wanted to be sure.

I couldn't think of anything else to say, so simply said, 'OK, Jamie, thanks, you take care of yourself.'

He snorted down the phone. 'Yeah sure, Andy.'

I was left listening to dead air.

CHAPTER THIRTY

A few days later I had my final meeting at Perennial Mutual. Pauline came and took Amy away for the morning, and said she would bring her back later in the afternoon.

The lack of any response from Molly made me sad but what could I expect? I had some time to kill before I went into Perennial Mutual for my final marching orders so I made a cup of strong coffee and opened the new iPad I'd managed to buy. I logged on to the oracle that was *Men Like Women and Women Like Shoes* to see if it had any pearls of wisdom relating to my situation.

There was a section entitled 'When All Else Fails'. I reckoned that I had pretty much reached that position so I opened up the link and started to read.

When you have tried everything you can think of to win over your sweetheart, it is time for a GRAND ROMANTIC GESTURE.

I wasn't sure what a grand romantic gesture entailed, but thankfully the site clarified this for me.

Romantic gestures come in many different guises. See the list below for some ideas:

- A hot-air balloon ride over Paris.

I was scared of heights so that was a non-starter. Having a jelly-kneed, gibbering idiot beside her on such a venture was unlikely to endear me to Molly.

- Scatter rose petals in her bedroom and in her bed.

That was unlikely to work on several levels. Firstly, I would have needed to gain entry to her flat and I wasn't a competent house-breaker. I could have asked Amanda who was adept at the art, for help, but I didn't think she would have been a willing assistant. I was also fairly sure that Molly was a hay-fever sufferer, so if I didn't freak her out by breaking into her flat she was unlikely to thank me for inflicting a runny nose and itchy eyes on her.

- Write a love poem.

I wasn't very good at that sort of thing. I could do a pretty good limerick, maybe something like:

There was a young man called Andy,
Who was so incredibly randy,
He dated those blondes,
Who dared correspond,
Named Ellen, Terry, or Mandy.

I knew Amanda wasn't blonde but allowed myself some artistic licence. When I read back my effort I decided that it was also unlikely to endear me to Molly who wasn't even mentioned – plus it wasn't very good, so I moved on.

The website also suggested that I write her a song, post her a copy then stand outside her home and sing it to her. My attempt at song-writing would, in all likelihood, be similar to my limerick and the thought of standing outside her flat (which was in a block of about forty) singing in my tone-deaf baritone was unlikely to win her over.

In fact, when I started to discount all the website's suggestions of 'grand romantic gestures' I started to feel completely out of my depth. *Men Like Women and Women Like Shoes* tended to have that effect on me.

Finally the site advised that if you cannot think of anything original yourself you could perhaps emulate the movies and steal an idea. One of the suggestions was to stand outside her house with a series of boards telling her how much she means to you whilst playing her favourite song (thank you *Love Actually*) but my issues with that were similar to the song in that forty other flats would also get the benefit of my gesture. It was possible that some other female might like the effort and feel sorry for me but that would only complicate my life even further and I didn't want that. I sighed and turned off my iPad. I didn't think any of the approaches from *Men Like Women and Women Like Shoes* would help me. Maybe something would come to me later.

I'd felt a headache coming on so after I'd donned a clean shirt, tie and a new suit I swallowed a couple of aspirin tablets, left my flat, took the lift to the basement and jumped in my car. I had decided that my sore head wouldn't tolerate public transport. I had also decided that the meeting was likely to be relatively short so the parking costs would be worth the convenience of having my car handy.

I was right about the meeting. They simply handed me some official paperwork and confirmed what I would receive in 'compensation' as they put it. I said little and left

247

the meeting sad that I would never set foot in my office again.

Very few of my former colleagues were around to bid farewell, so I headed down to the main entrance. I managed to avoid going anywhere near the HR section where Molly worked. On a whim I had one last glance at the staff noticeboard. It was supposed to be restricted to information about impending meetings and company updates but over the years had developed into a kind of Perennial Mutual Gumtree. If anyone had anything to sell, swap or get rid of, this was the place they usually posted it.

My eye was drawn to a small blue card placed by Carol Davis who worked part-time in the Accounts Department. I knew her reasonably well as she was the woman who had the dubious pleasure of approving and signing off my expenses each month.

Her cat had recently had kittens and she was offering them for sale at £5 each. Given that the price was so low I assumed her cat was not a pedigree breed and her attempt to sell them was maybe more of an effort to divest her house of kittens rather than to make any serious money.

Suddenly I had the germ of an idea and phoned her on my mobile. She picked up on the third ring and in the background I could hear the excited scream of young children and the unmistakable screech of a cat in distress. I remembered that Carol had in total four children, all girls - aged two, four, six and seven. I could only imagine the chaos added by the introduction of some kittens into her home.

She shouted down the phone. 'Carmen, stop chasing Candy, she doesn't like getting her tail pulled.'

Intuition told me that Candy was the mother cat and not some mutant daughter with a tail. The non-mutant daughter would be Carmen. I briefly considered how much more complicated my life would have been had Lindsay and I been given time to produce more than one child. It almost certainly would have curtailed my ability to go on Internet dates and, given my current dilemma, that might not have been such a bad thing. Before I could ponder more on the multiple children question Carol asked impatiently, 'Who is this? I'm kind of busy right now.'

'Hi, Carol, sorry, I know it sounds chaotic in there. This is Andy Hunter from the risk management unit, well former risk management unit. I read your card on the staff noticeboard . . . about the kittens?'

Carol's tone was calmer when she replied. 'Oh, sorry, Andy, I just thought you were one of those sales call things.'

I considered passing on my wisdom of how to deal with sales calls, but decided to reserve that for a later time.

'I'm sorry to hear about you losing your job,' Carol continued. 'It must be tough on you, with a wee one and all?'

'Yeah I know but it's OK, I'll get something else,' I said more confidently than I believed. 'Listen, Carol, I know you've got your hands full just now. Is there a better time to phone you back?'

'About the kittens?'

What else would I want to phone her about? To chat about my impending redundancy? The weather? My Internet dating experiences? I kept my sarcastic side in check.

'Yeah, I'd like to buy one of your kittens.'

'Just one?'

'Yeah, just one.'

'I could do a bulk discount.'

'How many kittens do you have?'

'Nine.'

'Nine?'

'Yeah, nine.' She sounded depressed when she said nine. I wasn't surprised. Four young kids and nine kittens.

'How did that happen?'

'Fuck knows.'

I didn't press for any more details. 'To be honest, Carol, I really only want one. Could I come over just now and maybe pick one out?'

'I'll need to round them all up.'

I wasn't sure if she was talking about the kittens or the kids, maybe both.

'Where do you live?'

'Blackhall Drive in Trinity.'

I did a quick calculation in my head. 'It'll take me about twenty minutes to get there. Is that enough time for you?'

'Yeah, that'll be fine, see you soon. Our house is number eight. You'll find us by the noise.'

When she opened her front door to me twenty minutes later, I realized Carol hadn't been kidding about the noise. I was met by a cacophony of cries and screeches and couldn't tell if they belonged to the kids, the cat or the kittens – probably a combination of all three. A flustered and tired-looking Carol ushered me into her cluttered kitchen. Carol was very thin with light brown hair. She was reasonably pretty and wore very little make-up. She probably got very little time to spend beautifying herself.

Huddled together in a basket beside the cluttered kitchen table were four kittens. I assume the other five were doing kitten type things elsewhere in the house. One of them raised its head and mewed quietly. It was a small tabby with a wet nose and clear blue eyes. It was gorgeous.

I smiled. 'It has to be that one.'

Carol smiled back. 'That's Trooper. We called him that because he was the smallest and last to be born and the only tabby amongst them all.'

I had been working on my plan during the drive over

to her house and then made my slightly unusual request. 'I have a confession to make. The kitten isn't actually for me, it's for a friend – someone who has always wanted a cat. Can you hang onto him until later today and I will come back and pick him up?'

Carol looked puzzled but was pleased to be getting rid of one of the kittens and didn't raise an objection. 'Yeah, no problem, I'll be in all day anyway, what time will you be back?'

'I'm not sure yet, I'll phone you with a time as soon as I can if that's OK?'

Carol shrugged. 'Whatever.'

Glad to be out of the noisy household I drove a short distance and then pulled my car over and executed part two of my plan. I looked up the details of Colin Spark's agent on Google and dialled his phone number. The phone was answered almost immediately by a grumpy sounding male.

'Yeah?'

'Is this Paul Burns, Colin Spark's agent?'

'Yeah.'

'Hi, my name is Andy Hunter, I was wondering if Mr Sparks would be able to do me a small favour. . . .'

'He's stopped doing nineties nights.'

I was slightly taken aback, I hadn't even made my request yet. It also occurred to me that nineties nights – given that this was the era of his fame – would probably be the bread and butter of his livelihood, but then maybe the much publicized bankruptcy was exaggerated.

I continued. 'Well, I wasn't actually looking for him to do a nineties night—'

His agent interrupted again, 'He doesn't do kid's parties, fetes, supermarket openings, beach parties, summer festivals, hen parties, retirement dos, twenty-firsts, thirtieths, fortieths, fiftieths, sixtieths or sixty-fifths.'

I smiled and suddenly realized why Mr Sparks sat playing games all day. 'What about seventieth birthday parties?' I asked mischievously.

His agent, obviously lacking a sense of humour, said, 'I'll need to check with him.'

I knew it would probably immediately be added to his list of prohibited activities. 'Look don't bother, I don't want him to do that anyway, Mr Burns. What I'm looking for is something a little . . . well . . . different. More personal.'

'He's not gay, despite what the press says.'

I laughed down the phone. 'I didn't think for a moment he was. Do you think I could speak to him personally about it?'

'About being gay?'

'No, about my request. . . .'

'Which has nothing to do with gay activities?'

'No, it's about a girl I like. . . .'

'Is she gay?'

I immediately got a mental picture of Molly in a soft-focused pornographic lesbian scene. I shook my head to get rid of the image.

'No, she's not gay.' I suspected Paul Burns had some kind of homophobic thing going on.

'Right, well if it has absolutely nothing to do with anything gay he might be interested. What's it about?'

I gave him a rough outline of my plan and the agent agreed to put the proposal to Colin Sparks.

I sat in my car for twenty minutes waiting for a call back. Eventually my mobile rang, the moment of truth. I answered before Katy Perry finished the words 'You're a', which in old money was about one and a half rings.

'Mr Hunter?'

'Yes.'

'Paul Burns here, Mr Sparks is intrigued by your request and wants to talk to you in person. Can you go to his flat and I'll meet you there in about half an hour? You're sure you're not gay?'

I laughed. What was it with the gay thing? 'No, Mr Burns I don't have a gay bone in my body.'

'OK then the address is 12 The Quadrant, Fountainbridge.'

I shivered involuntarily. That was the same block of flats where Carrie lived. I wondered if they knew each other, I hoped not. I couldn't remember the number of Carrie's flat because I wasn't paying that much attention to detail the last time I was there.

'Fab, thanks. I'll see you there.'

I started the engine and drove through the busy streets, cutting through Holyrood Park on my way.

I parked outside Colin and Carrie's block and noticed with relief that Colin Sparks's apartment was on the opposite side to hers.

I pressed the intercom buzzer to his home and after a few seconds he buzzed me in without asking who it was.

I climbed the stairs to the third floor and the door to number twelve was slightly ajar. I was nervous at the thought of entering the modest home of a once-famous pop star. It occurred to me that someone who had been idolized by thousands of screaming girls, sold out huge arenas across Europe and made umpteen TV appearances, should live somewhere a little grander than this.

A gravelly Glaswegian voice called out, 'Come on in, I'm just in the toilet having a shit. Go into the living room and I'll be there in a minute.'

I smiled. That first sentence to me from the former pop legend made me think that maybe he was in the right place after all. I closed the front door quietly and walked along the short hall into the living room. The room was surprisingly tidy. For some reason I'd expected it to be some kind of clichéd den of iniquity, with used syringes and empty whisky bottles everywhere. Instead it was sparsely furnished with a cream leather couch, a small chair and a modest flat-screen TV mounted on the wall opposite the window. His flat didn't have a balcony like Carrie's, but then he was on the other side of the building overlooking a busy road rather than the canal.

I sat on the edge of the couch and waited for Colin Sparks to finish his ablutions. He came through and held out his hand for me to shake. I grasped it and hoped he'd washed it.

'So, you've got women trouble?'

I laughed. 'Yeah you could say that.'

'Something I know all about, well *knew* all about. These days it's only middle-aged harlots with bad breath and huge arses that seem to fancy me.'

I smiled. I liked Colin Sparks's self-deprecating sense of humour and immediately thought 'you can take the boy out of Glasgow but not Glasgow out of the boy'. I sat back down on the couch and said, 'Well I guess the middle-aged women were the nubile teens when you were singing.'

Colin didn't answer me. Instead he glanced longingly at the Xbox sitting blinking quietly in the corner. Then he moved his gaze to me and stared at me for a moment, his green eyes sparking with more intelligence than perhaps I'd given him credit for. 'So, this girl of yours, is she likely to be swayed by the appearance of a washed-up rock star?'

'I thought you were a pop star.'

'Same difference.'

'Not really,' I answered. I didn't want to upset him, but I got the feeling that sucking up wouldn't work.

Colin narrowed his eyes, as if reappraising me. 'What's the difference then?'

I smiled. 'Credibility.'

He laughed out loud – not a reaction I was expecting. 'Maybe you're right.'

His mobile chimed, and he fished it out of his pocket and took the call. He grunted into the phone and hung up. 'My agent's not coming, got something more important to do. I'm way down his list of priorities these days.'

'Is that because you won't do much personal appearance work?'

'He gave you the list then?'

I smiled but didn't answer.

Colin obviously felt he needed to offer me an explanation and sighed. 'It's depressing.'

I nodded but didn't push for any more details. I could see in his face and demeanour that his soul ached for the past, for something he could no longer have. I knew the feeling well and didn't want to have that conversation with him.

I tried to distract him for both our sakes. 'Will you help me?'

'I used to be her hero, you said?'

'Yeah, and she's not middle-aged with bad breath.'

'Big arse?'

'Lovely arse.'

Colin grinned. 'That would make a nice change.'

'How much would it cost? Your agent didn't really give me any info, he was more obsessed with whether anyone was gay or not.'

Colin nodded. 'Yeah, he has a few problems with that. He's also not great at fee negotiation either.'

I had thought that was what agents were for but kept my opinion to myself. I waited for Colin to sell himself.

'I reckon I could do it for . . . oh I don't know . . . a grand?'

I shook my head. 'Five hundred.'

'Seven-fifty?'

'Six hundred. I really can't afford any more,' I lied. 'It's for a good cause.'

Colin Sparks smiled. 'OK then, six hundred quid but I want it in advance, and if she wants me instead of you, no hard feelings?'

I smiled, to cover the doubt that was nagging at me. Molly used to adore this man sitting in front of me and she was vulnerable right now. It was a risk but I needed to take it. I reached over and shook his hand. The bargain was struck.

I then outlined the details of what I wanted him to do.

'Kittens!' he exclaimed. 'I need danger money for kitten scratches.'

I laughed. 'It's a kitten not a tiger.'

Colin was serious. 'Have you ever had a cat?'

I nodded. 'Yeah, years ago.'

'I had a cat until last year, died of cancer, was glad to be rid of the fucking thing. Vicious little bugger, used to leap at me when it was dark and dig his claws into my scalp.' He rubbed his head at the memory.

A thought occurred to me. 'Have you still got a cat carrier and litter tray?'

'Yeah somewhere but that'll be an extra fifty.' He smiled, waiting for me to haggle him down.

'Deal. As long as we leave in ten minutes, we can pick up the kitten then swing by her work and you can brighten up her afternoon.'

'Yeah, OK, I've got nothing else on anyway, but remember I might brighten up more than her afternoon.'

I nodded. 'That's a chance I'll take.'

'You've got it bad then?'

I puffed out my cheeks. 'Maybe.'

I phoned Carol Davis and arranged to pick up Trooper.

Colin insisted on coming into Carol's chaotic household with me. She opened the door and beckoned us in.

She barely glanced at Colin, but once in the kitchen she narrowed her eyes and gave him the once over.

'You remind me of someone,' she said. 'Did you used to be on the telly?'

Colin grinned. 'Sometimes; I was a singer with the band Laser Lights.'

Carol smiled in recognition. 'So you were. I never liked your music much. It was too,' – she frowned searching for the right word – 'poppy.'

Colin stopped smiling. 'We were a pop band.'

'Exactly, that was what I didn't like. There was no substance to your songs – all throw-away lines and forgettable tunes.'

Colin tried to defend his artistic integrity. '"Lost in Your Eyes" was a huge hit and people still use it for their first dance at weddings.'

Carol shrugged. 'I preferred the Biggles Bakery version to be honest.'

I laughed out loud. The Scottish bakery firm had used the tune in a TV advertising campaign a few years earlier, changing the words from 'Lost in your Eyes' to 'Lost in our Pies'. It had been a huge success.

Colin was not amused. 'Yeah, the record company only told me about that a week before it started, still the royalties came in handy.'

While Colin had been talking, Carol had picked up Trooper and, after kissing his nose, placed him in the carrier I had given her.

'So,' she said, 'who is the lucky new owner of Trooper? It's not for you, is it?' She scowled at Colin. He was obviously not used to that kind of reaction and looked uncomfortable.

I intervened. 'No, it's for a friend of mine. . . .'

Colin Sparks interrupted. 'He's got the hots for someone called Molly at his work, and reckons that the combination of me and this kitten will get her in the sack.'

Carol turned to me. 'Molly Jenkins in HR?'

I nodded sheepishly. I thought about trying to contradict what the washed-up pop star had said but decided that might just make me look worse.

Carol was puzzled. 'I thought she lived with her boyfriend?'

I shook my head and said, 'Not any more. I didn't know you and Molly were friends?'

She shrugged. 'We're not really, I just know her to talk to. So what happened to her boyfriend?'

I shook my head. 'It's a long story and probably now's not the best time to explain.' I rolled my eyes towards Colin Sparks.

Carol relented, 'OK no probs, I'll get the goss another day.' She turned towards Colin. 'Are you doing this out of the goodness of your heart?'

Colin smiled. 'No, for the money.'

'How much?'

Colin glanced over at me for approval. I nodded.

'Six hundred quid.'

'I hope you're not going to sing?'

He flashed his smile at her. 'I might if asked.'

Carol was obviously not at all impressed by the thought of having a celebrity in her kitchen and turned back to me. 'Are you sure this is a good idea?'

I shook my head. 'Not really, but I can't think what else to do. I guess I've reached desperation stage.'

Carol laughed. 'Yeah you must have, to employ this aged Lothario.'

'I'm not that old,' exclaimed Colin.

Carol looked him up and down. 'You're at least forty-five, right?'

I smiled and bet Colin wished he'd stayed in the car.

'Don't be ridiculous, woman, I'm thirty-nine.'

Carol frowned, not liking the way 'woman' was emphasized. 'Really? I was actually being kind, I thought you were nearer fifty.'

I could tell Carol was winding him up. Unfortunately Colin couldn't and stormed out of the room.

I laughed, thanked Carol and followed the ageing Lothario into the street. Once we were safely seated in my car Colin glanced quizzically at me. 'I hope this Molly girl is not as mean as her friend back there.'

I shook my head. 'No, Molly is an angel with a heart of gold.'

'And a nice arse?'

I laughed. 'Perfect arse.'

That seemed to pacify Colin Sparks and with the promise of meeting the perfect arse we hardly spoke on our way to the Perennial Mutual building. It was nearly four o'clock when I pulled the car to a stop outside the main door and explained to Colin what he needed to do.

'Just go to the reception desk and ask for Molly Jenkins. The receptionist will buzz her and she'll come down to see you.'

Colin nodded. 'Would it not be more of a surprise to go and see her in her office or whatever?'

'Yeah probably, but they wouldn't let you in without a pass, especially carrying a cat basket.'

'Could I not use your pass?'

I smiled. 'I don't have one anymore, just lost my job.'

Colin regarded me strangely. 'Not having a lot of luck at the moment, are you?'

I sighed. 'Not really, no.' He didn't know the half of it.

Colin nodded. 'OK, just you shoot off, I'll do my bit and phone you later and let you know how it went. Don't worry about me. I'll get a taxi home.'

Reluctantly, I left him to it and drove home. I parked in my underground space and took the lift up to my apartment. As soon as I opened the door I knew instinctively that something was wrong. Nothing looked out of place. My new iPad wasn't broken, nor was there any shattered plates or glasses strewn about the room, but something was definitely amiss. Then I realized what it was, I could detect a faint scent in the air, I recognized it but couldn't quite place it.

I shook my head and blamed my overactive imagination. I kicked off my shoes and went into the bedroom to change out of my suit. It might be a while before I got to wear one again. When I opened the wardrobe to take out a coat-hanger I leapt back in shock.

All my suits had been shredded. Every one of them had both the sleeves of the jackets and the legs of the trousers cut off. I opened my other wardrobe but only my suits had been attacked. I had meant to get the locks changed as I'd promised the detective sergeant, but hadn't got around to it.

I turned, sat down on my bed and stared at the mess. Then I noticed an envelope sitting propped up against the lamp on the bedside table.

It was small and pink and on the front in neat-handwriting was my name. I picked it up and detected the same scent I'd noticed when I came into the apartment. It was Amanda's perfume. Bitch.

The note inside was brief.

Dear Bas-turd, (I like that – not bad for a dyslexic girl huh?)

I had to give her credit for spelling dyslexic correctly anyway.

I almost had you down as marriage material as well. I will need to readjust my criteria for that I think.

Anyway I hope you like the adjustments I've made to your

suits, not that you'll be needing them anytime soon – fucking loser!

I enjoyed myself this morning, almost as much as I enjoyed organizing your last little surprise. Despite the fact that you humiliated me I've decided to let you off lightly. I won't be visiting your apartment again and I might even forgive you eventually – but I doubt it. My change of heart has nothing to do with you, but I reckon you will find out the reason soon enough. In the meantime, Mr Hunter, please take this as a warning not to mess with women's emotions, especially psychotic Irishwomen LOL.

I hope your life turns to shit.
Love Amanda
XXXX
PS your keys are in the fridge

I re-read the note a couple of times and then walked through to the kitchen. There in the fridge, beside a carton of apple juice, were my keys, wrapped in a pair of red panties (Amanda's, I assumed).

I removed the keys from the panties and put them on the worktop. The panties had obviously been worn and had a certain crispiness to them which hinted at dried bodily fluids. I tossed them in the bin and washed my hands. I know some people pay money for used panties and stuff but that wasn't my scene. Besides, in Amanda's case they could just as easily have been laced with anthrax or something as equally unpleasant. I shivered and took the black bin bag out of the bin, tied a knot in it and put it outside the apartment door to take down to the rubbish bins later.

I considered phoning a locksmith in case she had copied my keys, but decided to leave that for later as well.

I then broke my golden rule about not drinking alcohol

before 5 p.m. (unless on holiday or now if I was subject to break-ins by psychotic women) and poured myself a glass of red wine. My mood was sombre and I flopped down on the couch and stared out of the window. My gaze wandered over the windswept bay and I wondered what would happen next.

CHAPTER THIRTY-ONE

I didn't need to wait long as my phone started ringing (or rather the Perry started singing). I didn't recognize the number but answered it anyway.

'Andy?'

I recognized the Glaswegian twang of Colin Sparks. My heart skipped a beat. Anxiety or excitement? I wasn't sure. Maybe both.

'Colin. How did it go?'

There was a slight pause. 'It went well, she's an absolute honey.' His tone was very upbeat and that made me nervous.

'And. . . ?'

'Well, I've got good news and bad news.'

'OK good news first.'

'She loves the kitten.'

'And the bad news?'

'Well there's no bad news really – well, not for me anyway – I'm taking her out tonight for dinner, but I guess that's bad news for you. Sorry, Andy, you knew the risks. I was her teenage idol and I guess you can't really compete with that, huh?'

I felt hot tears burning at the corner of my eyes but I

263

wasn't about to let this prick know he was getting to me. 'Yeah Colin, I knew the risks, just be nice to her, OK?'

He laughed, 'Oh I'll be very nice to her, don't you worry about that, oh, and one more thing.'

'Yeah?'

'You were right, she has a perfect arse.'

After he hung up I slumped down on the couch and drained my glass of wine. After a moment I got up and refilled it again and walked over and stared out over the grey ocean. I was trying to think of something to do that would take my mind off Molly when my mobile pinged signifying a new text.

Hi Andy. Lindsay here. Just sent u another email – read it when u get a chance. U might want 2 have a drink to hand before u do.

Well, that was handy, I put my full glass onto the table and logged on to my email account.

Love Byte 6 – 29th December – Hospice
Hi gorgeous husband

It's 5 a.m. and I'm sitting in bed typing. I can't get out of bed at all now, my legs are too weak. They've stuffed a tube in my fanny today to collect urine – well not in my fanny exactly but you know what I mean. The last degradation which is fucking uncomfortable. Anyway enough about that – details you don't really need to know. It was lovely to see you earlier, even though I was a bit dopey. That happens just after they give me my meds. My brain is much clearer now but the pain is almost unbearable.

I'm glad I moved in here, the staff are great and I had to

take the pressure off you both. Besides, Amy is scared of me now, I look like some freak from a horror film and every time she looks at me her eyes well up with tears and it breaks my heart.

I must be really disrupting your life by now but as I've always said, I'm doing it for your own good and it helps me feel better too. I don't think I've explained why I decided to wait so many months before I sent you the first email and there's no real big answer. I just reckoned that by now you should have got most of your grieving out of the way and have your head clear enough to deal with me.

I hope you're looking after my little angel. God I miss her so much, I can't believe that soon I'll never see her again. It's so cruel that she'll never know me, the person who gave life to her. The mother who nurtured her for nine months and beyond will always be a stranger to her. How sad is that?

Sorry, Andy, I know this will be tough for you, but please indulge me a little more. This is probably my final email – the drugs are making me too woozy to do this much longer and I'd rather sign off from this life while I can still be lucid rather than with some garbled nonsense weeks from now.

After this you will probably never hear from me again, at least not in this world. Hopefully I'll always live in your memory, and please when you think of me from time to time remember the good times when I was well, happy and sexy. Don't dwell on the emaciated mess that I am now. That's not me, that's not who I am, you know that.

The last few months have been wonderful and hellish. I've tried to bear this the best I can but I wouldn't wish this disease on my worst enemy – not that I've got a worst enemy, in fact I don't think I've got any enemies (well none that I know of). I hope when your time comes, you are very old, very happy and you pass away peacefully in your bed or maybe on the toilet like Elvis. Then when you do die – if there is an after-life – I'll come and meet you. That'd be funny, wouldn't it? You'd be an old codger and I'd be young and gorgeous. I probably wouldn't fancy you anymore and I'd want to go dancing and clubbing and you'll probably just want to sit in a comfy chair, watch the Antiques Roadshow and drink Horlicks haha!

OK I know I'm wandering a bit but please, please, Andy, to be serious for a moment, I want you to focus on the times we had before Amy came. The holiday in Florida when we rushed around the parks like wide-eyed children. Then later drinking beer in that Orlando bar with the drunken Germans who thought we were Americans – do you remember how we pretended to be from New York and took the piss out of them for hours? Also you must remember the time we danced through that thunderstorm in Crete while the rain cooled our sunburnt shoulders, and then afterwards when we plunged naked into the ocean and raised our arms to the sky and shouted every dirty word we could think of.

Those are the memories I want you to take with you, that and the times after Amy came along and we didn't know what was wrong with her, and the wonder we shared together when she took her first steps, and spoke her first word. You remember her first word, don't you? It wasn't mummy or daddy, it was 'shoes'! God how we laughed. That girl takes after her mother – she loves her shoes!

Oh God it hurts, Andy. I'm nearly dead. This empty worn-out shell of a body can't take much more. I'm sitting here typing, crying and laughing at the same time. Such a bittersweet moment, and I'm all alone – you're not here to share it with me but that's OK, you and Amy will be sleeping and that's a good thing. You need to be strong for Amy, Andy. Even if my plan to find you a woman has worked, you probably still need to be a mother to her as well unless you've found a saint. You will be the only one who has that real connection to her. She is part of you, she's part of me too but I'm gone. I'm history, you need to be her world, Andy, and the good thing is I know you know that.

I try not to think about it but I'll not get to see my baby grow up and that hurts more than anything. So spare a thought for me when she has her first day at school – all excited and dressed in her new uniform, with that pang of remorse and realization you'll experience when she leaves you at the school gate for the first time and walks into a life where you are no longer the centre of her universe. Be easy on her when she brings home her first proper boyfriend and be there for her when she needs a shoulder to lean or cry on.

I was glad I made it to Christmas. My final thought, whenever that will be – but probably not too far away now – will be of her face on Christmas morning when she opened that doll my mum had bought for her, the one she always played with in John Lewis. She was so excited, so happy.

I'm scared, Andy, but to be honest I'm so tired. My body aches everywhere, even with the drugs. In a way I'm looking forward to the end now, the release from the pain. When it comes I hope you try to celebrate my life, the fun we had and the joy we gave each other. Don't dwell on the dark stuff – it's not worth it. Life's too short, believe me I know.

That's it. I'm too tired to type any longer. I'm going to log off for the last time. I hope you will be happy with whatever life you make for yourself without me. I wish you well, I hope you find another love as big and as strong as mine and if you do, babes, hold onto it for all you are worth.

Tell Amy how much I love her when she's old enough to understand who I was and what happened to me.

I love you Andy, I always will – wherever I am.

Your very tired wife
Lindsay
XXXXX

I poured myself another glass of wine, then another one, then another one. . . .

CHAPTER THIRTY-TWO

The next day dawned bright and clear, and I dawned dull and foggy with a splitting headache. The previous evening Pauline had stayed with me until Amy was asleep and I'd sobered up enough to be capable of looking after her if she awoke.

Pauline was not judgemental and attributed my drinking to the bad day I'd had with Perennial Mutual. The weird thing was that 'officially' losing my job barely registered in the overall scheme of things. I'd also left it too long to explain to Pauline what her dead daughter was up to – even that sentence would probably have her organizing a psychiatric evaluation for me. Then if I tried to explain about a psychotic Irish girl who cut up suits, wrecked apartments and left dirty knickers in fridges, she'd probably have had me sectioned.

I crawled out of bed and padded through to the kitchen, took two aspirin and made myself some coffee. I took the steaming mug over to the dining-room table and gazed out of the window. The white tops on the waves told me that it was still windy and probably cold. It was amazing what a difference a few days made to the Scottish weather, the warm front that had given Edinburgh a last tantalizing taste of summer had now been replaced by chilly autumn air. I flipped on the radio and listened to the dulcet tones of Angus Paul who had the drive slot on local morning radio. He was a minor celebrity who just happened to have a flat in my block. I wasn't sure if he'd bought the flat or just rented it like me. Given his indifference to everything at the residents' meetings I assumed he was just a renter.

Normally his chatter just washed over me, but today my ears perked up when he started to describe what had happened to his car.

'Early this morning I took the lift down to the underground car-park in my building – which is supposed to be secure by the way – and found my car covered in white gloss paint. Now whoever did it wasn't happy with just splashing paint all over my green Audi, no they had to write obscenities on the doors and the roof as well. And you know what the worst of it was? Whoever did it was semi-illiterate, half the swear words were spelt wrong. So please, whichever low-life did this, next time you decide to vandalize someone's private property, remember to take a damn dictionary with you.'

After he'd completed his rant he played the latest Rihanna song and I pondered over what he'd just said. I had an uneasy feeling in my stomach, it could have been the vestiges of the wine from the night before but I didn't think so.

I didn't have time to think about it further at that point as Pauline arrived to help me get Amy dressed and ready. She was taking her to see the Singing Kettle. It had slipped my mind, like so many other things recently. I really needed to snap out of it.

After they left I showered and dressed. I had made no plans so moping around the apartment all day felt like a good option. I had just poured myself another coffee when my phone started to ring. I really needed to change the ringtone; 'Firework' had only bad connotations now. I noted from the readout that it was Jamie calling me. I groaned and thought about not answering, but decided if he was phoning me after our last conversation it must be quite important.

'Jamie. How are you?'

'I'm good thanks – probably better than you are – but that serves you right.'

'Jamie. . . .'

'Yeah I know – listen I'm not one to argue, I just need to tell you something, I don't actually want to but I made a promise. How are your suits by the way?'

'What? How did you know about that?'

'A little birdie told me, well a little Irish birdie actually.'

For some reason I wasn't all that surprised.

'Anyway, Andy, I'm just calling to tell you that I'm now going out with Amanda. I hope you don't mind, but given recent events you have no moral ground left to stand on anyway.'

I could have debated the point but didn't have the energy. Picturing the two of them in my mind I could see why they would get on. They even had similar degrees, so their brains and temperaments were probably wired the same way.

'I don't mind, Jamie. In fact, I think the two of you are well suited.'

Jamie missed the joke, I barely got it myself.

'That's what I thought. We got together the day after the débâcle in your flat and it's been brilliant ever since.'

Despite our recent differences I was a little worried for him. 'Has she told you what else she did?'

'Yeah, sorry about that, but a few broken plates aren't the end of the world and I tried to tell her not to leave her panties there, but she thought it was a good reminder of what you would be missing.'

'I take it those were the ones she'd been wearing after you'd been shagging?'

There was a moment of silence then. 'Yeah, I think so, sorry.'

'It doesn't matter Jamie, I binned them anyway. Listen did she say anything else about me or her plans?'

'No, just that she was finished with you and didn't want anything to do with your life anymore. Honestly I didn't know she was going to do that to your car either but she's promised to leave you alone now that—'

'My car?' I interrupted.

Jamie was silent.

'Jamie?'

'I'm still here,' he said quietly.

'What about my car?'

'You've obviously not seen it yet.'

'My car's fine.'

'It can't be. Amanda poured paint all over it, white gloss I think she said.'

I started laughing, 'She's a stupid cow. She didn't pour paint over my car she poured it over Angus Paul's car.'

'The DJ?'

'Uh huh.'

'How did that happen?'

'He lives in this building somewhere. He parks his car near mine.'

'He's got a red Audi too?'

'Nope, his is green.'

'Eh?'

'Amanda's colour blind Jamie, well she gets red and green mixed up, so that's what obviously happened here. Angus is pretty pissed about it too, he was ranting about it on his radio show this morning.'

'Are you going to tell him?'

I thought about that for a moment. I wasn't sure I wanted to try and explain the events that had led up to his car getting trashed and I wanted to have to explain it to the police even less.

'I don't know yet,' I lied.

'Look, Andy, I'll make sure that Amanda never comes anywhere near you again, OK? Let's just leave things as they are.'

I sighed. 'Yeah OK Jamie, just make sure she makes no more uninvited visits to my flat.' I was planning on changing the locks anyway. I didn't trust either of them. I'd had enough of the conversation. 'Good luck, Jamie, I hope everything works out for you.' My sentiment was genuine. Amanda might make Jamie change his ways, if not, at least he knew what was likely to happen to him. Maybe his parents would get the wedding and grandchildren they wanted after all.

'Thanks Andy, no hard feelings and I'll see you around.'

I doubted it but you never know.

Dead air again.

I put my phone down, lay back on the couch and closed my eyes. My hangover was easing but I felt tired. It's funny how you go out like a light when you are drunk, but the sleep you get is never good quality.

After a few minutes I sat up and wondered what to do to keep myself from thinking too much. I could have fetched my iPad and looked for jobs online, but then I might have been tempted to read Lindsay's email again and I didn't think I could have faced that without hitting the red wine. Instead I decided to clean out my wardrobe, I had a lot of suits that needed binning.

After I'd filled my third black bin bag, the intercom sounded and I sighed. I wondered who that could be. Pauline wasn't due back for hours. I picked up the receiver

273

but there was no answer, so I put it down. Then it buzzed again. I was getting annoyed and grabbed the handset. 'Hello?'

'Mail delivery,' a female voice said.

I pressed the green button. 'OK it's open.' I went back to work and a moment later there was a knock on my door. I opened it fully expecting to see the chubby overworked post-girl. Instead, standing there wearing a tight blue top, black jeans and a nervous smile was Molly Jenkins.

She was the last person I expected to see. I stepped aside. 'Molly. Come in, come in.'

Molly entered and I closed the door quietly. As she passed me her perfume opened another door to bitter-sweet memories and emotions. I slammed that one shut.

'This is a surprise,' I said, stumped.

Molly smiled and asked, 'A nice surprise or a nasty surprise?'

I smiled back. 'Oh definitely a nice one. I take it you are the mail girl?'

Molly laughed and nodded. 'Yeah, I wasn't sure you'd let me up if you knew it was me.'

'Don't be silly, Molly, of course I would let you in. I . . . I'm very pleased to see you.' I thought about my next sentence, it might be a make or break one for me. 'It also gives me the chance to say sorry. I know that probably sounds woefully inadequate after what I did, but I don't think there is anything else I could say that wouldn't sound lame.'

Molly sat on the couch and crossed her legs. She gazed around the apartment. 'The first time I was here was amazing, it felt exciting like the start of something new, something worthwhile. The second time . . . well, it was like someone had opened up a wound and poured salt in it. So I don't know if sorry is enough. I suppose it depends on how I feel about my third visit here.'

'How do you feel so far?' I asked.

Molly bit her lower lip gently between her teeth. 'I don't feel anything yet, why don't you come and sit beside me to see if that changes.'

Molly pulled her knees up to her chin and looked straight ahead as she spoke.

'First of all, thank you for Trooper, he is the most gorgeous thing I have ever seen. The delivery boy was pretty cute too.' She laughed and blushed. 'God, I so used to have a crush on him. When he was singing in Laser Light in 1997 I got right down to the front at one of their concerts at the SECC. I was only fourteen but had it bad for him. I used to have Laser Light posters all over my bedroom wall too, it drove my dad bonkers. He's still good looking. OK he's put on about thirty pounds, and is probably the wrong side of forty now but he's still got that boyish appeal. How did you manage to get him to deliver a kitten to me? Everyone in the office was gobsmacked.'

I was desperate to know what had happened with Colin Sparks, but at that point I was still unsure of my ground, or even if I had any ground so I simply answered her question. 'I phoned his agent and said I had a job for his boy. Colin Sparks spends most of his days playing video games so isn't that busy.'

'That's sad.'

'What, that he spends most of his days playing video games?'

'Well yes, but also that his life has been wasted.'

'He's not dead yet.'

'His eyes are.'

'Sorry?'

Molly smiled sadly. 'His eyes are dead, there's nothing there, it was the first thing I noticed when I saw him yesterday.'

'You still went out with him.' I couldn't help the

275

jealousy that welled to the surface of my voice.

Molly nodded. 'Yeah, he was less than honest with me.'

'How come?'

Molly laughed. 'He didn't tell me it was you who had organized the kitten delivery.'

'Who did he say it was?'

'He didn't.'

'Eh?'

Molly sighed. 'I just assumed it was Jamie being manipulative again, and he didn't contradict me when I said it was my ex-boyfriend trying to get me back.'

Relief washed over me, so Molly had thought Jamie was trying to worm his way back in with her – that made some kind of twisted sense. But I was puzzled.

'How did you find out it was me?'

Molly turned her head and fixed her lovely eyes on me. 'Carol Davis phoned me to make sure I was happy with Trooper and explained exactly what had happened. I don't think she's a great Colin Sparks fan.'

'Was that before or after you went to dinner with him?'

'During actually. It was good timing because I was trying to think of a way of escaping without hurting his feelings.'

I snorted. '*His* feelings?'

'Yeah, I think underneath all that bluster he puts on he's pretty insecure, and all he can talk about is the past which is a shame, and probably why he's alone.'

That echoed my view from yesterday. I said, 'I think he's stuck in the late nineties but maybe that's what happens when you have it all when you're young, it all gets burned out and there's nothing left.' My philosophical take on the little Scottish songwriter made Molly pause. I continued, thinking about a documentary on BBC Four I'd recently watched. 'A lot of great singer-songwriters write all their best stuff when they're young and full of angst, energy and hunger. As they get older they're less pissed at the world, don't fall in and out of love so easily and ultimately lose their edge.'

Molly smiled. 'Maybe you're right. It was nice to spend a few hours with someone I used to admire from afar, but I realized that sometimes the dream is better than reality, and of course I'm not fourteen anymore.' She paused and took some time to think before speaking again. 'Anyway, I appreciate the huge risk you took sending him to see me. After I confronted him with the truth he told me that he'd warned you about what might happen but that you carried on anyway – very selfless. I had been thinking about what to do, whether to speak to you again or not and then you go to all that trouble, and I felt like I had to come and see you, even if it was just to say thanks.'

I made a mental note to email *Men Like Women and Women Like Shoes* so they could add my romantic gesture to their list. I realized that it hadn't actually worked yet – so far it had only got Molly in my apartment again to say thanks – but maybe that would be enough.

I looked into Molly's eyes and suddenly needed to get away from her as I had an overwhelming urge to hug her and I wasn't sure she was ready for that.

'Do you want a coffee?' I asked, standing up and walking over to the kitchen.

'Yes please, just milk no sugar.'

Something suddenly occurred to me. 'Are you not supposed to be at work?'

Molly blushed. 'Yeah, but I phoned in sick.'

I already knew the answer to my next question, but had to ask. 'Why?'

'So I could come and say thanks to you.'

'Is that all you want to say?'

Molly sighed and patted the couch beside her. 'Finish making the coffee and then sit back down here and let's see what else we can find to talk about.'

So we sat. We talked, drank coffee and ate chocolate digestive biscuits. Conversation with Molly was relaxed and easy, and the thought of not seeing her again made my heart ache.

After a while our conversation dried up and Molly turned her body all the way round to me. 'Andy, I don't know how I feel about you right now. Part of me wants to be with you, and part of me wants to run away and hide in a dark place and never come out. At this point I don't know which part will win. When I saw you with that girl it was betrayal all over again. I was thinking "It's you Molly, it's your fault, you are made for people to treat you bad and break your heart. It's just what happens to stupid Molly Jenkins." I thought maybe I'd just be better living alone and never putting myself out there again, it was just too painful.'

She paused and tears welled up in her eyes. Again, I wanted to reach out and hold her, but instinctively I knew that was not a good idea. She needed to talk.

'Then later when I heard your daughter was really sick, part of me wanted to see you to make sure you were OK. Part of me knew – somehow – that you were a nice person and that you somehow had got into a situation you couldn't control. But that part of me also tried to excuse Jamie for all the hurt he had caused me over the years, so I only listen to it cautiously now. That's why I came to see you in the hospital that night, but it's also why I've not spoken to you until now. I needed to be sure.'

'Be sure of what?'

Molly sighed and dried her eyes with her sleeve. 'Firstly I needed to know that the Irish bitch was gone, and Jamie confirmed that to me this morning.'

'He's been a busy man.'

Molly smiled. 'He phoned you as well?'

I nodded. 'Yep.'

'Figures. He did sound like he was gloating. But that was part of it, I couldn't compete with her. I didn't want to.'

'Molly, it was never about competing. . . .'

Molly put her fingers to my lips. 'Sh! Let me finish OK?'

I shut up.

'Then more importantly I needed to be sure about me – what I wanted and what I needed from everything. Then having made my decision I needed to think about you. What do you want? What do you need? Could I cope with that?'

Molly paused and tears formed in her eyes again. I wanted to reach out and touch her but still I resisted.

'You see, Andy, you come as a package. There's you and there's Amy. I have to think "could I cope with that? Could I become a mother to someone else's child?" Amy needs a mother.'

'She's got me, Molly.'

Molly smiled. 'From what you tell me you do a great job, Andy, but some stuff you're just not very good at.' That sounded like Lindsay speaking, I wasn't sure if that was a good thing.

'Like what?'

'Answering her questions for a start.'

'I always answer her questions.'

'Yes, but from what you've told me the answer usually has something to do with poo or pee pees.'

I laughed nervously. 'OK, but Amy understands that kind of answer.'

'Yes, but you can't do that forever, she needs to have someone to confide in, a female who understands the way her brain is wired. You could never do that. I've no doubt that on your own you would do a great job of bringing her up, but there would always be something missing.' Molly sighed and sank back into the couch. 'But this isn't all about you and your daughter. It's about how I fit into that world, or even if I could. Also I don't know if Amy will like me.'

'She'd love you! Besides, at the moment she doesn't know the difference between a mother and a didgeridoo....'

'I'm sure she does.'

'Well yes probably, but my point is that she has no memory of Lindsay – I'll tell her all about her of course and explain what happened, but to her it will always be a second-hand memory. She'll only know who fits into her life in the here and now.'

'Yeah, Andy, I've thought about all that stuff and more than I can really explain right now, and tried to weigh everything up in my head.'

'What was your conclusion?'

Molly gazed into my eyes, searching my soul. 'I want to be with you, Andy – I feel it like a physical need – but I don't know if I can trust you. I know you've been through a lot in the last year, maybe too much to recover from. Then yesterday you go to all that trouble to get me something that is unconditional, something that would make me happy even if I never saw you again – and by that I mean the kitten, not Colin Sparks,' she said, laughing. 'But it made me decide to at least come and speak to you. I still don't know if you and I would work long term, or even short term.'

I didn't know either but felt this was a crucial moment, one of those crossroad moments in life. Most of the time you don't realize you are at a crossroad moment until much later, and by then it's usually too late to do anything about it. This was one of the rare occasions when I knew I was standing at the signpost. I knew which way I wanted to go.

I took hold of Molly's hands, they were trembling

slightly. 'Molly, I want to be with you, I want you in my life. I've been miserable the last few days thinking I'd lost you, especially last night when it seemed like I'd set you up with someone else. It's been an incredibly hard few months and last week when I nearly lost Amy too, well it just became overwhelming.' I could feel tears pricking at the corners of my eyes again but this time I didn't fight them. 'I hate being alone and dealing with stuff. I need to be part of something, something special I can grow with. I want you, Molly, you're kind and gentle and so strong, I know coming here today took huge courage and I really respect you for that. I know it must have been tough.' I leaned over and kissed Molly on the mouth, I could taste the salt from her tears. 'I don't think I can ever let you leave this apartment again.'

'I think I'll have to,' she sobbed.

'Why?'

'I'm parked on a meter and I don't want a sixty quid fine.'

So Molly left the building, but returned five minutes later and we drank more coffee and made plans – real solid plans. It was early days but I had a good feeling about it.

Later that day, Pauline brought Amy home and joined us for dinner. (We had to phone for a Chinese takeaway because as usual there was no food in the flat.)

After Pauline and Molly had consumed half a bottle of wine – I couldn't face any – Pauline turned to Molly and asked, 'So are you and my son-in-law going to give it a go then?'

Molly blushed, but was brave enough to answer Pauline's direct question.

'Yeah, we'll give it a go. I know I can't take the place of your daughter and wouldn't even try.'

Pauline sipped her wine and nodded. 'That's a good

start, but you're going to need some help. You and I should get our heads together and figure out a plan to sort out Andy and Amy.'

'Do I not get a say in any of this?' I asked incredulously.

They both turned, looked at me and burst out laughing. I didn't get the joke. I still don't.

EPILOGUE

It was 8.15 on a Sunday morning and I was sitting on a large boulder at the top of Arthur's Seat with the whole of Edinburgh set out below me. Although the view was slightly murky, due to the low cloud that threatened snow at any moment, it was still spectacular and the hike to the top had been worth it. I had lived in the city my whole life and yet had never been to the top of the extinct volcano which dominated the city's skyline. The best I had managed was about halfway up on that fateful bonfire night with Lindsay. That seemed like a lifetime ago now. I breathed in the earthy scent of grass and turf and enjoyed the rest.

It was 29 February and although the air was cold I was warm. This could be partly explained by the recent exertion required to climb the steep slope, but I think the main reason was that beautiful Molly Jenkins, whose crazy idea it was to come up here at this ungodly hour on a Sunday, was cuddled into my side. Her delicate perfume mixed with and accentuated the earthy scents.

Her cheeks were red with the climb and the smile on her face lit up the gloom.

'What are you so happy about?' I laughed. Her

happiness was infectious.

'Aren't you going to ask me why we're up here on this mountain?'

'I don't think Arthur's Seat qualifies for a mountain, I think you need to be a thousand feet up for that.'

'Eh?'

'I think mountains need to be a thousand feet high.'

'Andy, you need to spend less time on Google and more time in the real world', she laughed.

'Actually, I didn't get that from Google. It was that film with Hugh Grant where—'

Molly put her fingers on my lips. 'Shhh. I'm trying to tell you something.'

I shut up.

'Right, where was I? Andy you know I love you, don't you?'

'Of course, sweetie, and I love you too.'

'I know we've only been together a short time, but it feels like I've loved you forever. Maybe I have. Maybe I loved you even when you were married to Lindsay, but I just didn't know, or more likely I didn't let myself know.'

I hadn't realized any of this. All I knew was that Molly was the one, well, the second one. Lindsay would always have a place in my heart, but I now figured it was OK to let someone else in. Well, if I was honest, Molly had moved into my heart some time ago, spring cleaned it, rearranged the furniture and redecorated the place – to take the analogy to a silly level, which is what I was good at.

'Andy? You've drifted off into your own little universe again and I'm trying to talk to you.'

'Sorry, Mol, I was just thinking about how happy you've made me.'

'Well, hopefully I'm about to make you happier.' Molly moved away and turned to face me. She crouched down on one knee and looked into my eyes. I returned the gaze, getting lost in her gorgeous dark eyes.

'Andy Hunter, will you marry me?'

'Eh?'

'You heard me.'

I was conscious that my mouth was opening and closing like a demented goldfish again.

'Am I not supposed to ask you?'

'Andy, it's the twenty-first century and women can do things now you know. We've had equal rights and the ability to vote for some time. Also, it's the twenty-ninth of February so traditionally I'm allowed to do it. Are you going to answer me or not? My knee is getting wet.'

I wondered what *Men Like Women and Women Like Shoes* would have to say about all of this? I'd need to look it up later.

I laughed. 'OK, Mol. I don't want you to catch a chill, so of course I'll marry you.' I knelt down beside her and took her hands in mine. I put my forehead against hers and our lips met. We kissed. It was a nuzzling kind of kiss. In between kisses I said, 'I can't imagine ever being without you. I want to always go to sleep beside you at night, and the first thing I want to see in the morning is your beautiful face.'

Molly broke away and jumped up. 'Fab, well we'll need to get organized but that can wait.'

I reached for her, but she skipped out of range. 'OK Andy, that's what I wanted to ask you. Now I've got something to tell you.'

I sat back down on the boulder.

'First of all, now that I'm going to be your wife I have to tell you that considering what you've put me through during the last few months, you are so very lucky to have me here. But, I suppose nothing worth having comes easy.'

Molly moved back and sat down beside me. She smiled and turned her face up to me and I kissed her on the lips.

She then leaned into my chest. She took a deep breath and said, 'The main worry I've got about the wedding is getting a dress to fit me properly.'

Molly was a size ten. 'How come?'

'Well I'm probably going to put on a lot of weight over the next few months, Andy, because you're going to be a daddy again.'

I jumped up and Molly fell over, landing on her bottom on the cold ground. 'Hey, that's no way to treat a pregnant woman.'

I rushed over and picked her up. 'Sorry, Mol! When? How?'

Molly laughed. 'Well the "how" you should have worked out by now, the "when" . . . well sometime in December, I reckon. I'm not showing yet, but it's only a matter of time.'

I laughed. 'God, that's brilliant. I wonder if it'll be a boy or a girl.'

'Probably,' joked Molly.

I laughed again, I was feeling dizzy. 'It would be nice for Amy to have a little sister.'

'Well it's down to you really,' Molly stated.

'How come?'

'It's the male that determines the sex of the baby.'

'How'd you know that?'

'I Googled it.'

We both burst out laughing and laughed until the tears rolled down our faces.

As our laughter subsided it began to snow. A few flakes fell gently at first then more and more appeared in flurries blown about by the easterly wind. We gathered our thick winter coats around us and began our descent, taking care not to slip on the increasingly snowy path. I didn't want my perfect Sunday morning to end with a visit to A&E.

Initially we tried to walk together holding hands, but

the path was too narrow and steep so we walked down single file, with Molly in front. Halfway down my mobile pinged.

I reached into my pocket and opened the text. I was shocked to see it was from Lindsay. I was so distracted I almost lost my footing and fell on my face. I regained my balance and read the text. Her timing was almost super-natural. Maybe it was.

Hi Gorgeous ☺

I knew things would work out 4u. (Well OK - I'm taking a huge guess here)

BUT I reckon by now your life will be sorted and I can go 2 my grave content with my work.

I wonder if I'll miss u & my baby when I'm dead. I hope not – it's painful enough just now without having that for eternity.

I probably won't contact you again (I know I've said that b4) but – I think I've only got a few days left.

I love you, Andy, and for the last time, take care of my baby 4 me. I hope everything worked out for u in the end. I hope u r with Molly. If so, never let her go.

Your beautiful wife
Linz xxxxx

As the hill levelled out I caught up with Molly and took her gloved hand in mine. I was lost in thought.

Molly kept her eyes on the path to make sure she didn't slip. She asked, smiling. 'I hope that text wasn't from one of your other women. You'll need to tell them all you're taken now.'

I smiled sadly, thankful that the heavy snow meant she couldn't see the tears in my eyes. 'No, it was just an old friend wishing me well.' Silently I promised Lindsay that I would take her advice and would never let Molly go.

We walked more quickly as the snow got heavier. In the distance I could see the warm glow of an old traditional tea-room that would be very welcoming after the cold hillside and headed towards it.

I cuddled into Molly. I was happy now and I think I always would be.

I don't know if I believe in a happy ending, or even if there *should* be a happy ending, but I firmly believe that it is the possibility of one that keeps us all going.